HOMEBOUND

Falkirk Council Library Services

This book is due for return on or before the last date indicated on the
label. Renewals may be obtained on appl...

Bo'ness	01506 778520	Falkirk	503605	Gra...	504690
Bonnybridge	503295	Mobile	506800	Lar...	503590
Denny	504242	Meadowbank	503870	Sla...	851373

WATCH OVER ME

Eilidh Lawson's life is in crisis. At the end of her tether after years of suffering failed fertility treatments, a cheating husband and an oppressive family, she runs away to where she can find solace — her childhood home in the Highlands. There she reconnects with her childhood friend Jamie McAnena, who is trying to raise his daughter Maisie alone. After Maisie's mother left to pursue a career in London and Jamie's own mother, Elizabeth, passed away, he has resigned himself to being a family of two. But sometimes there's more to a story than meets the eye. Despite their reluctance, curious circumstances keep bringing Jamie and Eilidh together. For even when it seems that all is lost, help can come from the most extraordinary places.

DANIELA SACERDOTI

◆

WATCH OVER ME

Complete and Unabridged

CHARNWOOD
Leicester

First published in Great Britain in 2011 by
Black & White Publishing Ltd.
Edinburgh

First Charnwood Edition
published 2012
by arrangement with
Black & White Publishing Ltd.
Edinburgh

The moral right of the author has been asserted

British Library CIP Data

Sacerdoti, Daniela.
Watch over me.
1. Large type books.
I. Title
823.9'2–dc23

ISBN 978–1–4448–1342–5

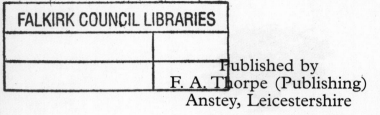
Published by
F. A. Thorpe (Publishing)
Anstey, Leicestershire

Set by Words & Graphics Ltd.
Anstey, Leicestershire
Printed and bound in Great Britain by
T. J. International Ltd., Padstow, Cornwall

This book is printed on acid-free paper

To those who watch over me
from the other side of reality.

And to the ones who stand beside me:
Ross, the earth, Sorley, the sky,
and Luca, the sun.

Acknowledgements

Thank you Ross, Sorley and Luca, for everything.

Thank you to my family, Ivana and Edoardo Sacerdoti, and to my dearest father Franco and grandmother Caterina, who watch over me.

Thank you to the Walker clan, especially to Beth and Bill, my second Mum and Dad.

Thank you Irene, the best friend anyone could want.

Thank you to the people of Caravino, in northern Italy, the real Glen Avich . . . a place full of ghosts, which I was taught, in my long, sunny childhood, not to be afraid of.

Thanks to Sorley MacLean and to Martyn Bennet, whose interpretation of 'Hallaig' sowed the seeds of this story.

Thank you to everyone at Black & White Publishing, for believing in me.

Thank you to Alexander McCall Smith and Alison Rae, for encouraging words that I'll never forget.

And forever thank you, my windswept, dark, warm, complicated, beloved Scotland, my home.

Prologue

Persephone

The strangest, most amazing day of my life, the day that changed my perception of life and death, started like any other. I woke up in the world I've always known, I went to sleep wrapped in a mystery.

All our lives we make ourselves busy, trying to ignore the fact that darkness will come, one day too soon, to get us. Infinity can't fit in our lives the way it is, too frightening, too huge. We have to cut it to size, doing all the million little everyday things that define the boundaries of our reality — using our five senses the way they're meant to be used, to touch things, to see things, things that are real and present and on this side of existence, the side of the living. We give the mystery a human face; we give a shape to something that's shapeless.

We invent rituals to define the passages, turn life and death into ceremonies, making them earthly and somehow easier to grasp, to comprehend. When a baby is born, we don't dwell on *why* that little soul is now here, where it was before, what it knows . . . The new mum comes back from her excursion into the unknown, taking the baby with her from darkness into the light, and both are cleaned and

1

dressed and made to look as if they never were beyond ... as if she hadn't just been underground, in the dark, where life and death touch and mix.

And when somebody dies, the family can mercifully occupy their minds with all the heartbreaking little things we need to do when it's all finished — the flowers, the food, what needs to be put away, what needs to be given away — while tears fall on the objects left behind: a pair of slippers, a mug, a dressing gown. We comfort each other, holding on to a solid arm, clinging to a warm hand where the blood flows strong, we feel it underneath the skin and it sings so loud, so clear, that it banishes death away.

How could we, even for a second, face what *really* happened — the way someone was there and then she was not, gone forever, gone into non-existence — without falling on our knees and screaming in terror, thinking one day it will happen to us, that we'll close our eyes and never open them again? How can we ever be so brave as to gaze into the deep, senseless darkness that awaits us and still keep on living?

If darkness is what awaits us.

Because I know now that it isn't.

The day that started like any other day is the day all the frills were stripped away and I looked straight into the mystery. I saw someone whom I thought was gone, and she was there, standing in front of me. I saw a soul without a body and she smiled.

Maybe I'm naive, maybe a whole lot of proof

2

and science and thought stands before me to say I'm wrong, but I believe what my gran told me many years ago — that love never dies and that what awaits us is the love we felt when we were alive. That beyond the fear and pain, love is there to catch us when we fall.

This is what I learnt, one spring night in the woods, and since then, I am not afraid.

1

A Lost Baby

Eilidh

The day I lost my baby, the weather was so gorgeous, so sunny, that half the town was out, with sunglasses on and a smile on their faces.

I had gone for a walk, wearing my big flowery maternity top. I was only ten weeks gone, it was way too early to wear maternity clothes, but I just couldn't wait. I had also picked up some groceries, some bizarre combination, sardines and cashew nuts maybe, because I kept telling myself I had this craving or the other. I didn't, really. I just wanted to be finally able to say things like 'I'm living on mango and HP sauce and I chew on elastic bands. You get such awful cravings when you are *pregnant*!'

Pregnant.

I really was pregnant. It seems impossible now.

I wanted to experience the whole of it; I wanted every sign, every little symptom — the morning sickness, the swollen ankles, the tops that look like tents, the sleepless nights. I wanted to laugh at how huge my underwear had got and check the likelihood of having a boy or a girl on some silly test I found in a magazine. I wanted to pour over name books, choose the nursery furnishing and discuss the advantages of a sling over a baby carrier. I wanted to buy the little vests, the little babygros, the hats, mittens and socks. All white, until the twenty-week scan, when I'd know if it was a boy or a girl. Tom and I would watch the screen in awe, saying to each other, 'Look, he's waving! He's saying hello!' We'd call our friends and relatives to tell them what we were having. We'd frame the scans and put them on the mantelpiece. Tom would bring one to his work, where the other doctors and the midwives and the receptionists would coo over it and say, 'He . . . or she . . . looks like you!' You can't really tell, of course, you can't see anything in these pictures, it's just one of those silly things, the sweet nonsense that people say to each other because it feels so good to be talking about them — the babies on their way to this world, all the hope and joy they carry.

But the thing I wanted most of all was to feel the baby kicking inside me. They'd told me it was like little ripples, like a butterfly flying in your tummy. I wanted to have Tom's hand on my bump, see the pride on his face and the tenderness for me, his wife, giving him a son or a daughter.

I'd waited so long, so long for this, while everybody else got pregnant and carried their lovely bumps around like a crown, and me in my size ten jeans and a flat stomach. I hated the way I was growing thinner instead of round and full and serene.

I desperately wanted to be *them*, the pregnant women: my sister, my girlfriends, my colleagues, my hairdresser. Even the postman — well, postwoman — inflicted her bump on me every morning, as I watched her waddle her way up and down our street and clumsily climb into the red post van. Until she told me they were changing her duties, health and safety you know, she was going to sit at the parcel collection desk behind the post office and watch her bump grow. She said to drop by, to say hello.

I'd scrutinize women's tummies obsessively, to see if they were swollen in that lovely, taut way you get right at the beginning, when your bump is barely there but already visible. I'd torture myself, convince myself that everybody, *everybody* was pregnant except me.

Whenever I crossed ways with a pram, I'd look away. I didn't trust myself to not have that look — that longing, lingering look that mothers recognise, so that they pounce and say with their eyes: 'This baby's mine.'

I wanted to be like that. I wanted other women to look at my baby with shining eyes and envy me, and feel like the queen of the whole world, the luckiest woman on earth.

Like my sister. She's an expert at doing that.

Katrina is three years younger than me. We both love babies, we both wanted to be mothers since we were little girls. We used to play house, look after our dolls, feed them, put them to bed, take them for strolls in their little pink prams. Not surprisingly, we both decided we wanted to work with children: she became a paediatric nurse, and I became a nursery nurse. Well, a child development officer, they say now.

She got married early, barely out of college, and within six months she was pregnant. She had a boy, a lovely boy, my dearest nephew Jack. By the time Katrina gave birth yet again — to twin girls — I'd been trying for over three years. As I watched her holding them both, one under each arm, with their pink babygros and little pink hats and scrunched up faces, I felt sick with sorrow.

After Isabella and Chloe — while I was going through the second IVF attempt — came Molly. She was the baby of the family, the apple of our eye. More congratulations, more celebrating, more get-togethers, with my mum and dad joking that one daughter was providing enough children for them both.

Except they weren't really joking. They know about my struggle, it's just that my family is not very . . . how can I put it . . . tactful. Some would say they are a bit cruel. Well, with me anyway. My sister in particular. She is quite merciless, constantly reminding me how fertile she is, how abundant her harvest of little faces and little hands and little toes is, how much they love her and cling to her and make her . . . worthy.

While I am worthless, barren, my arms sore with emptiness. Empty arms, empty heart.

'If you had any kids, you'd know how I feel!' she pointed out, crying, on Jack's first day at school.

'They just want their mum don't they? An auntie is not the same!' she'd laugh, as one of the twins bypassed me and ran to her with a scraped knee.

'Sorry, it's not like I don't want you to, it's just that she settles better with me,' she'd say if I asked to put Molly to bed.

In the meantime, her husband was giving Tom the same treatment. Including cruel jokes about firing blanks, which wasn't even true — they had already found out, after extensive tests, that the problem lay at my door. Tom would pretend to laugh, but would then become very, very quiet. He soon started finding excuses to miss family gatherings. I couldn't blame him.

Tom is a doctor; he's a few years older than me. It wasn't a crazy passion or anything, we were good friends, we got on and we both wanted children. Tom was well over thirty and wasn't close to his own family either, so we hoped to make a little family of our own and not be alone anymore.

We started trying for a baby just after our honeymoon. Ten years, a lot of tests and five IVF attempts later, it worked. I was pregnant.

But by then, our marriage was in tatters. Tom was seeing someone and had been for a long time. I was so worn out by the hormone injections and all that went with it, I didn't have the strength to discuss it, let alone fight.

I had left my job two years earlier. The treatment was making me an emotional and physical wreck and I couldn't keep taking time off. I worked with children all day, I had to smile

9

and be cheerful and loving when my heart was perpetually bleeding.

Not to mention the pregnant mums I had to deal with. They'd come to collect their children, struggling to bend down and take the children's sand shoes off, to which I'd say, 'There, I'll help you,' and they'd laugh and say, 'Thanks, sorry about that, I'm getting bigger by the day!' patting their rounded stomachs. And me, nauseous with envy, exhausted by hormone treatment, worn out by sleepless, sweaty nights, having to smile back.

I quit. I wanted to keep all my energy for my only goal, the only thing that mattered.

Four times they tried to put our babies into me — they called them embryos, I called them babies. Four times it didn't work.

It's not like they tried to latch on but then I miscarried. Not even that. Nothing happened, not even a bit of swelling, or some sort of feeling . . . different. I felt nothing, as if it had never happened, as if it had all been a dream of mine, those four babies-in-waiting. A dream that would vanish in the light, like dreams do. As if they were never there.

I would cry and cry for hours, sharing a glass of juice — wine was off limits during treatment — with my best friend Harry. His friendship saved my sanity. We met in school when we were thirteen, went out for a few weeks when we were sixteen and then decided we were better off as friends. A year later, he came out as gay, shocking his dad to the core. He went to stay with his aunt for about a week, until his dad turned up at his door and tearfully asked him to come home. After that minor upheaval, Harry's life rolled on smoothly. He met his partner Douglas when they were both at college and they're still together now.

While I was going through hell on earth, Harry and Doug provided a safe harbour for me and many a night was spent watching the soaps and some soppy film, eating prawn crackers and Singapore noodles.

I used to cry in Harry's arms and he'd say, 'Come on, come on, you'll be fine, you'll be fine . . . ' and I was so grateful my heart would overflow with fondness for him. He's like a brother to me.

When I told him that Tom had a girlfriend, he reverted back to his old self, before he came out, and asked if I wanted him to go and punch him. Then he came to his senses and suggested we'd post his profile, complete with mobile number and email, on a gay dating website.

'No, thanks. I think I'll just ignore it. Pretend it's not happening.'

'That never works.'

'I know . . . but I can't stop now. The treatment is booked in two months time, I can't possibly cancel, it might be my last chance!'

It worked. The fifth time, it worked.

As I stared at the blue cross on the pregnancy test, one line vivid blue, the one across hesitant and timid and barely there, I slipped down along the tiled wall onto the bathroom floor, closed my eyes and tasted the greatest happiness I had ever known.

Four tests later, four blue crosses later, I was

out of pee and dizzy with excitement.

Tom was overjoyed. For a while, he didn't work late anymore, he didn't have any weekend conventions and meetings and overtime to do. I was in a bubble of happiness but didn't dare to prepare for the baby yet. It was too early, I didn't want to jinx it. Mine was classed as a high-risk pregnancy, I had to have constant checkups, so I couldn't relax.

One day, Tom came home with a beautiful cradle, made of wrought iron and painted white. It was gorgeous.

'It was Eva's,' he said, carrying it carefully inside. Eva is his best friend's, and our best man's, little girl. 'You know how they don't want any more kids, so he gave it to me. They got it up in Scotland, some small place in the Highlands. I thought you'd love it.' He was smiling. Those days, he looked like the old Tom. The man I married.

'I do! It's beautiful! And it comes from Scotland!'

I lived in Scotland for several years as a child, when my parents separated. My mum, my sister and I went to stay with my gran Flora in Glen Avich, in the northeast of the country.

'The only thing is . . . ' I started, hesitantly.

He made a puzzled face.

'Well, they say it's bad luck to put the cot in the nursery too soon. Maybe we could put it in the loft.'

'In the loft? It'd get spoiled. And anyway, all that stuff about cots in nurseries and black cats and ladders, it's a lot of rubbish, you know that.'

12

'Of course, of course, I know.'

But I wasn't sure. My brain was saying, 'Come on, Eilidh, don't be silly,' but my gut was saying, 'Why chance it?'

'Eilidh,' laughed Tom, lifting the cradle to carry it upstairs, 'since when are you superstitious?'

'I don't know, it's just . . . ' I shrugged my shoulders. I had no words to explain.

'Nonsense. Come on, come and see.'

He carried it up the stairs and through the landing, the cradle that was never going to be filled. He placed it carefully in what was to be the nursery, the room that had been waiting for years.

'There. Doesn't it look perfect?'

I nodded, and smiled.

I tried not to be afraid, but I was.

★ ★ ★

It wasn't the cradle, of course. I'm not superstitious enough to think it really was that. It wasn't the cradle, it wasn't carrying the groceries home on a hot day either, it was nothing I'd done, the doctor said.

I shouldn't blame myself, he said.

But I do, oh I do, I blame myself, for not having been strong enough to carry the baby full term, to give him a chance to live. I let my baby down and now he's dead.

That lovely sunny day, three months ago, a lifetime ago, I stopped to chat with my neighbour for a few minutes, before saying goodbye and turning back to cross the road, towards my house. As I walked on, I heard my neighbour's hurried footsteps behind me and felt her arm go around my waist, as if to sustain me.

'Let me get these, Eilidh, darling, there's a good girl,' she said as she gently took the shopping bags from me and led me into the house, her arm still around my waist. I slowly realised that there was something wrong and then I felt something trickling down my legs, and it wasn't sweat, and I looked and it was blood.

★　★　★

Had I had a boy, I would have called him Harry. Had I had a girl, I would have called her Grace.

When I finished crying, three months later, I got up from the sofa, had a long, warm shower, got dressed for the first time in weeks and made myself a cup of tea. I sat at the kitchen table with my phone, a spiral pad and a pen.

Tom was on a weekend away. Some convention, he said, as if I didn't know the truth, as if I were stupid.

I wrote two notes:

Mum, Dad,
    I'm going away for a while. Don't worry, I'll be fine.
    I'll phone as soon as I'm settled.
    Eilidh

Tom,

Our marriage is over. I am sure you know why but your girlfriend is not the only reason. It's been over for years. I'll be in touch with my parents when I'm settled, they'll be able to reassure you I'm ok. Don't look for me.

Eilidh

Then I picked up my mobile and texted Harry:

I'm going away for a bit. Don't worry about a thing, seriously, I'll be fine. I'm leaving my phone behind, but I'll get on the net as soon as I can and e-mail you at once. xxxx
E

I left the notes and the phone on the kitchen table, and packed a few of my belongings carefully, deliberately.

I felt empty. Like a shell, a dried-up shell with nothing inside, nothing left to give.

I got into the car and started driving, not having the slightest idea where I was going. I just knew I had to go.

On the motorway, I started seeing signs that said 'North'.

North.

Suddenly, I realised where I was headed. Where the deepest, most secret part of me wanted to be, so that I could heal. I kept driving, on and on through the afternoon and the early evening.

The light was lilac and the pinewoods black against the sky when I got to Glen Avich. The sight of the whitewashed cottage and its red door made a million happy memories flood back. Had I been able to feel anything, it would have been relief. But I was numb.

I knocked at Flora's door. She wasn't there anymore, she'd been dead a long time — but my great aunt Peggy still lived there. She opened the door and gasped to see me so pale, so lost, so thin.

It was twilight, the hour when shapes seem to lose their definition and blur a little, as if they were beginning to vanish into the darkness. I was one of those things that were vanishing. I felt like Peggy could have opened the door and found a little cloud of blue cold air where I should have stood.

Peggy smiled, hugged me and led me in, made me a cup of hot, sugary tea, and spoke to me in the best accent in the world, the way my gran used to speak. By then, the night had fallen and it was pitch-dark, as we were deep, deep into the heart of the Highlands.

Peggy took me to my bedroom, the one I had shared with Katrina when I was a girl. I barely had the energy to put my pyjamas on and slip into bed. She brought me a cup of tea and left it on the bedside table. I whispered a thank you but couldn't move, every bit of me felt like lead. I closed my eyes.

Slowly, slowly, Scotland started to seep into me. She enveloped me and held me — her sounds and scents comforting me, as they did when I was a child.

I fell asleep, under clean sheets and a duvet

16

that smelled musty, but in a good way, like grandmothers' things do.

I slept for a whole twelve hours, after weeks and weeks of white nights. When I woke up the next morning, at first light, I felt like life was bearable.

Barely bearable, really, but bearable.

I felt like maybe, in the nick of time, I had managed to stop the vanishing process. Maybe I wasn't going to disappear and cease to exist.

Maybe life was giving me a second chance.

2

A Lost Mother

Jamie

I knew she was gone when I saw that the painting was missing from the living room wall. All her things — the canvases, the paints, the paintbrushes, the bottles of white spirits, her cloths and aprons — it was all still there. But the painting was gone.

She wasn't coming back.

It was the picture of a young girl, wrapped in winter clothes, her cheeks red from the cold, skating on a frozen lake. Janet had somehow managed to convey it all: the sense of joy on the girl's face, the apprehension of skating on thin ice, the defiance that said, 'I dare.' The cold and crisp air, the magic of the winter scene, with the icicle-covered branches, the pink-yellow sky, and the black silhouette of the winter trees in the distance . . .

That painting showed all of Janet's talent, her promise as an artist. It was part of her final exhibition when she had graduated from Slade in London. Everybody knew that Janet Phillips was one to watch, the one that would make it.

And sure enough, she did.

Three years after graduating, she was in great

demand, owned a flat in an upmarket area of London and was swamped with work. Her work was true and honest and amazing.

Her art meant everything to her; she would paint through the night and fall asleep at dawn on the sofa in her studio, among her canvases. When she was working on something, she couldn't think of anything else, she couldn't see anything else.

But after three years of this life, she started to feel the strain. Although happy, she was exhausted and physically drained. Her twin sister, Anne, convinced her to take a holiday in Scotland with a group of friends.

And that's when we met and both our lives were turned upside down.

I walked into the pub one night after work. They were sitting at the counter, all wrapped up in the high-tech fleeces, water-proof trousers and walking boots that seem to be the uniform of people coming here from down south, several whisky glasses in front of them.

You know that thing about love at first sight? People debating whether it exists or not?

Well, it does.

I swear, it took me about a second to fall in love. And I'm not even the romantic type. You know, quiet and all that. Shy. Brought up to hide my emotions as deep as I could, in the best Scottish male tradition. I wasn't even that interested in having a relationship, back then.

And still, there she was, there I was, everything changed in that second and it was never the same again.

We started talking and three hours later we were still together. Anne and their friends went back to their hotel, we went for a walk on the beach, among knowing smiles and innuendoes from the girls. We didn't care. I didn't even care about the people in the pub, most of whom had known me since I was born, and how tongues would start wagging. I didn't care about anything, except not leaving her side.

I watched her blonde hair on my pillow. It was the colour of ripe corn, of golden fields in the summer. I watched her face as she was sleeping, I watched over her all night.

She went back to London a few days later, leaving me in a grey world, in a lifeless world where I wandered in a daze, not knowing what I was doing, where I was going.

I burnt my hand very badly. I am a blacksmith, like my father, and in my line of work, you better watch what you are doing or you end up hurt.

As she was bandaging my arm, Dr Nicholson smiled. The whole village knew about Janet and me. That is how things work in Glen Avich.

'You are not the first and you won't be the last,' she said.

I looked at her.

'To do something silly like that. You know, the day I met John, about thirty years ago, I missed my stop on the train back from university and ended up on the coast. My dad had to drive two-and-a-half hours to come and get me. There, *this* will heal in no time.'

A few stunned weeks later, after many a

late-night session in the pub to drown my sorrow — and many a hungover day — she came back.

I opened the door and there she was. Golden hair, cornflower eyes, like the princess in fairytales. She had driven up from London with a small case full of clothes and laden with paints, canvases and a few paintings.

She looked scared. She clearly didn't know how I'd react. I could feel the tension in her body as I held her and kissed her, and then I felt her relaxing in my arms. She looked at me, her face flooded with relief. She could read on my face that I was overjoyed to see her.

She looked relieved, but she didn't look happy.

She wasn't even in the door. We were still standing on my doorstep as she told me.

'I'm pregnant.'

Everything spun around me and before my rational mind could process what she had just told me, I broke into a smile. She didn't smile back. She didn't look happy.

She was pregnant and she wasn't happy.

★   ★   ★

We settled down to this new, unexpected life. At the beginning, it was like being under water, everything was surprising, fluid, unplanned. I cleaned and painted the spare room and turned it into a studio for her. She tried to work but morning sickness — all day sickness really — made it so hard. She was constantly exhausted, lying on the sofa or throwing up in the bathroom. She soon gave up on painting.

21

My mum was a godsend. She made Janet feel welcome, she did her utmost to help her settle in. Janet took to her and they became good friends. They would go for tea and a scone in the local cafe, up to Aberdeen shopping, or just sit in my mum's kitchen and chat while I was at work.

The local girls had been quite taken aback by the sudden appearance of this London woman, her blonde hair, her designer clothes. They weren't as ready as my mum to befriend her. My sister Shona pointed out to me that it wasn't nice for them to see one of the few eligible bachelors in the area snatched by a newcomer. Of course, I hadn't thought of that. My sister commented that men are useless that way — they never notice these things. My mum seemed to be the only person that Janet truly trusted. It goes against the stereotype of the wicked mother-in-law, I suppose.

Still, Janet was miserable. It was as simple as that.

I could see it, my mum and sister could see it, everyone could. People would wonder what on earth she had to be so miserable about — a man who adored her and couldn't wait to marry her, a baby on the way, a lovely home.

But I understood. The pregnancy had taken everything out of her; the baby was sapping every ounce of her strength. Because her art required all her energy — emotional, physical, and mental — the two things just couldn't co-exist, for her. She was drained.

I didn't know much about pregnancies, I had only seen my sister whenever she was down from

Aberdeen, and apart from being a bit tired and nauseous, she seemed fine. Happy. I didn't want to start discussing Janet behind her back but I had to ask my mum for advice. I was at a loss.

'It happens sometimes. I was fine with you but with Shona . . . I was sick throughout, as big as a house and totally exhausted! She was my first — I just wasn't prepared. But then, when the baby came, I was so happy I forgot all about it. Sometimes your dad and I tried to stay awake all night just to look at her . . . '

It didn't happen that way for Janet. When the baby came, she didn't seem better. Maisie was born after more than twenty-four hours of labour, she was in so much pain and I couldn't help her. When it finished, Janet was exhausted, but rules were that I had to leave her there and come back the next day. Maisie must have been quite traumatised by the ordeal too, so she wouldn't settle in Janet's arms or at her breast. I left her holding the baby, sitting upright in her bed on the ward, and when I came back the following morning, she was in the same position, holding Maisie, with blue shadows under her eyes and looking like she was going to collapse. She told me she had held her all night because whenever she put her down, Maisie would start crying. She was so scared to nod off and drop her that she had pinched herself over and over again, so much that her arms were full of purple bruises. I couldn't believe it.

'Did the midwives not help you at all?'

'I didn't ask.'

As I held Maisie, my beautiful, sweet,

23

wonderful wee girl, I didn't know which feeling was stronger: happiness for her birth, or fear over her mother's state of mind.

A fraught few months followed. Janet looked as if she was doing her duty to Maisie but not enjoying it much. Maisie was fed, changed, held — she was very well looked after — but Janet just didn't seem . . . well, as enraptured as we were. Myself, my mum and Shona. And the rest of the village, really. Maisie was so pretty — she still is. The same blonde hair as her mum but not her cornflower eyes, she had inherited my own grey ones that were my father's too.

Janet started leaving Maisie more and more often, with me, whenever I wasn't working, or with my mum. She even tried to arrange for Maisie to stay over in Aberdeen with my sister for a few days — but I said no, she was only three months old, it was too early to leave her.

Even when someone else looked after Maisie, Janet still wouldn't paint. I'd come home to a chaotic house and Janet sitting at the window in her studio, her apron on, but no painting done.

It was breaking my heart. I felt so terrible, so terrible that something that happened with me, one night of passion, had made her so unhappy. I knew it wasn't my fault, and I knew I was doing my very best to try and make her better, but it didn't help the guilt.

I felt like she was this beautiful tropical bird and I had caged her, though unwittingly, and now she was dying.

One night I couldn't take it anymore and I

told her so. She burst into tears and held my hands.

'No, no, it's not your fault.' She was sobbing, she was distraught. 'It's not your fault, it's not Maisie's fault. I'll do my best, I'll try harder. I just don't know who I am anymore. I try to paint and nothing comes. I'll get better, I promise.'

In the next year or so, things improved. All of a sudden, she came back to life. She started painting again. She would paint all day, then on and on through the night. The colour came back into her face. She would sit down to dinner with us for ten minutes and then run back upstairs to her canvases. I missed her, and it seemed such a shame she wouldn't spend any time with Maisie and me — but it warmed my heart to see her happy again.

Maisie was now a toddler with golden wavy hair that curled around her face like a halo, a sweet little face and those beautiful grey eyes that I would lose myself in. She always asked for her mum, she was forever trying to cling to her and stop her from going upstairs. I could see how much she missed Janet — but she was generally a happy little thing and didn't seem to be overly upset by her mother's continuous absence.

Janet started driving down to London every month or so, to take new paintings down to galleries, or attend events, or just see friends. One time, she was offered an exhibition and spent five weeks down south without ever driving back, and she kept finding excuses for us not to visit her.

I grew terrified that she'd go and take Maisie with her. I couldn't sleep at night for fear that I'd awake and find them gone.

'We can all go down to London. I can get a job. If that's what you want, if it would make you happy . . . '

'Oh, Jamie. You would hate London. You know that very well.'

'But if that's where you need to be . . . '

'Stop it, Jamie,' she snapped. 'I don't even want to talk about this, it's not an option.'

I knew what she meant. She didn't want me with her.

★   ★   ★

She did go, just like I feared she would. But she left Maisie.

She took a few clothes, her painting and her cat. She took her cat and left her eighteen-month-old daughter.

I was relieved and distraught and horrified all at the same time.

That day I decided that it was going to be Maisie and me. We'd be a family. We didn't need anyone. Of course we had my mum and my sister and all our friends in the village, but the two of us were a wee unit in ourselves and would not allow anyone to come in and hurt us.

At the beginning, Maisie asked for her mum over and over and over again. Then, slowly, Janet's memory faded from her mind and she asked less and less. Then she stopped. I didn't give her an explanation. Maybe I was a coward, I don't know, but what could I say? 'Your mum left you because she was so unhappy here, she wanted to be in London and be a painter and yes, she could have still been a painter here, or take us to London with her, or even only you — as much as it would have destroyed me — but she didn't. Why? Because she didn't want me with her, and she didn't want you either.'

I decided that if Maisie ever asks, I'll find an excuse for what Janet did. Not to protect Janet but to protect Maisie.

The funny thing is, Janet's selfishness and cruelty in leaving Maisie behind meant that I could keep her, so in a strange, twisted way, I am grateful.

Now it's just us. Since my mother died unexpectedly three years ago, we are even closer. She is my life.

But when Maisie is in bed and the fire is dying, I sit looking at the embers with a glass of whisky and I feel a coldness inside, a loneliness that seeps into my bones. I feel myself withdrawing from life, rejecting it like something too dangerous, something only a fool would take his chances on.

I am frozen and I intend to stay that way. It's safer and I have a daughter to think of. Nobody will ever break our hearts again.

3

Mother and Son

Elizabeth

I've been dead three years now, to measure time the way you do.

Time feels very different when you are dead, an eternity is condensed into a second, nights and days pass in eternal twilight.

It was such a wrench to have to go, to leave Shona and Jamie behind.

I was sixty-five, not that old really, but not that young either. I had a happy life, I did all I wanted to do, but what hurt me so much, so much, is that I had to leave my children to fend for themselves.

I know, they are adults, but are our own children ever really adults? Are mothers ever ready to leave them? So much of our world is defined by our parents being alive, a barrier between ourselves and our turn to die. When our parents go, there's no more protection. We are on our own, exposed.

And Maisie. I didn't want to leave Maisie, poor wee mite, motherless. Well, she has a mother of course, but a mother not overly concerned about her. Or not concerned at all, really.

I suppose I should hate Janet but I don't. It's difficult to have these sort of feelings, anyway, when you are dead and you feel peaceful, at one with everything, safe.

But to be fair, I didn't even hate her or resent her before, when I was alive. I'd been incredibly relieved when she left without Maisie. I'd spent night after night awake, fearing she'd take Maisie away, and we couldn't have said no; it was her daughter and clearly Janet wasn't happy up here, with Jamie. But how could he have moved down to London? It would have been like trying to take one of our trees, the lovely mountain pines that grow all around us, and replant it in some suburban garden. Jamie would have been miserable. But still, he would have gone. She spared him this painful choice; she went and left Maisie to us. She hadn't been that interested in her anyway, since the day that little life started inside her.

Maybe I should say she's some sort of monster, that she's unnatural, without motherly instinct. But life taught me compassion. Who says all women should be mothers? Who says all women know how to be a mother, or want to be one?

One night — one night was all it took for Janet, and I remember how it feels to be young and reckless and have life flowing through you so strongly that you have to live it, live it deeply and fully. One night of love at first sight, and whisky, and the beauty of the Highlands all around her, and her life was turned upside down.

29

Who are we to dictate she had to be happy, that she had to take to motherhood like a duck to water, like I did with my children and Shona did with hers? People pointed their finger and despised her, as if they didn't know how many women *pretend*. They pretend to be happy, they pretend to want this life, of wife and mother, because that's what's expected of them. They bend and break themselves to fit the mould they were handed down from their mothers. Misery handed down from mothers to daughters, a life of self-denial.

Janet couldn't do that. She's an artist. Like you would say, 'She's a human being,' or, 'She's a woman,' — the very basic qualities that define her essence — you would also say of Janet, 'She's an artist.'

I knew someone like her before. A boy I went to school with, who used to think of nothing else but playing the violin. His dad played too, his mum was a beautiful singer, and they loved music. But with him, it was different. He was consumed — I'm sure that had they taken his violin away, he would have withered and died. He went on to be a famous musician and composer, he lives in Glasgow now. He has three children. Because you see, he could keep playing the violin ten hours a day and travel the world and live his music as deeply as he wanted, while his wife raised the family. He could have both, because he's a man. But a woman artist, if she wants children, she has to stop, she can't be consumed by it, she has to put her art in a slot to fit in with the biggest slot, the most important one — her babies. Some are willing to do it; some, like Janet, are not.

I don't know what that feels like, to feel forced to give up your passion, your very reason for being. I can only imagine it is like some sort of death of the soul. I saw it happening to Janet. How can I judge her? The only passion I've ever known is my family, James and the children, and my home, this little-known corner of the world, and all its beauty. I don't know what it feels like to have to give up your own soul.

Since I died, I am at one with my home. I am the loch and the silver fish that swim in it. I am the wind and the leaves and the mountains. I am the particles of dust twirling around in the rays of sunshine, seeping through the windows of my son's workshop. I am the moon that shines in a pool of silver light on Maisie's floor, as she lies asleep. I am the wind that caresses Shona's face, and her girls', whenever they come home.

When we die, we can choose to go and be reborn. Or if we still have things to do, things to be seen to, we can stay, although not forever.

At first, I didn't want to go. But now I do. I feel myself dissolving, I feel myself drifting more and more, every day another bit of consciousness leaves me and I am less and less myself. If I don't go, if I don't walk into the new life that has been chosen for me, I'll just disappear. It will be painful to go into the new life, because I'll have to forget all about them. James and my children and grandchildren, and all my friends, and

31

everything I knew in this life. But I must go.

The one thing that really keeps me here is Jamie.

He's lost. I watch him and fear seeps even into this peace I feel in death. I suppose not even eternity can stop a mother from worrying. I'm worried sick that he'll keep freezing up until it's too late and he can never come back. Maisie keeps him going but not much else. He speaks to people but he doesn't say anything. He smiles and functions through his days and ends them with a glass in his hand, and another, and another. He seems to thaw a little when he's with Maisie, but she'll grow and build a family of her own, and Jamie will be one of those men you see in pubs up here, a whisky in their hand, not wanting to go home to a cold, empty house.

He has shut the world out.

My lovely son, who has so much to give. I am determined I will not go until I've helped him.

★   ★   ★

One night I was sitting on the rocks, listening to the water lapping at the shore, when something startled me. A wave of sadness washed over me, like a shiver, from my forehead to my spine. It was as if I'd been looking out to sea and suddenly saw a distress signal, cutting the sky in a burning arc.

As a ghost, there are a million souls floating in mine, a million voices whispering their thoughts, their memories. That voice, I knew.

It was Eilidh, the granddaughter of my

childhood friend Flora McCrimmon, crying out her sorrow in her sleep. But she wasn't calling me, she was calling Flora.

Flora couldn't hear her — she had rejoined the sea of souls and she's not Flora anymore. But I could hear her, and I would *listen*.

I closed my eyes and called her.

I called and called, picturing the child that Eilidh used to be, the sweet girl with thoughtful eyes, so different from her brazen sister Katrina. Kind Eilidh . . .

Walking home from school in her blue uniform . . .

Dancing at the village ceilidhs, her brown hair flowing . . .

Eilidh on the swings . . .

Eilidh helping in Flora's shop, in her little maroon apron . . .

Sitting on the stone wall at the edge of the play park, daydreaming . . .

Sitting in our kitchen, chatting to me as I baked, Jamie coming in from fishing and them exchanging a few awkward words, the way children do when they are nearly teenagers and don't see each other with the same eyes anymore.

Memories of Eilidh kept flooding back as I called her, trying to seep into her dreams. I finally found her consciousness amid the million minds that floated in mine and stepped into it.

I recoiled. Such pain and sadness, it broke my heart.

'Come home, Eilidh, come home child . . . Come to Glen Avich . . . ' I repeated over and over and over again.

I'm not sure she heard me. I hope so because she needs to come home.

And maybe, just maybe, she could be the answer to my prayers.

I'd never been much of a matchmaker when I was alive, I never meddled in other people's business, I was always too reserved, too quiet for that. Flora and Peggy, out of all the women of my generation, were the born matchmakers.

However, here I am now, trying to set my son up. Life can be surprising. And as I'm finding out, death can be quite surprising too.

4

Life After Hope

Eilidh

The next morning, I woke up to a silent house, as the muted, milky light of autumn seeped through the curtains.

For a few seconds I didn't know where I was. I looked up at the low ceiling and around me. The wooden wardrobe, the old-fashioned dressing table, the paintings of fields and whitewashed cottages on the walls and, finally, the patterned carpet.

My gran and my aunt's house, still unchanged since I was a wee girl.

I waited for the usual pang of grief and sadness, the one I got every single time I opened my eyes, after a fitful sleep, since I lost my baby.

It came, but it was somehow less sharp, less cruel. As if something, or someone, was standing between me and the terrible pain I felt. Like it was being cushioned off, softened.

When you are a child, no pain is so harsh that the ones you love, the ones that look after you, can't ease it. Even the worst of days look up when someone tucks you in, brings you a cup of warm milk and a biscuit, and sits at the edge of your bed to read you a story. You look at their

35

well-known faces, breathe in their familiar scent, listen to the voice that you have heard since you can remember, and something inside you just unknots. For some of us, the person to do this was their mum. For me, it was my gran.

And that deep comfort and peace, the sense of safety, the childhood illusion that they'll always be with you . . . all that I had felt again since I had stepped into the house.

I felt Flora was still there.

And of course there was Peggy, my dear aunt who had been widowed a few years before, just after Flora's death. Peggy's daughters live in Canada and in the space of a few months, Peggy had lost both her husband and her sister and had been left to live alone. Strange, I had never before thought how lonely she must have felt — all this had happened while I was undergoing the first IVF treatments, and after a few years of trying and trying to get pregnant. I was so worn out that I could only see my own predicament, my own quest, and had no energy or time for anybody else.

I must have been so blind, blinded with the intensity of my desire, with the endless frustration of it never being satisfied.

I looked at the alarm clock on the bedside table, beside the untouched cup of tea and Tunnock's wafer that Peggy had left the night before. The biscuit made me smile — Flora was so fond of those wafers, she always put one in my lunchbox and produced them whenever she had visitors. Tunnock's wafers, custard creams and teacakes were her staples.

I blinked as I saw the time. And again. I couldn't believe it. Half-past nine.

I had slept twelve hours. Non-stop. Without Diazepam and all that anxiety and depression medication I had been prescribed and that wasn't helping me at all. I had put the lot into a plastic bag before I left, sealed it and dropped it in the bin, banging the lid for good measure, because what good was numbing the pain, numbing my brain, ignoring the storm instead of facing it?

My struggle's finished anyway. There's no hope left.

When you let go of hope, you have nothing.

And that's when there's a choice to be made.

You end it all.

Or you keep going, somehow. You try and try to fill the emptiness with something else and, through trial and error and sheer stubbornness, sooner or later you find the way out of darkness.

What I know now is that hope doesn't always spring eternal but there *is* life after hope.

★ ★ ★

That morning, I was going to face the emptiness and see what to do next. I wasn't scared. It couldn't possibly get any worse. No babies, no house, no husband, no job, hardly any money — the only way was up.

I got up to open the curtains and the view took my breath away. The grey, dramatic sky; the drifting clouds galloping like wild horses; the misty hills below, brown and orange and dark

37

green, soft and velvety and moist; the pinewoods, still and silent and solemn.

I opened the window and let the cold air embrace me, laden with that mixture of damp earth and leaves dissolving on the ground that is the scent of autumn.

To me, autumn smells of sleep. It was the perfect season because all I knew had gone and died, just like the leaves. It was a good time to be grieving, waiting for spring to bring life back.

I shivered and put on my dressing gown. The house was freezing. It does have central heating but it's terribly expensive. Most of the heating is provided by the stove in the kitchen and the fire in the living room.

I went downstairs and found that Peggy wasn't there. There was a tray on the table with a teapot, a cup, some bread, a butter dish, a jar of her home-made blackberry jam and a note: 'I'm at the shop. Help yourself to breakfast and get settled, then you can come up to the shop and we can have a chat.'

After a cup of tea and two slices of toast and jam, the drowsiness from the long sleep subsided. I had a quick, freezing shower, dried my hair and got dressed in jeans, a jumper and trainers.

Before I reached Peggy at the shop, I had something to do.

I picked up the phone, making a mental note of apologizing to Peggy for using it without her permission, and I dialled my parents' number. My mum answered immediately. I felt a pang of guilt thinking that Tom had probably told them of my disappearance the night before and that she must have been so worried.

'Eilidh! Where are you?'

'Hi Mum. In Glen Avich with Aunt Peggy. I'm fine. I left Tom.'

'I know, he told me. I asked him why and he didn't answer. I think I can imagine it, his silence sounded guilty. We are furious. My poor wee girl . . . ' Mum's Scottish accent and expressions always come back when she is upset or emotional and override the Southport one. 'Are you sure you are ok? Do you want us to come and get you? Or at least can we come and see you?'

'Please don't. I need some time by myself. Some time to think.'

A short silence followed.

'You won't do anything stupid?' she said in a small voice. Poor Mum, what I must be putting her through.

'Absolutely not. No way.' I meant it. I am not saying that for about three weeks after the miscarriage I hadn't thought that ending it all would have been preferable to all that pain, but then I had come to my senses. Probably my aforementioned stubbornness. I wasn't going to give up.

'Ok. Ok. Keep in touch . . . If you need anything . . . '

'Thank you.' My eyes welled up. 'Thank you.'

'Give Peggy a hug from me. Oh, Eilidh, we didn't sleep a wink here. I am so relieved you are home.'

Home. I smiled to myself. Scotland is not a

country you can ever tear out of your heart. My mum had spent the last thirty-five years in England, apart from the short while she had separated from my dad, but she still called Scotland home. I put the phone down and took a deep breath, drying my eyes.

I threw on my jacket and scarf and I stepped out of the house. I started walking to the shop that Flora and Peggy had minded since they were young women. It sells just about everything: food, newspapers, toys, bits and pieces of camping and hill-walking equipment, souvenirs for tourists. It even sells babies' clothes, knitted locally by the now eighty-years-old Boyle sisters.

The shop had suffered since more and more people could drive to the small supermarket in Kinnear, and especially since the big Tesco had opened on the outskirts of Aberdeen, forty-five minutes away. But it still did good business. It's not only a place to shop, it's a place to catch up on everybody's lives. Flora and Peggy loved a good blether and people knew that they could rely on them for a daily chat. But they didn't allow any nasty gossip, only good-natured conversation, and they especially took great pleasure in following the young ones' love lives. Having both been happily married, they loved matchmaking, and I know for sure that they had played a role in a few marriages in the small community of Glen Avich.

Neither of them thought that Tom was right for me. They were too delicate to say it to my face, but I knew. I suppose they were right.

I walked down the street and across the tiny

play park where I had so often played as a child. I turned onto the main street, past the chemist, past the church, past the tiny hairdresser's and up to the shop.

I stopped at the window. It looked lovely, clean and well kept. Peggy was nearly seventy now but she was still working very hard.

'Oh, hello Eilidh, did you sleep well?' Her face lit up when she saw me. She was neatly dressed, as ever, with a light blue shirt, a navy cardigan and a brown woollen skirt. Her dark grey hair was short and tidy, and her eyes a clear, light, startling blue, like Flora's, like mine.

'I did, thank you. Thank you for letting me stay. And for breakfast. I phoned my mum, I hope you don't mind.'

'Not at all. How is she?'

We were skirting around the edges. It was a formal dance before I'd have to give her an explanation of my turning up there alone and quite in a state.

'She's ok. She was worried for me. But she was happy to hear I'm here with you.'

'Did she not know, pet? Did she not know you were coming here?'

Pet. How I had missed being called that. I felt my eyes well up again. Oh no, here we go, the tears again. I'd had nothing but crying for the last three months.

'Oh, Eilidh, come on, come on dear, come through . . .'

She led me behind the counter and through the tiny storeroom into the room at the back, which they used as a kitchen. It was just like I

41

remembered, warm and cosy with the gas range, the table and chairs and the cooker in the corner. Here, Peggy and Flora would have their meals and endless cups of tea. They also used it as some sort of informal counselling centre, as anyone in need of a chat would be taken there for tea and sympathy. If those walls could talk . . .

'There, there. Let me put the kettle on. Have a good cry, you'll feel better.'

A lot of tears and a cup of tea later, I was ready to tell Peggy everything. Some things she knew already, my mum had told them bits and pieces through the years. She had certainly suspected there was something seriously wrong, as every time I'd been up, including the time of Flora's funeral, I'd been a little bit thinner and a little more miserable.

I told her about the baby I lost. And about Tom's girlfriend, or lover, whatever you want to call her. I told her that there was nothing left to keep me in Southport, that I needed a fresh start. She knew that the relationship with my parents and my sister was strained.

'Poor you, poor wee lassie. What a cross to bear. You can stay with me as long as you need, as long as you want.'

'Thank you. But I don't want to be a burden. I really want to pay rent. I mean, help you out. For the few weeks I'm here. I've got some savings . . . '

'Don't be silly, dear, I've got enough for both of us.'

'But Peggy, the extra bills and food. I can't let

you support me. I know it's only for a few weeks, but . . . '

'You are very thoughtful, Eilidh. You have always been. But honestly, it's fine.'

'As soon as I'm better I'll find a job, and . . . ' I sighed. 'It all seems so complicated.'

'Don't think about it now. You are exhausted and you can't think straight. Stay here as long as you like and have a good rest. You need to get back on your feet first.'

'I can help. In the shop, I mean. I can keep house for you and help you here.'

'Actually, I would be so grateful. You won't believe this, Eilidh, it's like a sign! A few days before you came, Mary Jamieson, remember Mary? She went off to New Zealand to see her sister. She was helping me in the shop, because you know, I'm just too old now, the deliveries and everything, it's too much for me. Did she not go and win a scratchcard, one of those lottery things we sell . . . and well, she hadn't seen her sister in years, and she was off like a shot! I couldn't find anyone else, had it been in the summer, but now . . . her nephew Paul is taking a year off to work before going to university in Glasgow, but he found something at the factory. And then you appeared.' She laughed. 'What a stroke of luck!'

'Of course I'll help. That's brilliant, thank you.'

What a coincidence. Someone was looking after me. I had a place to stay, for a while at least, and a temporary job. All I had to do was find the will to live again.

One thing is certain. What's ahead of me is a life without babies, which is heartbreaking, and most definitely a life without a man to hurt me and deceive me.

It's just me now. Nobody, nobody, is ever going to break my heart again.

5

A Family of Two

Jamie

So this is our life now. It's Maisie and me.

It's a balancing act. I work long hours but save time to be with her as much as I can. Every morning I take her to school, every night I go and collect her at Mary's, a cousin of mine who has no children and dotes on her. Maisie used to go to my mum's after school, but since she passed away, Mary has helped no end.

Maisie was only two when my mum died. Everybody rallied round, Shona stayed for a few weeks and I took three months off — I just couldn't bear to be parted from Maisie after all that happened — and we muddled through. In spite of the sadness of that time, I still smile when I remember the well-meaning women, coming to the house thinking they'd find chaos, and instead finding a clean, tidy place, Maisie nicely dressed and playing away and dinner in the oven. I felt I owed it to her, and to my mum, to keep everything ticking.

I didn't need their covered dishes or for them to do the housework but I certainly needed company. Those first few weeks it dawned on me — it was only Maisie and me left in the village, with Shona back in Aberdeen. It was so good, so consoling, to have people spending their evenings with me, sitting up to watch TV or chat in front of the fire. By the time they left, I was so tired after the day with Maisie — she used to wake up at five in the morning and have boundless energy all day long — that I'd just go straight to sleep.

That is how I survived the grief and loneliness until the sharp edge of the pain went away and I could see a new life, a life without my mum in it, but still a life.

Maisie started to spend her days at Mary's while I worked. When she turned three, that October, she started going to the local nursery for three hours a day, from half-past twelve to half-past three. Mary would normally take her in and collect her but sometimes I would walk up from the workshop so that I could take her myself. I loved walking with her wee hand in mine, her head bobbing up and down as she skipped happily, her long blonde hair in a ponytail, her pink waterproof jacket with flowers on it that her aunt had bought for her. I would peg her jacket up, put her sand shoes on and help her to sign her name. She would run up to her friends, without a care in the world, a joyful, lively child whom everybody loved. And when I could take time to collect her, she would run to me and hug my legs, and I would lift her up and look into her face and not see Janet, in spite of the resemblance, just see Maisie, my daughter, my family.

She's now in school, Glen Avich Primary. I

take her in the mornings and watch from the school gates as she runs in with her wee uniform on: a grey pinafore, navy cardigan, navy tights and black shoes with little pink flowers on the side. Shona and her daughters, who are ten, eight and six, took her shopping in Aberdeen before school started. I went with them but didn't do much really, just sat in changing rooms surrounded by shopping bags, looking vaguely around, the way men do when dragged to the shops. My nieces seem to be really in the loop when it comes to girls' fashion, thank goodness, because I wouldn't have a clue. We went to Marks and Spencer, Next, Debenhams and all those places that frankly make me lose the will to live but they seem to enjoy no end. Maisie got spoiled rotten. Dresses and tights and shirts, and the black ballerinas with the pink flowers, which she loves so much, she can't be parted from, and a pair of pink wellies. A navy duffel coat and a scarf, hat and mittens set, which I chose — all pink, that much I know. And a flurry of accessories — assorted hairpins and hair bands. She needs her hair away from her face in school or it'll fall all over her jotter, Kirsty explained, being a veteran of school herself — a big Primary Two. I treated everybody to lunch and Shona and I watched the girls giggling and chatting, like four sparrows.

When we parted at the train station, I couldn't say how grateful I was. I hugged my nieces tight and then Shona, and looked into her kind face. I wanted to say, 'Thank you,' but it didn't come out. Well, not in words — she could read it in my eyes.

I still get *that* look from the local mums — the one that Shona calls 'the *aaaaawww* look'. They seem to think it's incredibly endearing to see a single dad looking after his daughter. It's just my life, really. I don't particularly care if it's *cute*. All I want is for Maisie to be happy, loved and secure. Even if her mum left and then, unwillingly, her granny, I want her to feel that the world is a safe place, that the ground we walk on is steady and can't rumble and shake under our feet until we fall and can't get up again. She has plenty of time to find that out when she grows up.

For now, I want her to know that whatever happens, our home will always be safe and warm and lovely, that I will always tuck her in at night and wake her in the morning, that she'll always be loved and cherished. That she's the best thing that ever happened to me.

★　★　★

I hardly ever think of Janet but when I do, I realise that, in a weird way, I actually miss her. Strange, isn't it. She clearly didn't want to be with me, had she not got pregnant she probably wouldn't have even come back. When she was here, she was mostly miserable. And then she disappeared. Still, I miss her because she's the only woman I have ever loved.

A few months after she left, she phoned me. I felt my knees giving way, for fear she was

48

phoning to say she wanted Maisie. But no. She told me she didn't want to explain or justify herself. She said she couldn't be a mother, she wasn't the type. She just wanted to leave the details of a bank account where she'd make regular payments for Maisie. She said if I needed anything, I could draw from it.

It was hard — very, very hard — not to shout at her. I knew that if I started to shout, I wouldn't have stopped and horrible things would have come out, things that in a roundabout way might have ended up poisoning Maisie. So I stayed silent.

'Do you have a pen and paper?' she said.

'Janet, Maisie doesn't need your money. You know I do fine well.'

'I know. But I need to do something for her.'

'Are you saying that this would make *you* feel better?'

A pause.

'Yes.'

'Ok, then. Send me a letter with the details. I've got to go now.'

'Wait.'

'What?'

'How is she?'

'She's fine. Don't worry. I'm taking good care of her.'

'I know you would. I wouldn't have left otherwise. I know she's better off with you . . . '

'Janet, please. Let me go. I want to get off the phone and get on with my life.'

'OK, OK . . . Jamie . . . '

'What else Janet? What else is there to say?'

'I just wanted to ask about your mum. How is she?'

'She's fine.'

Another pause.

'Does she hate me?'

I could have lied. I could have said yes, she does, and so do I. I could have said that just to hurt her.

'No. She actually understands, believe it or not. The whole village thinks you are a monster but she doesn't.'

She was silent for a moment.

'Thank you. Thank you for looking after Maisie. For not hating me . . . '

I put the phone down.

★ ★ ★

There is someone. There has been for a few months now.

Her name is Gail. She's twenty-six, ten years younger than me. Apparently, she's had her sights set on me since she was a wee girl, or so Shona says.

We go for drinks sometimes, not often, as I like to be at home with Maisie in the evenings. We had Sunday lunch together at the pub a couple of times but I tend to avoid that. Her parents and wee brother were there too, and so was Maisie. It looked like . . . it looked as if we were an item, as if we were officially together, and I don't want that.

I know it sounds terrible, like I'm stringing her along, but I don't want to. It's just a friendship thing really. That's all I want. But I know she wants more.

After I walked her home from the pub one night, she put her arms around my neck and kissed me. I would lie if I said I didn't respond, if I said I didn't enjoy it. I'm only human.

So now whenever we walk home from the pub, we kiss. She hinted a couple of times that she would like to come up to the house. That she would stay the night. But I keep finding excuses. I am not ready; I can't possibly sleep with her. I can't sleep with her without making some sort of commitment and the truth is, I'm not in love with her. Which is better, because when you are in love with someone, they hold all the power, and I don't intend on that happening to me ever again.

So it would be perfect, really. I'm not in love, but I like her. She's kind to Maisie, she's funny, she's . . . uncomplicated. So different from Janet.

She really is lovely. It's not her, it's me. I know how it sounds but it's true. It *is* me. I don't want a relationship. I don't want anyone in my life. I don't want to let a twenty-six-year-old girl get involved with someone who doesn't love her because she deserves better than that. I tried over and over again to tell her but words are so difficult for me. I don't talk easily — I stumble, it doesn't come out right. Maybe I'll write her a letter.

I'm due to collect her from her work in Kinnear; we'll just go for a quick bite to eat before I drive her back. She'll probably come up to the house on Saturday afternoon to see what

51

we're doing and we'll take Maisie to the play park. On Sunday, Shona is coming down with Fraser and the girls, so we'll probably run into Gail and her family somewhere.

Oh God. I can see where this is going.

I can't do this. I don't see myself falling in love ever again. I don't want Gail to hope and be let down. I don't want her to spend the rest of her life with someone who doesn't love her, I mean properly love her, not like a sister or a friend — just because it's convenient, just because our families get on so well, just because it's perfect for everybody.

I can't wait until next week, I'll speak to her on Friday night, when I go and collect her from work. I can't possibly write her a letter; I have to tell her to her face.

But then a letter would be easier.

Oh, I don't know what to do.

I know what's going to happen. On Friday, she'll run to me and put her arms around my neck and she'll look so delighted to see me. We'll go for coffee before heading home, she'll take my hand under the table and look trustingly into my eyes. She'll take out a small parcel from her bag, a wee bracelet or a notebook or a fancy pencil, a treat she'll have picked up for Maisie.

And I won't have the heart to say anything.

Maybe it is better for everybody.

Maybe it is the right thing to do.

Maybe I can allow myself to feel a warm body beside mine, to fall asleep with my arms around someone, not alone and cold and, honestly, quite lost, like I've done for the last five years. In five years, there hasn't been anyone, not even a drunken one-night stand, nothing. I've been . . . frozen.

But would she take the loneliness away?

Gail was the first woman I kissed in all that time and it felt so different from Janet. Like I could part from her after that and be ok. Like I could easily turn my back and go home. Not like when you are in love and you just have to be with each other, and when you part it's like a limb has been cut off and all you want is to be with her again. I was kissing Gail and somehow, that sense of being lost, cold and lonely didn't really go away.

It's wrong and I know it but I know it's bound to happen if I don't stop it in its tracks.

I'll end up letting it happen. Next time when she says, 'I don't feel like going home, maybe we could stay up for a bit,' meaning she wants to come back to the house, I'll say no and the following time I'll say no again, finding excuse after excuse . . . until one night, I'll give in and I'll hold her hand and lead her through my door, upstairs, and we'll be very quiet, not to wake Maisie. And the next morning, it will be a new world, a world where it's Gail and Jamie like everybody hoped and I'll never, never tell her I'm not in love with her, and I'll never leave her because this is who I am, this is the way I've been brought up. Old fashioned, I know, even Janet said it was as if I came from another time, another generation, but this is me.

I stop it now or I stop it never. And something tells me I'm just too lonely to stop it now.

6

Lives Past

Elizabeth

The scratchcard was a stroke of genius, if I may say so myself. I found a way for Eilidh to stay and at the same time I did a good deed because Mary hadn't seen her sister in a long time.

It takes a lot of energy for me to do these sort of things, to intervene in the life of the living. I've been floating around for a while after that, too drained to do anything else.

When I came round, I saw Jamie and Gail.

Gail, whom we used to babysit when her mum worked nights at the nursing home in Kinnear. Her dad is a lorry driver, so whenever they were both out at night Gail used to come and stay at our house. I could see it, that she had a crush on Jamie. But she was just a child, still in primary school when Jamie started college in Aberdeen. I didn't think anything of it and then Jamie moved to Glasgow for his Masters, only coming home for the holidays, and not paying much attention to her. She used to giggle a lot. Not say much, just giggle.

Gail is clearly smitten with him, I can see it. But Jamie still seems far away. When he's with her, it's like he could easily be somewhere else and it wouldn't be any different for him.

The problem for Jamie is not the lack of women who are interested, it's the fact that since Janet left, he doesn't seem to be able to reach anyone. Apart from Maisie and Shona, he's all wrapped up in himself and Maisie and doesn't let anyone in.

Including Gail.

She's so crazy about him that she can't see it. She doesn't seem to see the faraway look in his eyes, the way he seems distracted, the way he keeps finding excuses not to meet more often. Jamie is letting himself be carried by her into this relationship and I don't know what to think. Part of me hopes he'll finish with her and part of me hopes that he'll fall for her and settle down with a nice girl, from a nice family, who clearly adores him. What mother wouldn't want that?

But deep down, I know he won't. Jamie's very quiet but behind that there's a strong mind, and a complicated one. A girl like Gail will not satisfy that side of him in the long run. I've always known, since he was a teenager, that he could only fall for someone a little bit unusual.

Eilidh was different from everyone else. She was a reflective, thoughtful little girl. She had a peaceful, self-contained, confident quality and was mostly quiet. And then, all of a sudden, she would be taken over by emotion and her passionate nature would spill out for everyone to see. She felt things deeply — a song, a beautiful sight would move her to tears. I suppose you could say about her that still waters run deep — like her mother used to say about her, yet somehow critically. Eilidh made me think of someone who lived before, as if her emotions came from somewhere well beyond her years. Once she did a reading in the community centre, at a charity do organised by her school. It was a beautiful poem by Sorley MacLean, 'Hallaig'. You could see the emotion running through her body, the intensity of her feeling. The hall fell very quiet and still, I felt tears well up, and as I looked around I noticed that quite a few people had shiny eyes.

Nothing in Eilidh's nature seemed to be grey or lukewarm — she was either black or white, scalding or icy. I could see why she adored Flora: they both had a reserved exterior and a passionate, warm nature, and shared a love of books, music and nature. All this seemed to have skipped a generation: Rhona, Eilidh's mum, is completely different. She's somehow lacking in warmth, especially physical warmth. I know that Rhona loves Eilidh, in her own way, but I could see how hard it was for them to understand each other. Eilidh was so hurt by her mum's coldness. Katrina was loud, lively, chatty and loved to be the centre of attention. She always made a point of reminding everybody that she was prettier, more likeable and all-round cleverer than her sister. She and her mum were as thick as thieves and Katrina couldn't put a foot wrong in her eyes. Don't get me wrong, she's not nasty or anything — she's just wearisome and the way she'd constantly put Eilidh down irritated me to no end.

With Eilidh, there was so much bubbling

56

under the surface. There was something about her, something vulnerable, yet strong . . . if you saw it then you could never look away.

It wasn't long after she moved to Glen Avich that her and Jamie became friends. Jamie started looking for her after school; they'd do their homework together in my house or go to Flora's shop to sit in the back room with a bag of sweets that Flora would invariably treat them with. At that age, it's not easy for a boy and a girl to be friends: when they are younger, nobody gives a second thought about it, but at eleven, it all appears under a new light.

For Eilidh and Jamie it didn't get to that stage, because very soon after the beginning of their friendship, to everybody's dismay, Eilidh left. Jamie had made her a wee keepsake in his father's workshop, a necklace with a pendant shaped like a deer, Eilidh's favourite animal. It was beautiful. Jamie was — he *is* — incredibly talented. He never gave it to her, though. I asked him why, but he just shrugged his shoulders. I never saw the necklace again.

Jamie had a few girlfriends on and off while at university but since he came home and took over his father's business, there wasn't anyone for a long time. He had a lot of friends and they would happily live as bachelors. Then one by one, his friends settled down and started to have children, and Jamie didn't seem interested in anyone, though quite a few girls were interested in him.

When Janet came on the scene, I wasn't surprised — she had something about her that was strong, uncommon and . . . poetic. What I couldn't see then was that as much as Janet seemed perfect for Jamie, Jamie wasn't perfect for her. For her, it turned out to be little more than a holiday romance with life-changing consequences.

Which is why I'm suspending my judgement now. Maybe Gail seems like a safe harbour now, after the storm of Janet.

Then why does he still look so lonely?

Now that Eilidh is back, anything could happen. Especially with a little help from me.

She looks so withdrawn right now, like she doesn't want to let anyone in. She is so thin and frail, her eyes are haunted. When I saw her standing in front of Peggy's house, trembling with nerves as she waited for Peggy to open the door, I so wished I could have put my arms around her, like a long lost daughter. Hold her in my arms like the wee girl she used to be.

I can't believe her life turned out the way it did, after so much promise. I know that she never got on with her mum and her sister, and didn't have much of a relationship with her father, but she seemed so happy when she first got together with Tom. She brought him up to meet Flora and Peggy — handsome man, smartly dressed, and a *doctor*. Everybody was impressed, except the very people he was there to meet, Eilidh's gran and aunt. They weren't convinced. They didn't say but we've known each other since we were all in our prams, so I could see it. I'm not sure why. It turns out they were right, it didn't work out at all.

Throughout her marriage, Eilidh didn't come up to Scotland for a long time and when she did, it was hurried and somehow fraught. Rhona and Simon, on their own or with Katrina and her family, come up more often. I thought it was strange because Eilidh had been so happy here, so settled, I didn't understand why she wanted to stay away. I know now. She was simply too unhappy to come up and let everyone see her like that. Flora and Peggy would tell me once in a while about her failed IVF and her deep sadness but not the full extent of it. My heart went out to her.

But I had never seen her like this. She's still very pretty, with that lovely, silky chestnut hair and clear blue eyes, but so worn and with that lost look in her eyes, as if she were a ghost, like me. The miscarriage was the last straw for her.

I know it sounds naive, but I think that for a start, more than anything, Eilidh needs good meals and lots of sleep. After a few weeks of Peggy's cooking and peaceful, silent nights with no traffic or lights from the city through the window, she'll get stronger. She'll put a bit of weight back on and start to smile again, that smile that used to light up a room. I know she will recover. I have faith in her.

Time for Eilidh and Jamie to meet again.

7

A Memory of Me

Eilidh

I'd been in Glen Avich for just over a month. October was nearly gone. I would have been about five months pregnant. But I tried not to think of that.

At the beginning, everything was like an echo of things from the past. Everywhere I went I was met by the ghost of the wee girl I used to be. I could see myself, my hair in braids, my grey and navy school uniform on, sitting on the swings at the play park, walking down the high street, doing homework in the back room at the shop.

I still *was* that wee girl — minus a lot of dreams, plus a lot of experience and an empty heart. Thirty-five years old, nothing to call mine, and all to play for.

Since I'd come back, I'd met countless relatives, young and old. In a village like Glen Avich, everybody is somehow related and when you walk down the street, or into the pub, they ask each other in a whisper: 'Who's her people?' and they dissect your ancestry, your parents, your grandparents, and where they're from. If any of them come from anywhere else, even a nearby village, that gets specified, as it means

60

you are not *really* from Glen Avich, not completely, anyway. I knew that for the first few weeks, everywhere I went, my ancestry would be recited in a low voice, like a passage from the Bible or some ancient saga: 'Eilidh, daughter of Rhona, daughter of Flora McCrimmon.' I know this would annoy a lot of people, that they'd feel like they were living in a fish bowl. But I enjoy it, like I did back then, when I first arrived with my mum and my sister, because it makes me feel like I belong.

To see the people I used to know again had been lovely and painful, all at the same time. The painful bit was having come back with nothing and admitting that my life hadn't amounted to much, or that's how it felt.

Every single conversation came, sooner or later, to the dreaded question: 'So, how many children do you have?' Then, accompanied by the usual feeling of being stabbed in the heart, came my rehearsed answer, trying to keep my voice steady: 'They never came.'

To which they'd say, awkwardly: 'There's still time,' or, 'There's more to life than children,' or, 'Your time will come.'

Next question. 'And how is Tom doing?'

Oh dear. More embarrassment, them trying to find something supportive to say: 'All marriages have their ups and downs,' 'It'll sort itself out,' 'You're still young,' and the best one: 'Who needs men anyway?'

And to round it all up, 'How's your job going?' That was the nail in the coffin.

'Oh. Oh well. I suppose you are back here

now, that's all that matters.'

By then, we both needed a cup of tea.

I actually felt quite sorry for them. It must have been really hard to hear of all the devastation, to see the pain etched in my face, find out the reason and still try to keep the conversation going. It wasn't long before the whole village knew about my quest for babies, of my one and only chance to have one, how it had been lost and I had ended up in hospital with a breakdown.

Sooner or later, all the girls I used to be closest to when we were children came to the shop, some for errands, some because they genuinely wanted to see me, some for a bit of juicy gossip they could spread on. Alannah came with her boys, two tall lads of thirteen and eleven. She'd married young and stayed at home to look after the boys. Sharon and her twin sister Karen, both of them hairdressers in the small local salon, one boy each, came together and finished all each other's sentences. Mary, a solicitor in Kinnear, mother of two girls, came on her way to work, power-dressed, hair perfectly blow-dried. She'd married the most unpopular boy in the school, Michael, known for bullying the younger ones and looking down on just about everybody. As she mentioned him, I could guess that their marriage was less than happy. Sylvia, a teacher in Glen Avich Primary, came with her wee girl Pamela, who has Down's syndrome.

And Helena, sweet, softly spoken Helena, my childhood best friend. In school, we always sat together. She was one of the bridesmaids at my wedding. She came in a hurry to stock up for a long car journey. They were driving down to London to see her husband's family.

'Eilidh! It's so good to see you!' she exclaimed, a big smile on her face, her eyes sparkling.

'Helena! You look lovely,' I said honestly. She did look great — happy and as pretty as always, with her wavy dark-blonde hair and her dark eyes.

'Come here.' She gave me a big hug and I could feel by the way she held me that she was aware of all that happened, that she felt for me.

'Is this Calum? And Euan? I can't believe it! Last time I saw you, you were toddlers!'

'I know. Time flies, doesn't it? We need to run now, we'll be away for a couple of weeks, but when we come back we'll catch up properly. I met Margaret at the hairdresser's — she filled me in. I'm so sorry for your loss.'

I nodded.

'And how's your mum and dad?' she said quickly. 'And Katrina?'

'They are fine, they are all fine. And your parents, and Gail?'

'Same here, all fine. By the way, you won't believe who Gail's seeing now.'

'Who?'

'Jamie. Jamie McAnena — remember him?'

Jamie. I remembered Jamie very well. We'd been close friends for a while, just before I left. I suppose I used to have a crush on him, when we were children. In the past few years, every time I'd come up he seemed to be away to study or otherwise engaged and we kept missing each other.

'Yes, of course, Jamie. He's going out with Gail? Goodness, how old is she now? In my mind, she's still a wee girl!'

'She's twenty-six. Can you believe it? Anyway, how long are you staying?'

'I'm not sure. A few weeks I suppose. Until I get back on my feet.'

'Is there no way back for you and Tom?' she said in a low voice.

I shook my head and looked away.

'I'm sorry. How awful. You've always been strong, Eilidh, you were by far the most determined of us all — so self-sufficient and independent. You'll get through this.'

I looked at her, surprised. Strong? Me? Self-sufficient and independent? Is that who I used to be? I can't remember the last time I ever felt strong. Of all the memories of myself I've had since I've been back, the one of strength was the most remote.

Helena went away with the promise to drop by as soon as she was back.

The same day, on my way home after Peggy had come to relieve me, I saw him.

Jamie McAnena.

I froze. At last, I thought — and then wondered where this thought had come from, as if since I'd arrived, I'd been waiting to spot him, hoping to bump into him.

He was standing in the play park, beside a climbing frame. Sitting on top of the climbing frame was a girl of about five, wearing a pink coat and a pink scarf, her flaxen hair blowing about in the breeze. She was pretending to be riding a horse, or so it seemed, because she was sitting upright, her hands holding imaginary reins, her feet kicking the sides gently. Her cheeks were red and she was smiling. She was so pretty, so endearing, that I couldn't help but look at her for a minute or two. Who could she be?

Then it dawned on me. One of Shona's daughters. Shona was blonde too. She had three, as far as I could remember. I didn't know Shona well, she is a few years older than me, but I remember their mum, Elizabeth. She was very close to my gran and always so kind to me.

Jamie spotted me. He raised a hand and waved. I waved back, wondering if he'd recognized me, if I should go and say hello.

I stood there frozen, not really knowing what to do and not knowing why I felt so awkward.

He started walking towards me, a smile on his face, so I crossed the road and walked through the wee gate into the play park.

'Eilidh!'

'Jamie! How are you?' We stood in front of each other, not sure of what to do. A hug? Not the Highland way. A kiss? Not in a million years. Shake hands? Continental but acceptable. We did that, awkwardly, laughing.

'How are you? How long have you been in Glen Avich?'

'About three weeks now. I moved back. From England I mean.'

'And how's Tom?'

Oh, here we go.

'Jamie — to save both of us time and embarrassment — Tom and I separated.'

'I'm sorry, Eilidh. I'm so sorry to hear that. My mum told me that you were having trouble . . . that you couldn't . . . ' he stumbled, 'you know . . . '

'Have children. Yes.'

'I'm sorry. I didn't mean to . . . '

I shook my head, 'It's ok. Really. I've had all this since I came back. Sooner or later everybody will move on, the commiseration will stop and I'll be just Eilidh again.'

Jamie smiled.

His black hair, his blue-grey eyes, his fair skin . . . Apart from a copper-coloured five o'clock shadow, he looked just like the boy I used to know.

The wee blonde girl had climbed down and was now on the swings, her lovely long hair floating behind her.

'And how's your mum? I haven't seen her yet, Peggy hasn't mentioned her either.'

The smile faded from his face.

I blushed. I knew what his expression meant.

'Oh, Jamie . . . ' I started.

'She died three years ago.'

'I'm so sorry. Oh, I'm so, so sorry.' I felt my eyes well up. Elizabeth, gone.

A sudden memory came into my head. A vision of the past . . .

I was sitting at the McAnenas' kitchen table. Jamie and I were doing our homework and Elizabeth had just made us toast and jam. She

66

stood behind us to check our maths assignment and put her arm around my shoulders, and I, not used to a mother doing this kind of thing, had soaked up the affection like a flower soaks up water.

Elizabeth.

I blinked, once, twice, to dry up the tears.

'All we've been saying since we met is 'I'm sorry'!' smiled Jamie. 'There, this will cheer you up. Come and meet Maisie.'

'Oh, sure, which one is she? She must be the third, I think the eldest is about twelve now, isn't she?'

Jamie looked confused.

'What? The third . . . oh, I see what you mean! No, Maisie's not one of Shona's daughters. She's mine.'

'Oh . . . ' I was going to ask about Maisie's mum but the girl had run to us and was holding Jamie's hand. She looked at me with a smile.

'Hello,' she said. Now that I saw her face properly, I could see her blue-grey eyes, exactly like Jamie's.

'Hello, Maisie. I'm Eilidh.' I bent down and held out my hand. 'Nice to meet you.'

'I was riding on Rainbow,' she said, in her wee silvery voice.

'You were riding on the rainbow? How lovely,' I said.

'Nooo silly! Not on the rainbow! On Rainbow!'

I looked at Jamie, baffled.

'Rainbow, her imaginary pony,' explained Jamie.

'Oh, I see. You were riding your pony. Maybe one day we can go on a real one, you and me. I love horse riding. I used to do it all the time when I was your age.'

Maisie's face lit up. 'Really? We can?'

'If your dad's OK with it, I can take you up to the Ramsay estate.'

'Can I, Dad? Please please PLEASE!' She started jumping up and down.

'Are you sure it's not too much trouble, Eilidh?'

'Not at all. I'm only working in the mornings right now, at Peggy's shop. I also keep house for her, help her with the housework, the garden and all that, but I have a lot of time off. Too much, probably,' I added, looking down. It was my way of telling him I would have loved to spend some time with that joyful, lively girl doing something we both enjoyed. I thought that maybe it would have helped me bleed a little less, breathe a little more.

'Well, if it's not a bother, ok.'

'Next week? Tuesday would be great. On Monday we get the deliveries in.'

'Perfect. You can collect her from school if you like. I'll let Mary know. She's Maisie's childminder,' he added, by way of explanation.

I wondered briefly why Maisie's mum hadn't been mentioned, but not wanting to pry, simply said, 'Will do. It'll be nice to see our old school again. We'll be a couple of hours but if you're not home yet, I can take her to Peggy's house for dinner.'

'Thanks but I think I'll be home. I'll make it

an early day. My house is up past the school, up St Colman's Way, near my dad's workshop. Well, my workshop. The white cottage with the blue doors. You'll see the sign on the garden stone wall, it says 'McAnena'. Very imaginative, I know.'

I laughed. 'A flight of fancy! Great. I'll see you then.'

Maisie was beaming.

'Say thank you to Eilidh.'

'Thank you!' she said, with another few jumps. I was beginning to think she couldn't speak without jumping or skipping, as if she was on springs. Sheer life force, flowing through her like lymph through a plant.

'See you next week then,' said Jamie, holding Maisie's hand.

'See you. Bye, Maisie.'

As I was walking home, I thought of her and the way her face lit up when I mentioned horse riding. I felt a strange, unfamiliar warmth fill my belly, a tenderness I didn't know anymore. It was the nearest thing to joy I had felt for a long time.

Again, I wondered where Maisie's mum was, if she was living in the village, how often she saw her daughter. I thought she was so lucky, so lucky, and somehow, I was absolutely sure that she didn't know she was. I don't know why.

The last time I'd seen Jamie, I told him I was going. We were both eleven and had just finished primary school. The summer was starting and we thought we had six long weeks ahead of us to play, chat and roam the fields around Glen Avich.

Then, unexpectedly, it was all turned upside down and I was going back to Southport, leaving Flora and Peggy, and my friends, and everything I knew. I had spent six years in Glen Avich and loved it. It was my home.

My parents were getting back together. My dad had come up to Scotland every single holiday — every Christmas, every summer — to spend time with us. Every single time he and my mum had fought like cat and dog. But he came anyway and she'd let him stay. My dad is not a bad person, he never mistreated my mum, let alone us — it's just that they don't get on, that's all. They still don't, after forty years of marriage and a six-year-long separation.

I was distraught, unlike Katrina, who had never taken to Glen Avich and was dying to go back to the city.

When I told Jamie, he didn't say anything. He said he had to go, he was meeting his friend John, they were going fishing. He avoided me for the next two weeks. The day before we were due to leave, I saw him standing across the road with his hands in his pockets. I wanted to go to him but my mum needed help with the packing. I waved from the window and he waved back.

That was the last I had seen of him, before today. I wondered what memory of me he has had all this time, if any.

My memory of Jamie was that he was talented, quiet, stubborn, kind and single-minded in everything he did. That was the wee boy I knew, that is my memory of him.

70

8

A Basket of Apples

Jamie

I'm finding it hard to concentrate on my work today. It just doesn't seem to be flowing like it normally does.

Work usually takes care of itself — I go to the workshop, put on the gear and away I go, job after job, until I'm finished. End of. Sometimes I give myself time to sit with a sandwich, outside on the bench if it's good weather, inside at the small table in the corner, looking out of the window, if it's raining. The view from the workshop is amazing, which is something that always delighted my father. He loved his work for the same reasons I do: we use our hands, we don't sit all day and we don't need to speak to anyone. I know, it makes me sound like a real misery guts, which I'm not. I love having people around, I just couldn't chat all day.

I come from a long line of quiet men. My father and my grandfather were both blacksmiths and both legendarily silent, even by Scottish standards. My mum used to always tell me how restful she found this quality of his, the way they would sit in peaceful silence, and how every time my father spoke, the whole family would listen

71

because we all knew he had something important to say. They both smiled when, one year at school, my teacher wrote in the final report: 'Jamie doesn't speak much but when he does, he always says something worthwhile.' I've inherited their love of silence and also their gift: my great-grandfather was a stable lad and a horse whisperer. His voice could calm and soothe the horses, when he spoke softly in their ears. I seem to be able to do the same but with people.

I'm deeply, deeply rooted in this place. Nobody was surprised when, after doing my Masters, I came back to live in Glen Avich. Well, nobody who knew me. I'd been offered a scholarship to do my PhD in London. I was all set to go, as if I couldn't help just walking on the path I seemed to have taken by accident — I hadn't expected to do so well — when it occurred to me that I desperately, desperately didn't want to go to London.

I was on holiday at home in between terms and I just walked over to my father's workshop and told him I wasn't going, that I wanted to stay in Glen Avich. That I wanted to help him in his job and eventually take over.

He said, 'Oh aye? Great.'

That was it. But I knew he was delighted.

My mum tried to talk me into finding some kind of academic post in Aberdeen or Edinburgh, or at least teaching. But I had decided I wanted to do what my father did, that every time I raised my head from what I was making, I wanted to see the pinewoods and the hills silhouetted against the sky, the clouds' shadows moving across the heather.

It turned out I had a talent. I'd always enjoyed it but when it became my full-time job I realised that I was quite good at it, that things took shape easily in my hands and they were beautiful. When my father got ill and couldn't work anymore, I took over completely and by word of mouth I became quite a hit with the tourists and hillwalkers coming up in the summer. I make ornaments, small objects and jewellery, all inspired by Scottish history and landscape, and they seem to be quite popular. Before I knew it, I was doing exhibitions in Edinburgh and down south, and orders were coming in from as far as America. From 'local blacksmith' I became 'a promising young artist', quoting from the *Guardian*, no less.

I bought my lovely home on the hill, up the winding road that leads to St Colman's Well, hoping to fill it with a family one day.

My work thrived but the right person didn't come along. All my childhood friends seemed to settle down, marry and have children, some happily, some less happily. I didn't. I had had a few girlfriends when I was a student, nothing serious, but by that time I was ready to settle down. I wanted to find the love of my life.

There just didn't seem to be the right woman around. Suitable ones, yes — ones that should have been perfect, the perfect choice for both our families. But I always found myself wanting more. I wanted to fall in love, and truly, truly feel that the person you love is the one who's meant

73

for you. I believed you fall in love once and that's it — that there's only one person out there, one person that we can call 'soulmate', that when you meet her, you just can't be away from her ever again.

Then Janet came. Then Janet went away.

And now I ask myself, do we really only fall in love once? Because I did, and now that she's gone, I wonder if I'll be alone forever. I hope I'm wrong, that you can love more than once, that there is more than one person out there for us.

And now there's Gail.

I truly don't know what to do. Last night, after we came back from the play park, she came in for a while. We were having dinner and I pulled up a chair for her. It was . . . nice.

Yes, it was really nice. She chatted with Maisie and we all watched *Charlie and Lola* together, then the time came to put Maisie to bed and she said she'd wait for me downstairs, make me a cup of tea.

I said I had some paperwork to do, some orders had come in and I had to look them over. Which was nearly true but not quite. She looked hurt, disappointed. I felt so guilty.

I am going to speak to her on Friday night, no more delay. I can't have Sunday lunch with her family and Shona. By Sunday, I want it to be sorted.

I met Eilidh Lawson at the play park the other day. I can't believe she's back. I never thought she would return. Probably she's just here temporarily, until she gets things sorted in her life, and then she'll go back south.

Funny, when I saw her, this memory came into my head: opening the door of my family home and her standing there with a basket of red apples for my mum. Flora had sent her to bring apples in exchange for eggs. I remember her wavy hair falling around her face like a halo and those startling blue eyes. I had gone to school with her for years but it was like I'd seen her for the first time. When she told me she was moving down south with her family, I was gutted. I went fishing every day for two weeks so I could be on my own and not talk to anyone.

She hasn't changed much, the same brown hair, now down to her shoulders, the same beautiful eyes. But she's so thin and she looks like she's been crying a lot. I know she lost a baby and that she'd been in hospital. My mum told me years ago that she was having a hard time, that she was struggling to have children and that her marriage wasn't so good. It seems impossible, that Eilidh couldn't have children, because I can't remember her wanting anything else. It even came up in school once. We were asked to write a short piece on 'What I want to be when I grow up'. She wrote that she wanted to have three children and to work in a nursery. I wrote that I wanted to be a fisherman — John and I were going through a stage where we went fishing all the time.

Maisie took to her immediately — she kept talking about Eilidh on the way home and how Eilidh would take her riding. Eilidh and her sister used to go riding a lot, up at the Ramsay estate, because the owners are cousins of theirs.

75

Anyway, can't think about all that now. I have to decide what to say to Gail.

But Eilidh was a natural with Maisie, anybody could see that she's been working with nursery children. I hope I haven't embarrassed her by asking too many questions, I hope I haven't put her on the spot. I wonder if she and Peggy will go to the pub for lunch on Sunday. I'll probably see them there. Eilidh will want to catch up a bit and Shona will be there, so she can see her as well.

To go back to Gail, I must talk to her in person. A letter just won't do. Oh, look, it started raining. I hope Eilidh is not out on her bike. She used to love cycling, we'd been everywhere on our bikes when she lived here.

I just burnt my hand.

★   ★   ★

Gail is sick with the flu. She didn't go to work. I can hardly go round to her house and speak to her now. It'll have to wait until Sunday, if she's well enough.

★   ★   ★

'Jamie!' Shona shouted from across the road, waving her hand. She was getting out of the car with Fraser and the girls. We walked up to the church, Alison, her eldest, holding Maisie's hand, all four of them looking so pretty in their Sunday clothes.

Shona slipped her arm under mine.

'How's things?'

'Aye, aye, ok.'

' . . . Yes?'

I laughed. 'What do you want to know?'

'You know fine well . . . ' she said with a smile.

'I am going to finish with her.'

'Good.'

'Good? I thought you liked her!'

'I do, very much. She's lovely, and Helena is a good friend of mine, and her mum and dad were good friends with our mum and dad, and blah blah blah. I can see the way you look at her.'

'How do I look at her?'

'Like you look at me.'

Unbelievable. Shona is so perceptive and she knows me like the back of her hand.

'Hi!' I felt a hand on my shoulder. Gail. She stood on her toes to kiss me on the cheek, elegant in a white trouser suit and full make-up on. I could smell her perfume — she always wore a lot of it.

'Hi Shona, and where are the girls? Here they are, hello! Hi Maisie!' she chirped, as bubbly as ever.

Shona and I looked at each other. I felt positively sick. I hate, absolutely hate, making people upset. No, really. It's just awful.

We sat beside each other in church. I had a nice chat with her mum and dad, her mum touching my arm affectionately. I could feel my resolve dissolving.

After the service, we all walked to the pub for lunch and sat on the red couches beside the fire. Myself and Gail, Gail's mum and dad, Shona and Fraser and the four wee girls. I went up to get drinks for everybody.

As I was standing at the counter, I could smell something lovely, something fresh and sweet. I turned and she was behind me.

She smelled of clean, she smelled of shampoo and of apples. Well, maybe the apple bit was just my imagination. She smelled of Eilidh.

'Hello.' My heart was in my throat and I was mad at myself for it.

'Hi Jamie. Is Shona here? Oh, Shona! It's been so long!' She went over to hug my sister. 'And look at your girls, all grown up! Gail, hello, I saw your sister the other day, it's great to see you again.' A flutter of greetings followed. Eilidh looked so fresh and simple, in her jeans and a black top that showed her shoulders, her hair shiny, her skin not quite as white as the girls up here but not dark — sort of buttery, somehow. Creamy.

I noticed that Gail wasn't smiling much. I thought that maybe she still wasn't feeling well.

'Are you sitting with us?'

'Thanks, that would be great, but I can't, Peggy and Margaret will be here any minute.'

'Come here beside me till they arrive then,' said Shona, patting the seat beside her. They sat and started chatting while I brought the drinks over two by two.

'I'll phone you during the week,' said Shona. 'We'll arrange something. Maybe you can come up to Aberdeen, I'll take you out for lunch.'

'Oh, Shona, I'm not great company these days,' she whispered, a shadow darkening her face. The haunted look again. My heart went out to her.

'Oh well, I'm never good company at all, ask Fraser!' They laughed. 'Seriously. It'd be lovely.'

'Ok. Ok, thank you.'

She hugged Shona, said goodbye to us and disappeared into the next room to find a seat and wait for Peggy and Margaret. I watched her walking away, following her lithe figure with my eyes, unable to look away.

When I looked around again, I saw that Gail was looking at me, Shona was looking at us both and Fraser was looking into his pint, typical bloke. The girls were debating who's the prettiest fairy in *Tinkerbell: the Secret of Pixie Hollow*, a film that I've seen so many times I could recite it back to you. I sat down, my cheeks bright red, and took a long, comforting sip from my pint.

After lunch, we all went back to my family house, where my mum and dad used to live and where Shona stays when she comes down. I had been there that morning, to light the fire and switch the heating on. We spent the afternoon chatting while the girls played, until it was time for Shona and her family to drive back to Aberdeen.

'Take care. Let me know how it goes,' she whispered in my ear as she hugged me. I watched her drive away, the girls waving from the back seat.

'Can you come up to the house? I need to talk to you,' I said to Gail while locking the door.

Her eyes lit up. Oh God.

We spent a painful hour chatting and drinking

79

tea. I couldn't speak to her when Maisie was around, of course.

Finally, five o'clock came crawling and it was time for dinner, bath and bed. Gail insisted on helping while I bathed Maisie and sat on her bed while I read her a bedtime story. When Maisie was finally tucked in, we went back downstairs.

'Why don't I cook something nice?'

'Gail, we need to talk.'

Her face fell. She could see from my expression that something was wrong.

'What? What's wrong?'

'I'm sorry, I really really am, but this is just not . . . right. I can't have a relationship right now. I just can't . . . '

Her eyes welled up and she started crying. Oh no, oh no, oh no.

'Gail, I'm so sorry, I don't want to hurt you — '

'As if I didn't know! As if I didn't notice!' she said angrily, jumping up from the sofa.

'What?'

'Helena told me to watch out for her. I knew it!'

Eilidh. Shit. I didn't want her involved.

'What are you talking about?'

'You know very well! She sat across from us in the pub! On purpose! And you kept looking at her . . . She keeps going to the workshop to see you, Helena saw her walking up the hill!'

What?

'Gail, who are you talking about?'

'As if you didn't know! That German girl, that

80

flaky one with the pottery business. Silke. I saw the way you were looking at each other!'

Oh God almighty.

'Gail, Silke comes up to the workshop because we have business together. I don't fancy her. I don't fancy anyone and I don't want anyone, for me or for Maisie. Please, Gail, try to understand — '

'Rubbish. Maisie and I get on like a house on fire. There must be someone else.'

'There is no one else. But you are right, it's not just because of Maisie. It's true that I don't want a relationship. But it's also true that I'm not in love with you.'

More howling and sobbing. My stomach was in a knot. I felt so bad, I just wanted her to stop crying.

'Come here . . . there, there . . . '

'Don't touch me!'

'Gail, please, calm down. It's OK . . . it's ok . . . ' I stroked her hair.

She relaxed in my arms and I held her, like a little girl. For a second, a split second, I felt it would have been so much easier to keep holding her and to kiss her, and maybe that awful freezing cold I had felt in my bones for years would go away.

But I had to do it.

'Gail, you need to go home. I'm sorry. You'll be fine, believe me.'

She looked at me, a long, sad look. She wasn't angry anymore.

'It might not be the proud thing to say but I'm in love with you,' she said and the young girl

81

suddenly looked like a woman, a woman who knows her mind.

'I'm sorry.'

Without another word, she left. I sat in my armchair by the fire, a glass of whisky in my hand — then another one, and another one, something that's happening more and more often. I thought of a poem I read once that called whisky 'the smiler with a knife'.

I can't stop drinking alone at night, I don't know where else to turn.

I can't stop drinking.

I sat until late and looked at the flames.

9

Listen To My Heart

Elizabeth

I listen carefully to what Jamie says when he doesn't speak. I hear his words unsaid, I hear his heart calling, calling.

I know that if things don't change, if he doesn't take a turn in this path he chose, or maybe he was thrown on, something horrible will happen to him.

I watch him from the flames, I watch him from the darkness outside his window, as the glass gets refilled, over and over and over again.

Maisie is asleep upstairs, peaceful and serene. I touch her unwritten forehead, I sit on her bed, I watch over her while Jamie sits downstairs and drinks until the bottle is empty.

They couldn't see me today, sitting among them at the pub. The way he looked at Eilidh, the way his face lit up when he saw her. I feel so sorry for Gail, that poor girl, she has a bad crush on him or maybe it's love, I don't know. I could see her glaring at Silke, how wrong she was!

There are so many secrets in a village like Glen Avich and, being a ghost, I can unravel a lot of them. Silke has been seeing Fiona, Jamie's cousin from Innerleithen, but she's not telling anyone. Silke doesn't care what people think but Fiona is terrified about revealing that she's in love with another woman.

Strange how people seem to want to decide what's wrong and what's right for everybody else. Why would love be a sin, when it doesn't hurt anyone? I don't know. Now that I'm dead, I look back and realise how brief life is . . . It makes no sense to live a lie because when we die, and it always happens sooner than we think, our one and only chance to love is gone.

Silke is definitively not the one Gail needs to worry about. Well, she doesn't need to worry at all now because Jamie did the right thing. I'm relieved because it would have been so sad for her to spend the rest of her life with someone who is not in love with her, though she can't see that now. And I would have hated to see Jamie keep living in quiet despair, like he's been doing for the past few years. They both deserve better.

The more I look at them, the more I listen to their hearts, the more I think that Eilidh and Jamie could save each other. But I know they need help to find each other. They're both too hurt, too withdrawn to take the chance and jump into the unknown.

There are many, many ways I can help them.

When I saw Eilidh looking to the play park, I became a wisp of wind and whispered into Maisie's ear.

'Rainbow,' I said and she thought of one her favourite games, pretending to ride her imaginary pony. I knew that Eilidh would remember how much she loved horse riding and think of

84

the Ramsays and how she used to go up to the estate, and maybe with a bit of luck, she'd think that Maisie would love that.

It worked.

So that is settled now, Eilidh and Maisie are going horse riding.

There's something else I intend to do. But it's quite naughty and my conscience is biting. It involves someone suffering a bit, not much, just a tiny bit of physical pain and then she'll be as right as rain, but still . . . I really don't want to do this but I have to. It's just an ankle. Oh goodness, I can't believe what I'm about to do. Here I am, I sorted the first Mary, now I need to sort the second one.

Here we go . . .

10

Providence

Eilidh

We were just in the door and I was helping Maisie take off her jacket and scarf, when the phone rang and Jamie went to answer it.

'Mary? Hello. Oh. Oh, poor you. Oh no. I see. Three months? Seriously? No, don't worry. We'll be fine. What about you? Do you need anything? Fiona is coming to stay, that's good. Is she there already, do you need help tonight? That's OK then. I'll take Maisie up to see you as soon as you are better. Call if you need anything. Bye.'

Jamie sighed as he put the phone down and rubbed his eyes wearily.

'Sh . . . Sugar!' he muttered to himself, remembering that Maisie was around.

I stood in the hall awkwardly, not sure whether I had been invited to take my coat off and stop for a bit.

'Eilidh, come in, come and sit down. Sorry, just some stuff I need to deal with,' he added, gesturing to the phone. He turned to Maisie and smiled. 'Sweetheart, you're covered in mud, come and wash yourself off.' He took Maisie by the hand and led her into the bathroom.

'Did you enjoy it?' I heard Jamie asking her.

'Lots! I rided a pony! I was high up and going really fast. I got big boots and a helmet and Eilidh said I looked great. Can I go back tomorrow?'

I smiled to myself.

'You need to ask Eilidh, maybe she'll take you again.'

'Eilidh!' Maisie ran through. 'Can you take me again?'

'I didn't mean ask now!' Jamie intervened.

'I'd love to,' I said and meant it. It had been a magical afternoon. I hadn't ridden for so long, it was amazing to be on a horse again, and even more amazing to see wee Maisie loving it. She had been a real star, a natural, the breeze catching her golden hair as she was softly led on Sheherazade, a sweet mare they used for children and novices.

'You don't have to, I can take her,' said Jamie.

I was taken aback. 'Sure. If you prefer.'

'I don't want to put you under any pressure, you must be busy,' he said and looked away.

Which meant: 'Don't come too close to us.' I was stung.

'Would you like a cup of tea? I was just about to make dinner for Maisie.'

'It's ok, I'll let you have your dinner.'

'No, not at all, there's no rush — I'm sorry, I didn't mean it like that.' He looked genuinely embarrassed but I wasn't offended. I wasn't about to invite myself for dinner.

'Ok then, a quick one, then I'll be off.'

'Maisie, roni cheese for dinner?'

'Yes! Roni cheese! Do you like roni cheese, Eilidh?'

'I love roni cheese.' I laughed and looked at Jamie.

'It's quicker than saying 'macaroni',' he explained.

Jamie busied himself in the kitchen while I sat on the sofa. Maisie wanted to show me her My Little Pony collection.

'Look, you need to brush their hair to keep it soft. Like yours,' she said and ran her wee fingers through my hair.

All afternoon she had held my hand, sat very, very close to me and given me a few cuddles. Every time I had felt a tenderness, a joy that I hadn't experienced in a long, long time. It's one of many aspects of motherhood I long for . . . *used* to long for: the physical closeness and the contentment that stems from it. But all that is behind me.

'Then you can put them to bed,' Maisie went on. 'No wait, first you have to brush their teeth. There, you have the pink one. Brush her teeth.'

I took it obediently and pretended to brush.

'Now we are all ready. Night night!' she said, laying the ponies side by side on the sofa.

'Here's your tea,' said Jamie, handing me a steaming cup. He sat on the armchair across from us. I could see there was something on his mind and I thought of the phone call I had heard. I was in two minds whether or not to ask him about it. Then I noticed an angry red mark on his hand.

'Jamie! What happened to your hand?'

'Oh that, nothing. Just a wee burn — occupational hazard in my line of work. Nothing compared to Mary, anyway. The poor woman broke her ankle. She won't be able to look after Maisie until at least Christmas.'

'Poor thing! Is she in hospital?' I asked.

'She was but she's back home now. Fiona is down from Innerleithen to look after her.'

'I can put on my nurse outfit and go and bandage her leg,' Maisie said. I stifled a smile.

'That would be very helpful, Maisie, thank you, but the doctor bandaged her leg already. You can make her a card,' said Jamie.

'I'll make her a card with stickers and glitter. Then she'll feel better,' said Maisie solemnly and ran upstairs.

'Stickers and glitter! That will make her lots better!' I laughed. 'How are you going to manage? How much time can you take off?'

'A week, no more. After that I need to find someone else. Mary will be out of action for three months, it's a bad fracture. Probably one of the other mums at school . . . she has a best friend, her name is Keira, maybe her mum . . . ' He sighed. 'I don't want her to go with just anyone, you know . . . I trust Keira's mum, of course, but . . . '

'But three months is a long time. I understand.'

'They don't really know her. And what if they just do it as a favour but then it's a bit of a bother to have an extra child at home for three hours every afternoon and then she doesn't feel welcome?' He laughed. 'I know, I shouldn't be so anxious about things. I know I'm fussing.'

'Not at all, you are just protective. I'd be the same, if she was my . . . ' I stopped abruptly.

My daughter, I finished in my mind.

My daughter.

What was the baby I lost going to be? A little boy or a little girl?

I was never going to have a daughter. The old, familiar pang of grief.

'You're just protective,' I recovered quickly.

'I suppose. I'm sure it'll be ok.'

'What about Gail's mum? She's retired, isn't she?'

He looked away.

'I don't think that's a good idea. You know Gail and I . . . we were seeing each other. Sort of. But it wasn't working out. So I told her. I'm not really the Ritchies' favourite person right now.'

'I'm sorry to hear that.'

'Yes, well.'

Awkward silence. Desperately looking for something noncommittal to say.

Couldn't think of anything.

'Anyway, I better go. I'll let you get on.' I sprang to my feet.

'Thanks for taking Maisie riding. She loved it. Maisie!' he called in direction of the stairs. 'Eilidh is going!'

'Noooo! Eilidh, don't go!' Maisie came flying down the stairs. She had blue and silver glitter on her fingers and a bit on her left cheek.

'Have some roni cheese with me! Dad, can she stay for dinner? Eilidh, are you staying for

90

dinner? We can have a yoghurt afterwards and we can play ponies while I have my bath!'

'I'd love to, sweetheart, but I have to go. Another time?'

'Soon?'

'Soon,' I reassured her. She gave me a hug and spread glitter on my jacket.

'I'm sure it'll be ok, keep me posted,' I said to Jamie and walked out into the cold evening air.

As I stepped onto the road, I turned back and saw Maisie and Jamie waving from the window, Jamie's other hand resting on her shoulder.

Over dinner, I asked Peggy about Maisie's mum.

'Aye, yes, it's very sad. Her name was Janet. Well, her name *is* Janet, she's not dead, she's just gone. She lives in London. She came here on holiday and you know how these things happen . . . she stayed for a couple of years, then just up and went, without Maisie. That poor wee lassie, her mum just left her like that. Jamie is so good with her, you know? And now that Elizabeth has gone, it's just him.'

I felt the air being knocked out of my lungs with shock. Maisie's mother had left her. *Left* her. That woman had a daughter, a wonderful daughter, and she abandoned her and went away.

How could she? How *could* she!

I felt my hands trembling.

She had been blessed. She had a daughter. And she threw it all away.

I couldn't eat anymore.

91

'Ach, Eilidh, don't get yourself upset over that now, it all worked out for the best, Maisie is a cheery wee thing, they take such good care of her.'

But I had tears in my eyes again and they were tears of anger. She had a daughter and left her, and I wasn't even given the chance.

Later, I sat cross-legged on my bed and emailed Harry on my new laptop.

From eilidhlawson@hotmail.co.uk
To harrydouglasdesign@live.co.uk

Hi, silly me, got all maudlin tonight. Just one of those nights. Peggy had mince and tatties ready for me after horse riding — do you know what that is? Mince and tatties I mean, not horse riding. It's lovely and warming, but I really feel like having a Chinese with you and Douglas and watching a film with Jennifer Aniston in it, you know one of those. And drinking Bailey's. Like old times. I miss you guys. Had a ball today, the wee girl I told you about is so lovely, she reminds me of the twins, the things she says. She's really funny and sweet. Poor Maisie, she's going to have to be passed around for the next three months, her childminder broke a leg, sort of considered maybe looking after her, I'm free in the afternoons. Just to help out. Probably silly idea. Right. Going to go read a book. This house is very silent tonight. Bye guys.
  Eilidh

I had barely pressed the send button when the laptop beeped.

From harrydouglasdesign@live.co.uk
To eilidhlawson@hotmail.co.uk

Hi baby! You there? Give us a minute to read your mail.
   X

From eilidhlawson@hotmail.co.uk
To harrydouglasdesign@live.co.uk

Am here! Pjs, hot water bottle and all! Read, debate and respond at your leisure, boys. E.

After a few minutes sipping hot chocolate in a cup with Nessie on it, the computer beeped again.

From harrydouglasdesign@live.co.uk
To eilidhlawson@hotmail.co.uk

We say not a stupid thought at all, go for it, you miss working with children and you're great with them. Can't shut them out forever, you'd throw the baby away with the bath water, not a sensitive way of putting it but you know what we mean. This little . . . or should we say wee! The wee girl sounds great, bet she'll be good for you. Also good for you to be busy. We miss you too. Wish you were here. You put us in the mood for a Chinese. We'll have Singapore noodles and think of you. Bet there isn't a Chinese for miles around where you ended up. You probably have to go hunting. Ha ha. P.S. Glad you have a hot water bottle. What about a plaid? H&D

From eilidhlawson@hotmail.co.uk
To harrydouglasdesign@live.co.uk

You're probably right. Will ask her dad tomorrow. Love you lots xxxx
P.S. Very funny about the plaid. Things have moved on since *Braveheart*, you know? Also, there actually is a Chinese takeaway in Glen Avich, believe it or not. It's just that they are on hol. So there! ☺

From harrydouglasdesign@live.co.uk
To eilidhlawson@hotmail.co.uk

We are now thinking of Mel Gibson wrapped up in a plaid. Nice. Thanks Eilidh ☺

I was smiling as I switched the laptop off and lay down with my book.
I thought of Janet.
And then I noticed a bit of blue and silver glitter, fallen from my hair, shining in between the pages like stars in the night sky.

11

Means and Ends

Elizabeth

I can't quite believe I'm responsible for someone breaking a bone.

It doesn't always work for us ghosts to do these sort of things. I willed myself to become as solid as possible and I tripped her, seeing that she would land on her left ankle. She hurt the same ankle years ago, when she was a wee girl, so I knew it would put her out of action for a bit. I feel positively terrible about it.

Then again, if things go the way they should, it was worth it.

I'm exhausted now; the effort of becoming solid has been overwhelming. I feel myself thinning and thinning. I need to rest for a while, I'll go down to the loch and lose myself in the water and the mist. It's Jamie and Eilidh's turn to make the next move.

Jamie

I was at a loss. I had over fifteen orders to be dealt with, not to mention the local trade, and Silke was pushing for me to help her with the shop and the exhibition. I could hardly take a day off, let alone three months. There was no way Maisie could sit in the workshop with me; it's a dangerous place for a child, with melted iron and sharp things and scalding stuff all around. Maisie there for three hours, half-supervised while I worked . . . no, I couldn't even consider it.

I needed to think about things for a few days before I started asking around. The best way was probably to ask Keira's mum first, then maybe Rachel's. I knew they'd say yes but I just hated the idea of Maisie being passed around like that. Maybe the best thing was to look for a proper childminder, someone to rely on in these sort of situations.

Once again, I thought what a shame it was that Shona didn't live here. I'd phoned her the night before and she'd said to ask Eilidh but I couldn't possibly do that. Yes, Eilidh only worked in the morning, and she was great with Maisie, but she'd been back five minutes and she had so much on her plate, so much to sort out.

I was actually really surprised when Shona had suggested Eilidh; it hadn't even crossed my mind. Maybe mothers deal with these things better.

I suppose all this should have made me miss Janet even more but it didn't, not really. She used to do her utmost *not* to be with Maisie, she would have asked the bloody postman to take her on his rounds, so that she could paint. She would have been no use. My mum would have been the one to ask, except obviously she would have been looking after Maisie in the first place, she loved being with her.

So there I was, walking Maisie to school. No point in taking the car, the school was only five minutes away and parking was murder. It was a rainy, dark November morning and Maisie was wearing her pink Mac, matching waterproof hat and pink wellies with white dots all over them. She looked like a little flower, all pink against the dark backdrop of rain and grey skies.

That morning, as soon as I told her it was pouring, she started jumping up and down.

'Daddy! I can take my new *Charlie and Lola* umbrella!'

A wee girl's outlook on a rainy day.

The bell was ringing. I watched her running to Keira and her friends, their umbrellas closing one by one like popped balloons, as they went up the steps and into the school building, shepherded by the teachers.

I had to run, I only had about five hours' worth of work before I needed to collect her.

A thought came into my head: to go and ask Eilidh there and then. No point in dithering, and before I knew it the week would be over and I'd be stuck. On the other hand, I couldn't put her under pressure. I mean, who was I to ask her to look after my daughter every afternoon for three months?

I was getting soaked. I started walking up to the workshop, shoulders hunched against the cold and damp. I'd think about it there.

Eilidh

I had changed my mind.

Jamie would have probably said no anyway. Also, what if they came to rely on me? I couldn't possibly stay here forever. It was just temporary, until I started to feel a wee bit less wobbly and vulnerable. Then I'd go back to Southport. There wasn't really anything for me there but I couldn't rely on working in the shop forever or keep living with Peggy.

Although she seemed to love having me around — I could see she had been lonely before I arrived, she didn't like living on her own. Also, the more I worked in the shop, the more I realised how much hard work it was for a sixty-seven-year-old woman, even with Jim doing the odd jobs. But still — this was not my life, I mean, not my *real* life. I only intended to stay until Christmas, maybe a little longer.

On the other hand, that would have been enough to see Jamie and Maisie through until Mary got better. And Maisie was a wee star, it would have been so good to go and collect her from school and have the rest of the afternoon together. A bit like old times, when I used to work in the nursery, surrounded by children all day.

I kept talking myself in and out of it, I was exhausting myself. I decided to think about it over a cup of tea and some tablet. Tea and tablet is just the best combination. I'd been at the tablet a lot, these last few weeks. My jeans were a bit tighter around my waist and my face had lost some of its hollow look. Even my hair seemed that little bit shinier. I was eating more and nearly always sleeping at night, I seemed to cry a lot less and I felt a whole lot stronger. Strong enough for a full-time job, to keep my afternoons busy as well as my mornings.

I knew that Peggy wouldn't have wanted to give up her afternoon shift at the shop, she enjoyed seeing people and having a chat. Maybe it was time to look for some sort of part-time job in Kinnear.

Or maybe it was time to ask Jamie if he needed a childminder for a while.

If I found the courage.

Maisie

'Good work, everybody. Let me see . . . ' said Mrs Hill, sitting on her chair in the carpet area, with the Primary One boys and girls at her feet in their navy and grey uniforms.

She had a pile of sheets on her knees, all titled 'Today's News', in her lovely, careful handwriting.

'This is a great picture, David. Very tidy, well done. Would you like to show it to everybody?'

The children made room for David to take a few steps over tangles of wee hands and legs, until he stood beside Mrs Hill. He held up his sheet.

'Tell us what this is, David.'

'It's my dad's new van. It's green. Me and my sister went for a drive but she's only wee and she didn't wake up.' David's cheeks were bright red, his hair was standing on end and half his shirt was out of his trousers.

'That's a brilliant story, David. And look at this lovely writing. What does it say?'

'My. Dad. Has. Got. A. New. Van,' he explained, pointing proudly at the unintelligible, rune-like scribbling.

'Well done, lovely work, isn't it, children?' said Mrs Hill, passing the piece of paper to the classroom assistant, who blue-tacked it onto the writing display. David sat back down, all pleased with himself.

'Who else, let me see . . . Maisie. Tell me about your picture,' Mrs Hill said, handing her the sheet.

Maisie stood up confidently in her navy pinafore, white shirt and navy tights, her blonde hair kept tidy with two hairpins at each side of her face. She held her sheet for everyone to see.

'This is a horse. Not an imaginary one, a real horse. Her name is Shazad. I went riding yesterday and I had boots and a helmet. And this is Auntie Mary. She has a sore leg. She can't look after me. Eilidh will look after me and play with my mini ponies.'

'Well done, Maisie, and what a lovely horse. What does your story say?'

'It says, 'Eilidh likes roni cheese.' And here it says, 'Maisie'.'

Mrs Hill stifled a smile. 'There you are, Mrs McHarg, I think this should definitely go on the writers' wall.'

Elizabeth

Oh, for Heaven's sake, will you make a decision the two of you!

It's pouring today. I love being water, rain and loch, all mixed together. It's so peaceful.

Eilidh hasn't found it yet. She wore her jacket this morning. The black coat she had on when she took Maisie riding is still hanging in the hall, untouched. When she wears it again, she'll find it and hopefully return it.

And that's the last thing I will do for a while. They better sort themselves out; I can't keep going around tripping people down the stairs! Now it's up to them.

Jamie

I had a distraught child on my hands. One of the ponies was gone, her favourite, the pink one. She had looked for them as soon as we arrived home because she said they had to get their snack and do their homework. The lilac one was on her bedside table but the pink one had vanished.

She was now sitting in front of the TV, her eyes puffy from crying, clutching Bog the wee red dinosaur. She hadn't even touched her toast with jam. I had tempted her with chocolate buttons, the white ones that she loves, but — no joy.

I promised her we'd go to Kinnear at the weekend and buy a whole new set but she said it was no use, that Pink Pony was all alone somewhere, lost and without dinner. She was inconsolable.

Eilidh

I was brushing my coat, trying to get rid of the horse hair and dried mud — what possessed me to wear it while out riding in the first place? — when I felt something in one of the pockets.

One of Maisie's ponies.

I immediately realised the gravity of the situation. Maisie slept with the ponies. She'd told me she can't fall asleep without them. I had to return it right away. I remember once, when Jack was about three, he'd forgotten his Beddy Teddy at my mum's house. Katrina told me that he refused point blank to go to bed and they had to fix a makeshift bed for him on the living-room floor.

I threw a jacket on and walked up to the McAnenas'. Jamie opened the door.

'I found this in my pocket,' I said, handing him the pony. 'Sorry, didn't mean to steal it! I promise it was an accident!' I said smiling, standing on his doorstep.

A little blonde head appeared behind him. When she saw the pony, Maisie's face lit up, and before we knew it, she had brushed past Jamie and jumped into my arms. She held me tight, pressing her wee face into my tummy, her arms around my waist.

'Thank goodness. It was awful,' said Jamie, without a hint of sarcasm.

And then it just came out, before I could start thinking and analysing and stopping myself from living.

'Jamie. I was wondering if I could look after Maisie for you.'

12

This Side of Reality

Eilidh

My first appearance at the school gates to pick up Maisie was quite eventful. Keira's mum came up to me with a great, big, thoroughly insincere smile and a glint of curiosity in her eyes. I had never met her before, she'd only been in the village for a few years. I took an instant dislike to her.

'Sooo . . . you are Maisie's new childminder?' she said, eyeing me up and down. I suddenly felt quite unkempt, in my pale blue jacket, jeans and trainers, my hair loose around my shoulders and messed up by the wind. She was immaculate, her blonde hair — fake, I thought, and then was shocked by my own bitchiness — in a perfectly blow-dried bob, a stylish light pink cardigan, high heeled boots and manicured hands clutching her car keys.

'Temporarily, yes. I'm Eilidh,' I answered, offering my hand.

She took it limply and quickly.

'Sharon says you and Jamie are childhood friends,' she said, fishing.

'Yes, we went to school together.'

'And you are back here after your divorce,' she

added, with an exaggerated sympathetic look.

'Well, I'm not divorced yet, just separated.'

'How lucky for you,' she went on. 'In fact, Jamie could have easily asked me. It wouldn't have been a problem to help poor Maisie . . . '

Poor?

'Yes, well, no need now,' I cut her short and walked away. Heavens above. I'd heard about the so-called 'mummy mafia' but obviously never experienced it myself. Well, that was a nice introduction.

'Hello!' said a confident voice from behind me. I turned around and was faced with a smiling woman of about forty, holding a brown-haired toddler in her arms. 'I'm Ruth. You must be Eilidh.'

I nodded. Fresh from the encounter with Keira's mum, I wasn't going to give anything away.

'Nice to meet you. Helena told me about you. I'm Ben's mum. And this is Jack,' she said, juggling the wee boy who was trying his utmost to free himself.

'We must get together sometime. Maybe you could come up to the house one day?'

'I'd love to. That'd be good.'

'We get together quite a lot, we do these mums' gatherings where the kids run around and we can have a cup of tea and a chat — and vent!'

Mums' gatherings. With me as one of the mums? Strange. A glimpse of a world I always looked at from the outside but was never allowed in . . .

'Maisie was hardly ever there, you know with Mary being an older lady, she preferred to do her own thing . . . It's a chance for Maisie to come and play with Ben and the others . . . here they are!' she said, as the children started running out. 'I'll give you my mobile number . . . bye!' and she was gone, walking away with one last wave and a smile, a boy by each side, holding her hands. Well, Ruth had just reconciled me with the world of school gate mothers.

I watched the boys and girls run down the steps, giddy with freedom and pent-up energy, until I saw a wee blonde head bobbing up and down.

'Eilidh!' Maisie ran to me and gave me a cuddle. I waved to her teacher who was watching by the steps, checking that each child was safely picked up.

'Hi baby, how was your day at school? Come while I meet your teacher.'

I walked up to her, a kindly looking woman with grey hair and glasses.

'I'm Eilidh. Maisie's dad must have told you about me,' I said, holding out my hand.

'Yes, hello, I'm Mrs Hill, Maisie's teacher. Maisie's dad told me you'll come and collect Maisie for a few weeks. How's Mary?'

'Aye, doing ok, it'll be a while I'm afraid.'

'I'm so glad they found you, then. Maisie was so excited today, weren't you, darling?'

'Yes! Eilidh has a shop!'

'Well, not exactly . . . ' I began.

'And I can work in the shop today!' Maisie added.

'Well, not work in it, just sit there and do your homework,' I added hastily. God. They'll think she's going to be put to work. Child labour or something.

But Mrs Hill laughed. 'You'll be a great help for Eilidh, I'm sure! See you tomorrow!'

A chorus of bye-byes followed until we were alone on the steps.

'How was your day, sweetheart?'

'Good! We are growing frogs. But they look like commas. Lots of commas swimming. But then they have their lifecycles and become frogs. Like butterflies. Are we going to your shop?' She was jumping up and down with excitement.

'Yes, you'll have a snack, then you'll do your homework, then we'll walk up to your house and wait for your dad. Sound good?'

'Can I help in the shop?' she asked, excitedly.

I smiled. I used to love helping in the shop when I was a wee girl, it made me feel all grown up and responsible. To see Maisie so keen, it was like seeing a memory of me coming to life.

'Of course. Peggy will be grateful for the help,' I said solemnly.

She nodded, all serious. We held hands and walked in silent companionship, the wind playing with our hair, a hint of darkness in the sky already, in spite of it being just early afternoon. Winter was closing in.

'Hello!' I called as we entered the shop.

'Hello there, girls!' Peggy answered from behind the counter, her light blue eyes smiling at the sight of us.

'Can I help you? Can I wear a apron?'

We laughed. 'You sure can, pet, go and get your snack and Eilidh will get an apron just for you. Eilidh, it's like seeing you all over again!' she said to me, a wistful look passing on her face quickly, like the shadow of a cloud on the moors.

'I suppose you can do your homework later on at your house,' I sighed. I had been outnumbered.

She downed her jam sandwich at the speed of light, champing at the bit to go and help Peggy.

'A apron! A apron for me!' she said happily, as I fastened the strings behind her back. It was a bit too long and too wide for her, but not too bad. She looked so pretty, her hair held back with a white hair band, her wee legs in grey tights sticking out of the burgundy apron, her grey eyes sparkling with excitement.

'I'm ready!' she declared, stepping out into the shop.

'Very well!' said Peggy. 'Your first job is to tidy up this shelf,' she said, handing her a cloth. 'Look. You move the boxes, then you dust underneath and then you put them back, all lined up nicely.'

Their heads were bent together over the cereal boxes, a blonde one and a grey one, as Peggy crouched to show Maisie the ropes. I could see myself all those years ago, bending over the exact same shelf, tidying up cans and boxes.

The bell tinkled, once, twice. The door opened and a young woman walked in, a train of cold air following her.

There was something exotic about her that made me do a double take. She had short black hair, cropped in the back and longer in the front, with bright blue highlights, a multicoloured jumper that looked hand-knitted and a miniskirt over long, lean legs in bright pink tights. I had seen her somewhere before. Then I remembered. I had met her in the pub once.

'Hello, Peggy, hello,' she added, with a smile towards Maisie. Her voice had a foreign lilt.

'Oh, hello there, how are you, Silke?' said Peggy, standing up. 'Haven't seen you in a while.'

'Very well, thank you. It's been crazy, with the gallery opening and all that.' Her English was perfect, with just a hint of German behind her Scottish intonations.

'This is my niece Eilidh, I'm not sure you've met . . . '

'Not formally, no,' she said and extended her hand to me with a big, friendly smile. I took it. Her handshake was warm and firm.

'Jamie said you'll be looking after Maisie. Just as well, Eilidh, cause you must know, I'm going to put Jamie through his paces with the gallery project!' She laughed.

'How is it coming on?' asked Peggy.

'Great, thanks, it's brilliant. The opening is next month. There will be music and catering, and lots of fancy people from Edinburgh and even London. Will you come?'

'Ach, Silke, I'm too old for these things, but Eilidh . . . '

'I'd love to. It sounds great,' I said and I meant it.

'And you'll come for a bit, won't you,

sweetheart?' Silke added, bending to stroke Maisie's hair.

'Yes. I'll wear my fairy outfit,' Maisie said, perfectly serious.

'Cool! Do you have wings as well?'

'Uh-huh,' she nodded, 'and a wand.'

'Brilliant. Just what we need.' Silke was equally serious.

'Will you come as a fairy?' Maisie asked.

'No, I'm actually a witch. A good one though.'

'A witch?' Maisie's eyes were two round saucers.

'Yes. But don't tell anyone. Can I leave these with you?' she added, handing Peggy a wad of leaflets and a poster.

'Sure. We'll let everybody know,' said Peggy, going over a leaflet. ''Glen Avich Art Gallery' — it has a nice ring to it, doesn't it?'

'Thanks! Right, better run, I'm driving up to Kinnear to hand these in. Bye, nice meeting you,' she said and, with a last wave to Maisie, she went out into the twilight. With her bright blue hair and pink tights, she was a little beacon as she crossed the road and disappeared.

'Peggy? Is she really a witch?' asked Maisie.

Peggy laughed. 'There's no such thing as witches, pet. Except at Halloween!'

'If she's a witch, she's a good one. She seems lovely,' I said.

'Oh, aye. A great lassie. Very . . . unique.'

I smiled. Bet her blue hair caused quite a stir when she first moved to Glen Avich.

'We'll need to get a move on, my love, you still

110

have to do your homework and your reading.'
Homework in Primary One. I had my own
opinion about that but it had to be done.

'Ooook . . . ' she said sadly, giving the cereal
boxes one last pat. 'Will you keep my apron
safe?' she asked Peggy.

'I certainly will. Maybe you can come back
tomorrow? There's a lot to be done.'

'Can I? Can I, can I, CAN I?' she asked me,
imploringly.

'Of course. Come on, baby, jacket on, your
dad will be home in just over an hour,' I said,
escorting her to the back room.

A few minutes later, we were walking up St
Colman's Way. The air was purple, the sky
slowly turning to black, the smell of late
autumn in the air. Early November, the days
of the dead.

'Did you enjoy helping in the shop?'

'Loads. My granny was smiling too.'

'Your . . . your granny? You mean my aunt
Peggy. I'm sure you can call her granny, if you
like. She'll love that.'

'Nooo, not Peggy. My granny Elizabeth.'

I felt a chill run down my spine.

'Your granny Elizabeth . . . was there?' I asked.
My mouth was dry.

She nodded, skipping happily. I didn't ask
anything more. I wanted to be out of the
darkness, I wanted to be home in the light and
warmth, the TV on, the kettle on, all the safe,
prosaic sounds and sights of daily life around
me, to bring me back over to this side of reality.
I shivered, holding Maisie's hand a little tighter.

111

Jamie

When I saw the lights on in my house, my heart skipped a beat. Then I remembered Eilidh was there with Maisie. I stood at the window for a second and looked in. Eilidh was standing at the stove, stirring something, her back turned, her brown hair in a ponytail. Maisie was sitting on the sofa, clutching her ponies, watching a *Charlie and Lola* DVD.

So this is how it feels like. To come home to a warm house, the fire on, the lights on.

And someone there.

I was exhausted. It'd been an incredibly full day with no time for lunch or even a cup of tea. All I wanted was to put Maisie to bed and sit in front of the fire, with some mindless film on, and close my eyes.

'Daddy!' I felt the usual rush of joy whenever I saw Maisie after a separation, however short.

I looked up from over her head as she hugged me and saw Eilidh standing there, a smile on her face, but a shy expression, slightly awkward. Like the whole scene was too domestic, too intimate, for two people who, after all, hardly knew each other.

'The kettle's on. What do you take?' she said, with that soft, warm voice of hers.

And I said the wrong thing. Completely the wrong thing.

'It's ok, Eilidh, thanks, you must be tired. I'll make my own tea and see to Maisie.'

Why, WHY did I say that? When what I wanted to say was, 'Milk and one sugar, thanks, come and sit with me you both. Tell me all about your day.'

I could have kicked myself.

'Sure. Bye Maisie, see you tomorrow,' she said, forcing a smile.

'Are you not going to give me my dinner?' asked Maisie, clearly disappointed. 'And my bath? And a story?'

'Your dad is here now, baby, I'll get you tomorrow at school.'

I was speechless, overwhelmed by my own awkwardness. It was as if there was this invisible thread between them and I had just cut it, and they were suffering for it.

'See you, Jamie,' she said and was out the door before I could speak.

I slapped my forehead in frustration as Maisie sat back on the sofa, silent. I took my jacket off and went to make the tea.

On the stove was a pot of roni cheese. She had remembered Maisie's favourite dinner. The oven was on, too. I opened its door and a delicious smell hit me. A pasta bake, enough for one. My own dinner. My heart sank.

I went to get a mug, then I saw that Eilidh had two cups ready, each with a tea bag in.

I'm an idiot.

13

Light and Shadow

Eilidh

Days and nights fell into a pattern, a whole new life — a gentle, unhurried one. It felt so easy and natural, like I had never known any different. The mornings in the shop, the afternoons with Maisie, the evenings at home with Peggy or, very occasionally, out for a drink with Helena, Ruth or Silke.

The last couple of weekends, I had helped Silke with the opening of the gallery, unpacking artwork, cleaning, making phone calls and all the odd jobs that needed done. I had also been convinced by Silke's charm and Peggy's enthusiasm to do a reading at the opening. Silke had mentioned to my aunt that they had found a harpist to do a solo and a singer to perform some traditional Gaelic songs. To that, my aunt had mentioned my reading of 'Hallaig' all those years ago and how it reduced half of Glen Avich to tears, or so she maintained.

Jamie had asked me to read 'Lucy', a poem by George McKay Brown. I had chosen the one by Sorley MacLean, 'The Choice', a poem about love and loss that called to me.

Once that had been decided, I had to do

something very important: choose what to wear. I'd left all my nice clothes in the house that Tom and I shared and brought up only jeans, t-shirts and jumpers. I prefer to dress casually, it was Tom who liked seeing me in evening dresses, complete with make-up and jewellery, and go out to expensive restaurants or dinner parties. It felt like dressing up, literally. Like opening a chest full of fancy clothes and putting on a costume. I didn't enjoy it much.

However, I couldn't go to the gallery opening in jeans and a t-shirt. Even Silke was going to dress up, in a black mini dress and tartan tights, with her newly dyed pink hair. Not to mention Maisie and her fairy costume. No, I needed something.

'Shona? It's Eilidh, how are you? Good. Yes, all is well. It's a pleasure. She's a wee star, isn't she? Anyway, you know the gallery opening? You'll be there too won't you? Well, I'll be doing a poetry reading and I have nothing to wear. Yes, exactly. You guessed. Oh. Does he know? Good luck with that! Tomorrow? Yes, I can, but not if you are busy . . . ok. Ok. I'll text you the time. Thanks. See you then.'

Phew. Shona had it sorted already, of course. Is there something she doesn't think of or plan for? She said Jamie was going to get a new outfit, too. The idea made me smile. To prise Jamie out of his jeans, t-shirt and faded grey jacket combo was no mean feat, one that only Shona and her bossiness could accomplish.

★ ★ ★

The train arrived in Aberdeen station at 11.23 on the dot. Shona was there already, a Starbucks cup in each hand. She kissed my cheek with no arms, laughing, and pressed one of the cups into my hand.

'You need energy for our shopping expedition. Come on. Oh, Eilidh. I just love your hair,' she said, running a hand through my freshly washed hair. 'With hair and eyes like that, you'd look amazing in a rag. Not that we are going to buy a rag, of course. Debenhams first, I think, then we'll have a look in Hobbs.'

I was smiling as the cold Aberdeen air hit my face, the tall granite buildings all around us. We walked into Station Square, the neon lights shining on the polished tiles, the shop windows all lit up. It looked lovely. It was so good to be out and about again, thinking of nothing important, nothing deep. Just having fun with a good friend.

★   ★   ★

I stepped out of the dressing room with a bright red wrap dress. We both shook our heads. Then it was the turn of a deep green silk dress, then a black trouser suit — very job interview. Next, an empire style dress, so low cut that I would have been arrested — and I would have frozen to death as well, on a cold November night.

'Shona! I look like . . . I look like a . . . you know what I mean!'

I gasped, looking at my reflection in the dressing room mirror. I had a black corset on,

116

the tightest, tiniest, most revealing thing I had ever worn in my life. My breasts overflowed from it.

'You don't look like *that*! You just look sexy. My brother would have a heart attack,' she added under her breath.

'SHONA!' I said, shocked. 'What on earth . . . '

'Sorry!' She laughed. 'Right, get it off. Try this one.'

Half an hour later, still no joy, so we went for lunch in Debenhams.

I attacked my tuna and cheese melt like I hadn't eaten for a month, I was so hungry after all that hard work and the cold air.

'Goodness, Eilidh. You are nearly eating the plate!'

'I know,' I answered, a big smile on my face. 'It's like I haven't eaten in years. Actually, if I think about it, it's true. I haven't eaten properly in years.'

'Yes, I could see that when I met you that day at the pub. You were skin and bones. You look so much better now. Oh, Eilidh . . . I wish you had come to us earlier. I mean, for a change of scene, at least . . . '

'I wish that too. Well, I'm here now.' I was determined not to think of the past. It was too good a day to spoil it.

'So you are. And to be honest, it wasn't only good for you. Peggy looks happier, less tired, since you moved in. And as for Jamie . . . ' She took a sip of her cappuccino. 'Well, you know he needed some help.'

'Mary will be back on her feet soon.'

117

'Yes, I know. But apart from that. I mean, he needed help with Maisie. Not only practical help. They needed someone in their lives . . . '

I looked away. Shona sensed my uneasiness.

'That looks good!' she said, pointing at my carrot cake.

'Oh, it is. Carrot cake is just *gorgeous* with a hot chocolate.'

'You need to watch it, Eilidh, if you keep going on like this you might even become a size ten!' she said sarcastically. Shona is a curvy, full-bodied sort of woman and it suits her. Obviously, like most women, she doesn't see her own beauty. She doesn't see how luscious and soft her body looks, how lovely her wavy blonde hair, her milky skin and her light blue eyes are. She had inherited her fair, northern looks from Elizabeth, while Jamie got the black hair and grey eyes from his dad.

'Come on, go for it,' I said, cutting the cake in half and handing her the spoon.

'No, honestly . . . '

'Now, either you eat this or I'll go and order a piece of chocolate cake and put it right in front of you.'

She laughed. 'You leave me no choice!'

The cake was gone in just under two minutes.

An hour later, there it was. *The* dress. The one.

I stood looking at my reflection and I couldn't quite believe what I saw. I looked straight in my own eyes, in an intense moment that made Shona stop in her tracks. It wasn't so much the beauty of the dress, soft black silk-chiffon, with see-through sleeves and light blue embroidery — a bit gypsy-like yet sober all at the same time. It wasn't the high-heeled shoes or the fullness of my hair on my shoulders that enchanted me.

It was the woman looking back at me.

Her eyes weren't hollow. They weren't desperate. They weren't empty.

I looked . . . alive.

★   ★   ★

The train window was black. I could see the profile of my face as I leaned against it, under the bright lights of the carriage. The book I had bought to read on the way lay unopened in my hands, as I was lost in thought.

I had had such a great time, a day of sheer lightness and joy. I was laden with bags, one of which contained Jamie's outfit, a gift from Shona to be handed over tomorrow. I had also bought a few books and some brightly coloured pampering products from the Body Shop. I couldn't quite believe how much pleasure I found in my shopping session. All the little things that used to give me joy had been obliterated by my frustrated quest. I hadn't been fully enjoying anything for a long, long time.

I thought of Tom. How hard it must have been on him.

It had started dawning on me when I realised that I hadn't once thought of Peggy, when she was widowed and alone. That had made me see how single minded I had been all these years.

119

How unaware I'd been of anybody else's needs, including Tom's.

Our marriage was well and truly over, I knew that. It had faded away through years of neglect, of mutual isolation.

He had cheated on me, there was no excuse for that. But how lonely, how lost he must have been while I was so absorbed in myself, in my own, malfunctioning body, in my own self-pity.

Tom. I wondered what he was doing now.

The train slowed down and came to a stop, as the lit-up platform slid up beside us. I gathered all my bags and was making my way towards the door when I saw a girl standing at the end of the carriage, looking at me with a blank expression.

Gail.

I smiled and opened my mouth to say hello, but then she turned away, towards the door. I froze, surprised.

I walked onwards and stood just behind her, unsure of what to do. That was Helena's sister. And she was ignoring me. On purpose.

The train came to a stop, the door opened with a sound as if the air was being sucked out of it and we stepped down. Gail walked away, hurriedly, without looking back.

She had seen me, of course she had seen me. Actually — it dawned on me — she had been aware I was there the whole journey.

There was only one explanation, I thought, walking home in the dark. She wasn't over Jamie and she was jealous of my closeness with his family.

Well, she needn't worry. I had no intention of

becoming involved with him or anyone else. I shook my head. What a silly, silly girl. Better not mention anything to Helena. My life was complicated enough without adding to it.

I knocked at my door. I had the keys, of course, but I didn't want to startle Peggy.

'Eilidh! Eilidh, come on in, darling, here's Katrina on the phone.'

My heart sank. Katrina. Oh well, I hadn't spoken to her since I had moved up.

'Hi, Eilidh, how are you?'

'I'm ok, thanks. A lot better. And you and the kids?'

'We are all fine. Listen, I know it's a bit early, but I was wondering if you'd like to come down for Christmas. I mean, I don't know what your plans are but we'd love to see you.'

My heart softened.

'And with you not having any obligations, no children or anything . . . see, it has its advantages!'

It was like being punched in the stomach.

I couldn't believe it.

It couldn't just be lack of tact. I had just lost a baby, for God's sake. I couldn't have any children, it was the cross of my life, and she made a remark like that, in the same breath with a Christmas invitation? My eyes welled up.

'Thanks, but I'm staying in Glen Avich. Peggy is having Christmas dinner here,' I said, keeping my voice steady. I couldn't let her know I was hurt.

'Mum and Dad would love to see you,' she said reproachfully.

121

'I just spoke to them last week. I'll see you all soon. Thanks for phoning.'

'Oh well then, bye Ei — '

I put the phone down. Leave me alone, leave me alone, leave me *alone*!

I ran upstairs, a knot in my stomach.

'Oh, Eilidh! That girl, for heaven's sake, what has she said now? She always had a poison tongue that one!' Peggy exclaimed, loyally.

I was so angry. So angry with Katrina, and with myself for being so weak and silly, and crying instead of telling her to get out of my life, for good.

'Come on, pet, come on. It's just like when you were wee, isn't it? I remember very well. Come here, come and have a cup of tea . . . Did you have a good time in Aberdeen?'

I nodded.

The bell rang.

'On you go upstairs and wash your face, my love,' she said, as if I were a wee girl.

I ran upstairs with my bags.

'Oh, Jamie, hello, come on in, what a lovely surprise.' I stood on the landing, frozen.

'Sorry to bother you, I know it's nearly dinner time. My sister just phoned and said to come and collect something from Eilidh . . . something she got from Aberdeen today. Maisie is away for a sleepover, so I thought I'd just walk down . . . '

I panicked. I couldn't hide away. But surely he'd see that I'd been crying. Oh no . . .

I jumped into the bathroom to wash my face, tripped on one of the bags and landed flat on my face, banging my head against the bathroom door.

'That must be Eilidh,' I heard Peggy saying coolly, in spite of the horrendous noise.

I picked myself up. Ouch. Oh God, the embarrassment.

I washed my face, brushed my hair and went downstairs grumpily.

'Hi.'

'Hi.'

Jamie was sitting in the kitchen, with a cup of tea in front of him.

'There you are,' I said, handing him the bag.

'Thank you.'

Peggy looked from one to the other, Jamie, silent and shy, and me, silent and sulky with red eyes.

'Is Maisie away?'

'Yes.'

'Did you remember to pack the Rose Cottage?' Maisie's new toy. She wanted to show it off.

'Yes,' he answered and looked at me for the first time. 'Are you ok?' he asked, his grey eyes full of concern.

'Yes. Yes, of course.' I was monosyllabic like a teenager.

'Did something happen in Aberdeen?'

'No, not at all!' I shook my head vehemently. 'I had a great time with Shona. We had a ball.' I would have hated for Jamie to think I didn't have a good time, when Shona gave me the best day I had had in . . . well, I don't remember how long.

'Katrina,' said Peggy, as means of explanation,

and left the room before I could protest.

'Oh.' Jamie nodded. He knew her too.

We were alone in the kitchen.

'You must be tired.'

'Yes.'

'Otherwise I was going to ask you if you wanted to go for a drink.'

'I haven't had my dinner yet. Peggy has it ready.'

'I can come back after dinner, if you like. Drive up to Kinnear, maybe?'

'Not tonight, Jamie.' I hadn't finished crying. It had been my favourite pastime for months after all, it's difficult just to stop completely.

Also, I had this awful, awful feeling that if he came too close to me I would just put my head on his chest and close my eyes and just *stay there*.

And that, I couldn't do.

14

Calling in the Night

Jamie

I hadn't driven up to Peggy's house just to collect Shona's present, of course. I had driven there because my house was very silent, and very empty, without Maisie.

And because I wanted to see Eilidh.

More than anything, I wanted to see Eilidh.

When I saw her red, swollen eyes, I desperately wanted to make it better. Like when Maisie falls in the play park, or if something upsets her, and I dry her tears with my fingers, and I hold her until her heart slows down and she relaxes in my arms like a small bird. That's what I wanted to do for Eilidh — and I nearly did. I nearly raised my hands to take her by the shoulders and pull her against me. But then I didn't.

Sometimes, all this silence I was born with seems like a curse. But even without words, I still could have shown her how I felt, had I not been frozen.

I went home, my heart echoing with the words I hadn't been able to express. I wished she could hear me.

The whisky felt bitter in my mouth, burning

125

down my throat without comfort. I drank, and drank, and drank, looking for a relief that didn't come. Whisky to me used to be beautiful warmth, a sense of peace, a dreamy state . . . the amber-coloured purity, the smell of peat, the taste of the blood of Scotland itself . . . now it's only oblivion and it smells and tastes of loneliness, and nothing else. The smiler with a knife.

I looked at the clock on the mantelpiece: three o' clock, the deadliest hour. I stood up, slightly dizzy but perfectly lucid. I took the bottle, walked to the kitchen sink and emptied what was left, watching it swirl and swirl down the drain.

I opened the cupboard — *that* cupboard, the one I kept for my lonely evenings and nights. I took out the bottles — three of them. I opened them and stood them in a line beside the sink. One by one, I poured them away.

I stood there, clutching the sink.

Men don't cry.

Men don't cry when there's someone to see.

And then, something strange happened.

I felt something . . . someone . . . touch my hair, a light and gentle hand, like the dream of a caress.

I felt my hair stand on end. I turned around, slowly, fully expecting to see someone there, but there was no one.

And again, another caress, this time on my cheek.

I was frozen to the spot, sobered up at once. I swallowed. I could hear the blood rushing in my ears, my heart pounding and pounding like it would jump out of my chest.

Slowly, I walked to the chair before the dying fire and sat there.

The silence was unnerving, so I switched the TV on. Its flickering light filled the room, together with comforting voices and sounds. I sat, watching the screen without seeing it, and fell asleep.

I woke up at dawn, grey light filling the room, all the ghosts gone.

I saw the empty bottles lined up tidily, their contents washed down to the river and then the sea, and I felt light, lighter than I'd been in a long time.

I could stop, then. I thought I couldn't but actually, I did it. Thoughts of newness and hope filled me as I stood in the shower, warm water washing away the cold and silence and disappointment, to join the whisky on its way to the sea.

Eilidh

I lay there, looking at the ceiling. A wee crack on the left, a long one on the right, a bit further up, a tiny round missing bit of paint beside the light. Tossing and turning.

No use counting sheep, sleep wouldn't come.

I got up to open the curtains, to get some relief from the sense of claustrophobia. Black hills, black sky, no moon. I opened the window, hoping that the cold November air would blow away the anxiety, the panic that had taken hold of me since the phone call.

I don't even know why I felt that way.

Or maybe I do. I had been reminded that my life in Glen Avich was just a temporary respite, that sooner or later I was going to have to go back to reality. Face it all. My family. Southport. Tom.

A divorce.

No good. Not even the moist, sweet-smelling breeze was helping.

I had to get out.

I looked at my watch. Three in the morning. Oh well, no one will see me.

I threw a fleece over my pyjamas and slipped downstairs. I put my jacket and trainers on and stepped outside into the cold, black night.

I started walking, to the sound of the wind in the trees and the occasional call of an owl. A fox crossed the road, a few yards from me. She stopped to look, her yellow eyes shining in the darkness, then disappeared. I walked in the empty streets of Glen Avich, up St Colman's Way, past Jamie's house and up the hill.

I sat on the bench in the small garden that had been built around the well. St Colman's waters were said to aid fertility. How ironic. I'd have to drink the whole well before it worked, I thought bitterly.

I could see the whole of Glen Avich at my feet and the black hills behind it. On my right, the winding road that had led me up here, lined with houses — including the McAnenas' cottage. The light was on in Jamie's kitchen. I wondered why he was still awake in the small hours.

I had done the right thing, of course. The last thing I needed was a night out with him. One touch and all the loneliness and sadness would have come rolling out, and God knows what would have happened.

And that was all over for me.

Because who would want me, who would want someone who can't have children?

Which is why Tom had found someone else, a woman who functions properly, like women are supposed to. Women are not supposed to be barren.

There, I said it. The secret I couldn't disclose to anyone, because it would have given away the true depth of my self-loathing, the sense of my own worthlessness. I could never say this aloud, it's too raw, too cruel. If a friend of mine told me something like this, I'd be appalled. I'd say, how can you think like this, how can you hate yourself to this extent? How can you think that nobody will ever want you because you can't have babies? And yet, I thought that of myself, this awful thing that I will never speak aloud.

I believed it; I believed in my very bones that nobody would want someone like me. Let alone Jamie McAnena, him and his lovely, lovely daughter with all to live for, his success as an artist, his beautiful soul, his handsome face, his voice that flowed over me like warm waters, calming me and soothing me and making me feel that all is right with the world.

He was going to find someone . . . suitable. A real woman, one whose body worked properly.

Oh no, Eilidh, you won't start crying again.

129

You WON'T. I hid my face in my hands, then hastily looked up.

Laughter.

Laughter from the bushes and hushed voices.

Coming my way.

I dived off the bench and hid behind a pine, my heart pounding. Who could be out at this time of night — well, apart from me?

A black silhouette came out of the bushes, someone tall. A woman. Followed by . . . I squinted, peeking from behind a tree . . . another woman, a smaller one. They were whispering and giggling and holding hands. It was clear what was going on.

Oh well, times are changing in Glen Avich, too. I resigned myself to stay hidden until they went. I didn't want to embarrass them and also, I couldn't exactly give an explanation to why I was out in the middle of the night. At least they had a good excuse.

The two girls held each other and kissed. I felt uneasy, not because it was two girls, but because I was seeing something I wasn't meant to see.

There were tiny, solar-powered lights all over the garden, buried in the ground like shiny mushrooms. They gave a faint glow, like fairy lights dotted all over the place. The girls stepped on one of them in their embrace and I could see their faces: Silke . . . and . . .

Heavens above! Fiona Robertson! That shy wee thing, Mary's granddaughter. She blushes furiously if anyone so much as looks at her. Oh well, still waters, as my mum always says about me.

I really, really, really wanted to go. I felt so bad intruding on them like this. I took a big breath and stepped out slowly, on tiptoes.

Fiona and Silke were now facing each other, holding hands, lost in each other's eyes. The look on their faces was . . . amazing.

It was pure, unadulterated love.

No one had ever looked at me that way. *I* had never looked at anyone that way. Not Tom, that's for sure.

I stood in the shadows, holding on to the tree, looking at them looking at each other.

And I had two revelations.

One was: I have never loved and now it's too late.

And the other one was: everyone has a choice of how to live their lives. I don't have to go back to Southport. I can actually choose to stay, sort it all out, tie up all the loose ends, with Tom, with my family, and *stay*.

We all have a choice.

I want to stay, I want to be home. More than anything, I want to be home.

15

One Star in the West

Elizabeth

The excitement is palpable, even I can feel it flowing through my substanceless body as I sit on a wooden beam, up near the ceiling. I can see Silke, you couldn't miss her, so tall and striking with her pink hair. She makes me smile because she's brave, fresh and free. Girls of my generation would have never been so daring.

And there's my darling Maisie, chatting to all and sundry in her sweet, funny, confident manner. She's wearing her pink fairy outfit, so she did manage to convince her dad to let her wear it! With a little help from Shona, for sure. Jamie was worried that she'd be cold. He must have ruled that she could wear the fluffy, light dress in spite of the chill in the air, as long as she wore it over her pink long-sleeved top and stripy pink and purple tights to keep her warm. Really, my son is like a mother hen sometimes. Shona has smeared a bit of Kirsty's blue glitter on Maisie's wee cheeks and her lovely flaxen hair is loose on her shoulders like a golden waterfall. The whole effect is so pretty, looking at her from up here, I feel like a hand is squeezing my heart.

Jamie looks smart in his blue and white

checked shirt and dressy jeans. He's standing with a group of fellow artists, a beer in his hand, quiet and unassuming as ever. I'm so proud of him. His work is by far the most remarkable of all those displayed, a beautiful collection of medals, small sculptures and jewellery, all with a Scottish theme, the usual symbols — the thistle, the deer — reinvented and reinterpreted anew. I'm proud of his work, and proud of his decision last night. I'd been terrified for so long, seeing him drinking alone night after night, wondering when it would start spilling into his life, into his work and into Maisie's world. But he stopped it. When Jamie closes a door, it stays closed. He's like his father — indecisive, dreamy, dithering and then, his mind will be made up and there will be no going back. I couldn't resist touching his face last night, though I could see he was startled . . .

Eilidh just came in. She's truly beautiful tonight. She's turning a few heads, in her black dress and shining eyes, walking over to chat with Shona. Fraser and the girls have stayed in Aberdeen to attend Fraser's nephew's birthday party, and Shona is staying with Jamie. I can see how friendly Shona has become with Eilidh since she moved back up. The four-year difference between them was a huge gap when they were growing up but not anymore. Jamie hasn't seen her coming in. Wait till he sees her in that dress!

Oh goodness me. Mary's here. In a wheel-chair. I feel like I'm positively *dissolving* with embarrassment. Had someone told me years ago

133

that one day I would have been a ghost practically throwing an innocent frail woman down the stairs . . .

It did pay off though.

What am I saying? Elizabeth McAnena, you have no shame!

But it *did* pay off.

There, just like I thought. Jamie saw Eilidh. I smile to myself as I see his eyes grow wide with admiration, but he stays rooted to where he's standing, awkwardly. Men. Trust Shona to do the right thing, take Eilidh by the hand and walk over to him and his pals, John and Ally — there they are, the three scallywags. I remember the three of them, barely ten years old, sitting in my kitchen having a piece and jam before going fishing together. John and Ally are both married now, one is a teacher in Kinnear, the other works in a bank in Aberdeen.

Ally is looking at Shona when he thinks nobody sees him. He's always liked her and I think she liked him too, but then Fraser arrived on the scene and that was it. I've often wondered what would have been if Fraser didn't turn up one day, visiting his cousins in Kinnear, down in Glen Avich for the day. After about a year of long distance courting and wearing down the road between London and Glen Avich, he realised that if he wanted Shona to marry him, he would have to move up here, so he did. A wedding, a gorgeous house and three daughters later, neither of them has ever looked back.

Shona had wanted to be a nurse but she never made it because she got pregnant, and then

134

again and again. But don't we all have regrets and learn to live with them?

My regret is a secret. Nobody ever talks about him. To them, it was a blip, a 'thing that happens'. To me, it was a baby. Old enough to know his gender, too young to survive outside of me. I called him Charlie. Then Jamie came and everybody forgot. Everybody except James and me. They say that every woman has a baby story, one that she never shares or talks about. Well, that is mine.

Yes, we all have our regrets, and Shona is happy anyway, I can see it. She's been making enquiries again to see if she could go back to college, start training next year. She'd make a great nurse, caring and efficient as she is. Scarily efficient, really. She used to keep all three of us in line and she's still the only person that can boss Jamie around and get away with it.

The music is starting now. Jamie and Eilidh are sitting side by side in the front row, Jamie has Maisie on his lap. It will be Eilidh up next. Some of the audience will remember when she last stood in front of Glen Avich to read, over twenty years ago.

There she goes, standing in front of the microphone for a second, composing herself. She reads beautifully, her voice is like velvet as she leads the audience into sadness and loss and then to happiness again with the lovely poem for Lucy, Jamie's favourite.

A second of suspended emotion, then somebody claps and the spell is over. Eilidh steps down and Silke hugs her, mouthing 'thank you'.

135

Time for Maisie to go home, she's half asleep in Shona's arms. A flurry of goodbyes and then Jamie and Eilidh stand alone, one in front of the other. Until . . .

'Jamie McAnena? Hi, how are you? I'm Emily,' says the grey-haired woman in a blue pashmina and ethnic jewellery. 'I love your work.'

And Eilidh walks away.

Jamie

Tonight, everything's right with the world. The awful, awful worry in the back of my head, the sense of shame, the hidden threat that I knew one day would take over my life — all that is finished. I'm sure of it, there's no doubt in my mind — I'll never go back there. Once the whisky was poured away, that was it for me.

I am free now.

Eilidh is beautiful tonight. She always is, in her jeans and t-shirts and trainers, but tonight, with that dress, and her hair all wavy and soft . . . I wish everybody would disappear and leave us alone.

But I see sadness in her eyes again. The same sadness I saw when she first arrived in Glen Avich. I wonder what Katrina said last night.

'Eilidh . . . Thank you, you were amazing.'

'Oh, I'm just grateful I remembered it all!'

'Are you ok? You look a bit . . . ' I stumbled. Words. They are so . . . difficult.

She laughed. 'No, it's not me, it's my eyes. I've

136

got my father's eyes, you know — he's Jewish, they all have really sad eyes on his side of the family. Kletzmer eyes, he says.'

I didn't have the slightest idea what to say next. So I came out with, 'Your eyes are beautiful.'

Naff, naff, naff.

To which she smiled, blushed and took a sip of her white wine.

'Jamie McAnena? Hi, how are you? I'm Emily. I love your work.'

I turned to see a woman of about seventy, with grey hair and startlingly dark eyes. Like I care that you are Emily and that you love my work! I didn't say that of course. I nodded politely and took the woman's hand, and Eilidh walked away.

Then something strange happened.

Emily released my hand.

'Go after her,' she said.

What on earth was she talking about? I don't even know this woman! I stood, rooted to the spot.

'Go on, Jamie McAnena,' Emily went on. I looked into her face, there was a smile in her black eyes. 'We can talk about your work another time.'

She turned away, in a cloud of perfume and soft blue cashmere.

It dawned on me. Emily Simms! *The* Emily Simms. The sculptor and patron of the arts.

Shit!

Oh well, whatever. I looked around for Eilidh and found her chatting with a group of girls. I took a deep breath. Here it goes.

'Eilidh, would you like a walk?'

She looked up, surprised. 'Are you not meant to be working?'

'Yes. But I need some fresh air. Come with me.'

Eilidh looked around. 'But . . . the evening sort of . . . just started. Silke will kill us . . . '

'We won't be ten minutes. Come on. I need a word.'

'A word? That sounds serious.' She laughed. 'What have I done? Have I been feeding Maisie Irn Bru and Smarties for her snack or something?'

She grabbed her coat and without looking around for fear of someone talking to us and stopping us from going, we walked out into the freezing night.

'It's sooo cold!' she said. 'It's lovely though. I love it when it's really, really cold and you can see your breath like little clouds.'

'Eilidh. Listen to me now. Would you like to go out with me? This weekend? Just you and me?' Her face fell. Not what I was hoping.

'I . . . I can't, Jamie. I'm sorry. I can't.'

'You need to tell me why. You need to tell me that you don't want to go out with me because . . . because you're not interested in me, or because you're still in love with your husband, or whatever reason, you need to tell me.'

'Neither of them,' she whispered and looked away. 'Jamie, please. Please let me go now. I can't be with you.'

'Why?'

'Because I can't.'

'That's not a reason.'

'Why are you . . . tormenting me like this?' she shouted out. 'I thought you cared about me. Why are you doing this? What do you want me to say?'

I felt myself inhaling sharply, in surprise and dismay.

'Eilidh . . . I'm sorry . . . Please don't cry . . . '

She hid her face in her hands.

'I want to be left alone. I want to be *alone*!'

I took her by the shoulders and drew her to me. She didn't protest, she felt soft and malleable as she moulded herself around me, onto my chest, putting her arms around my neck and holding me tight. We held each other, I cradled her and stroked her hair and whispered in her ear that I was sorry, wishing she could melt into me, so that I would never have to let her go.

It only seemed to last a second, because it wasn't enough, it could never be enough.

Then we heard Silke's voice as she was saying goodbye to some guests at the door and the spell was broken.

She ripped herself away from me, or so it felt — like a part of me was being cut off. I held her face in my hands as she looked up to me and I saw she wasn't crying anymore. She looked peaceful. She looked . . . *resigned*, a voice inside me said.

'Why, Eilidh?'

'Because I'm no good,' she said, and walked away into the night.

16

Life is What Happens To You

There are two lines.

Two lines.

Two wee pink lines standing one beside the other.

I sit on the floor between the toilet and the sink, incredulous.

How on earth did this happen?

People have accidents, but really, *other* people have accidents, not me.

The pink lines dance before my eyes and I feel sick. Too early for morning sickness, this is just reaction.

Maybe it will all go away, as suddenly as it came over me. Things happen. It's really early, something will happen and make it all go away.

Yes, it will go away.

I open the bathroom door and step out, like I don't have a care in the world, like my world wasn't turned upside down in an instant, like nothing has happened.

Because *nothing* has happened, really, it will all go away, like a dream dissolves the second before you open your eyes, and my life will be normal again.

I wrap the test into a sheet of kitchen towel and slip it in the bin when nobody's watching, and there, it's done and dusted. Now I just have to wait until my period comes and all will be fine again.

Eilidh

'Eilidh! Hi darling! Hi Maisie!'

Great, I thought. Just who I wanted to see. Keira's mum.

'Hi Paula.'

'Can I have a word?'

Why was it that everybody wanted to have a bloody word with me?

'Sure.'

She gestured at Maisie with a look that said, 'Not when she can hear.'

Just leave us alone, will you? I thought, but nodded. At the school gates, diplomacy is key. Meetings of mums can be like UN conventions.

'Well, what I'd like to say is,' she whispered conspiratorially, 'we all take our girls to the dancing on a Saturday morning, there's Molly and Rachel and Alina, and Maisie is sort of the only one who doesn't take part. I mean, I can understand Jamie not wanting to do that, what with it being all mums and girls, but now that you're on the scene . . . '

I raised an eyebrow. On the scene? Ruth caught my eye for a second, I could see she wanted to laugh, but she kept her face straight.

'I'd love to take her to the dancing, Paula, but you must understand, I only work for them. The weekends are family time. Jamie wants to spend

141

time with Maisie, sort of on their own, if you
know what I mean.'

'Then *I* could take her. I could collect her and
drop her off again. Just so that she could take
part, that poor wee thing . . . '

I could feel my cheeks flushing. Thing is, I
tend to be quite sweet and gentle most of the
time, but I do have a temper on me, the
McCrimmon temper, though my mum says it
skipped a generation and went down from Flora
directly to me. She's lying, of course. She's the
worst of us lot.

'I can't see why you'd say Maisie's a poor
thing, Paula. She has a dad who adores her and a
lovely wee life. Prancing about in a pink tutu is
not everybody's idea of fun, you know,' I said
icily and walked away.

I didn't care about school gates diplomacy
anymore. I was *furious*.

'Come on, Maisie! Let's go.'

Ruth caught up with me.

'Goodness me, I'm glad I've got two boys,' she
said in a low voice.

I couldn't answer her. I couldn't speak yet. I
was still crimson, I could feel it, and breathless
with annoyance.

'You see, Paula can be a bit . . . well, a bit
overpowering . . . '

'You are always so PC, Ruth! She's not
overpowering, she's a bitch!' I whispered,
minding the children were out of earshot.
'Maisie is perfectly happy. Jamie's a great dad
and they've got better things to do than stupid
ballet.'

142

'I take your point, I'm sure they have lots of fun at weekends, but . . . well, it's true that all the girls bar Maisie and another one go to that dancing class. And while I know that Maisie's a happy girl, well, I've seen her face when they showed us the pics from last year's show. All the pretty costumes, it's a wee girl's dream. Maybe you could bring it up with Jamie.'

I sighed. 'I will. I bet he can't wait to hang out with Paula and her gang — or coven, I should say!'

Ruth laughed. 'You're always so . . . candid.'

'And you're always so kind,' I said, truthfully. 'I've never heard you saying a bad word about anyone.'

'I suppose I don't have it in me. Does Peggy expect you at the shop?'

'Not today, no.'

'Then come up to the house for a cup of tea.'

'I'd love to,' I smiled, looking at Maisie and Ben walking companionably side by side, chatting about the nativity play.

'I hope I'm Mary so I can wear the dress.'

'I hope I am a tree like in nursery so my mum paints my face and my hands and then I can touch things and make them green. Like my mum's coat.'

Ruth and I looked at each other and smiled.

She'd become such a good friend to me, though I hadn't known her long. Which was good because relations with Helena had grown positively frosty, to my frustration. Only recently, I met her walking down the road, leisurely enough, it seemed to me, but when she met me, she was suddenly in a hurry.

'Sorry, Eilidh, I really must dash. My mum has been a bit poorly, you know, all these flu things going round . . . '

'Oh, I'm sorry to hear that, I'll drop by to say hello,' I said, without thinking.

'No, no, it's ok, really, she gets tired easily.'

'Of course, sorry, I should have thought. I'll just bring her some chocolates or something, then, I won't stay.'

'No, honestly. It's ok, I don't think . . . ' She looked away.

A few seconds of silence, then I thought, what the hell, I've got the right to say my piece.

'Helena, I saw Gail on the train from Aberdeen last week. She ignored me. I think I know what's going on and you're wrong. There's nothing between me and Jamie, nothing,' I said vehemently.

'Oh, Eilidh, come on. Do you think it's a coincidence that he broke up with Gail when you came back? I mean, I thought it was Silke.' Oh, how wrong you are, I thought to myself. 'But then I saw the way he looks at you . . . '

'He can look at me however he wants. I'm not seeing him. Or anyone else. Helena . . . I've known you for many years. Don't let this come between us.'

'I'm sorry . . . I know it's not your fault . . . but Gail is distraught. She's devastated. She thought he was . . . you know . . . the one.'

'I'm so sorry. Gail is a lovely girl. I mean her no harm, or you, or your family. I'll stay out of the way,' I said, exasperated — as if it was my

144

fault that Jamie was not interested in Gail!

'I'll call you,' she said and practically ran away. Great. Just great.

Since then, Ruth, Silke and my e-mail correspondence with Harry and Doug have been my main social interactions. Shona hasn't been in touch either. I did wonder if Jamie spoke to her about what happened that night, but it wasn't like her to cut me out for that.

I haven't told anyone about what happened at the opening of the gallery. Not even Harry and Doug. I know what they would say, that I'm an idiot. I can't tell them the truth. I don't want anyone to know why I will not get involved with him. I could never say that it's because I won't put anyone through what Tom went through with me.

'So . . . have you decided?' Ruth began, interrupting my thoughts by handing me a cup of steaming coffee. Maisie and Ben were playing in Ben's room and Jack was building with Lego at our feet.

'So, I'm staying,' I answered, knowing instantly what she was talking about. I had confided in her about how I wasn't sure what was going to happen after Christmas, how I was dreading going back.

'That's great news!' she said, genuinely happy. My heart warmed to see her so relieved that I was going to stay. 'Have you spoken to Peggy?'

'I have. I've told her I can move out and look for a job, probably in Kinnear, but she said she truly needs a hand in the shop and she loves having me at the house. I know it can't last

145

forever . . . I need to make sure I work full-time and when Mary is back on her feet, she'll look after Maisie. But for now, both Peggy and Maisie need me, so . . . '

'And what about your family? And Tom?'

'My family are OK with it. Well, my mum and dad are. I suppose they're just relieved that I'm back on my feet. My sister is quite annoyed. She loved having me around for babysitting duties, errands and the likes, and just to gloat, really.' I smiled bitterly.

'She sounds like a nightmare.' I had told Ruth about my difficult relationship with Katrina.

'She's all right, really, just a bit tactless. At the end of the day, it's not her fault if she's so bloody fertile while I . . . I . . . '

Ruth put her hand on mine. 'Don't torture yourself. We all have a cross to bear, we all muddle through.'

I nodded. Ruth was going through a rough time herself, her marriage was on the rocks.

'And Tom?'

'My mum and dad told him. He phones them every week. I'll phone him after Christmas. I want things sorted as soon as possible.'

'It must have been awful for you . . . I mean to find out . . . '

'No, it wasn't awful, that's the thing. It upset me, of course, but there was so much else going on. I didn't want him to leave, that's all, because we had our IVF booked and all that . . . but I wasn't heartbroken. I wasn't surprised, either, really . . . Anyway,' I took a big breath, 'enough about me. How's things with you?'

146

'Well, stressed out at work, and Billy's saying he's fed up and wants to up sticks and move to Aberdeen . . . on his own.'

'Oh, Ruth!' I was shocked. I didn't think things were as bad as that.

She nodded, her eyes filling up. 'We'll see how it goes,' she said, chokingly. 'That's men for you, I suppose.' We both looked at Jack, happily banging his Lego together, looking impossibly cute in his denim dungarees. 'Apart from present company, of course!' she added and we both laughed, Jack joining in with his delightful chuckling, waving a piece of Lego over his head.

★ ★ ★

That night, I texted Shona.

U ok? Haven't spoken in ages.

Yeah, ok. Lots going on. U?

Ok ☺ *Can we talk? It's about Maisie.*

She ok?

Yes just need advice about something.

Sure. Will speak nxt wk.

Will speak next week? That is not like Shona. Normally, she'd be on the phone at once. I wanted to ask her what she thought about those

147

ballet classes, if I should talk to Jamie about it or if I'd better leave it.

Ok. Night.

I frowned.

'Everything ok?' Peggy and I were sitting together, watching *Eastenders*. I *love* the soap operas. I love spending an hour thinking of nothing but the entangled life of its characters, like some sort of suspended reality.

'Mmmm, suppose so. Just Shona being a bit strange.'

'Yes, she looked funny last Friday, you know, when she came down for the opening. She dropped by for a minute on her way to Jamie's house to get a few things and she looked a bit tired. Well, very tired really.'

That's Glen Avich for you. You can't as much as sneeze without everybody knowing. My mum loves telling this story: once, on her way to secondary school in Kinnear, she had got off at the bus stop before her usual one to look at the window of a clothes shop that was a bit out of the way. When she came home from school, Flora asked her why she had stopped there and not at the usual bus stop, closer to the school.

'How did you know?'

'May told me.'

'May? But she lives in *Canada!*'

'Well, Sharon saw you and told her mum, Agnes mentioned it on the phone to May and May phoned me from Canada to tell me. They

148

were all wondering why you got off at the wrong stop.'

So there you are, Shona wasn't feeling great on Friday. She looked OK at the opening, though I did notice that she was wearing a bit more make-up than usual.

On the TV screen, a woman in a leopard-print mini dress was standing at a market stall, screaming and shouting at someone.

'Dearie me. They're always arguing, aren't they?' laughed Peggy, taking a sip of her tea.

'So they are, it's a miracle the actors have any voice left by the end of the week. Anyway. There's *New Tricks* tonight, Auntie Peggy, you love that,' I said, looking at the TV guide.

I loved this sense of domesticity. It felt . . . safe. Settled. Like nothing bad could happen ever again. Like I was a wee girl again, sitting with Flora, the room dark but for the black and white TV in the corner, watching some variety programme while having our cocoa and biscuits.

It couldn't last forever; I knew that. But for the moment, it was making me strong again. I looked out of the window and I wondered if Silke and Fiona were meeting tonight. Silke was lodging with a local family and Fiona was staying with Mary — there was no privacy for them. I was rooting for them.

From harrydouglasdesign@live.co.uk
To eilidhlawson@hotmail.co.uk

Gay liaisons in Glen Avich? Fire and brim-stones! What were you doing wandering at

149

night anyway? Having illicit rendezvous of your own?

From eilidhlawson@hotmail.co.uk
To harrydouglasdesign@live.co.uk

No, just couldn't sleep. Silke and Fiona are keeping it a secret. I hope it all works out for them.

From harrydouglasdesign@live.co.uk
To eilidhlawson@hotmail.co.uk

Keep us posted. And how's you? How's the dashing Scotsman? That raven hair . . . He's the perfect height, bet you fit perfectly. Doug here is dying to come and visit. Since we got that pic of Maisie with Jamie in the background, he talks of nothing else ☺ ☺

From eilidhlawson@hotmail.co.uk
To harrydouglasdesign@live.co.uk

Please stop guys. I really don't want to hear any more of that. Do come up for New Year. I spoke to Peggy, she remembers you both from my wedding and says she'd love to have you.

From harrydouglasdesign@live.co.uk
To eilidhlawson@hotmail.co.uk

Sorry, didn't mean to upset you. We know you're very raw. All we're saying is, don't

150

shut the world out. Will def be up for Hogmanay, ach aye! Prepare yourselves for an awesome sight: white hairy English legs sticking out of a borrowed kilt. Doug is hearing the call of the ancestors. Ps We know you're allergic to new technology and we should be grateful you can actually switch the laptop on, but when will you get Skype? We want to see your face. Kisses XXX H&D

I smiled and switched the laptop off. I wondered what they were all doing, all my friends and my family back home.

I wondered what Jamie was doing.

That night, I had a strange dream. I'd heard my mum and my gran talk about local women having the Sight, but it runs in families and none of us has it. I certainly don't. And still, that dream was like a vision, a vision of the past. Except it wasn't *my* past.

I saw a wee boy, no more than two, toddling on a wooden floor. I was kneeling on the floor in front of him, but I wasn't myself — I was someone else. I could see my own legs, in beige tights and a woollen skirt, and a ray of sunshine coming in from the window, a million dust particles dancing in it. Somehow, I knew that the wee boy was Jamie. I opened my arms to him and he wobbled on towards me and into them. I held him and he looked up into my face. Our eyes met and I realised that in the dream, I was Elizabeth and Jamie was my son. I woke up with a sense of loss.

17

Thawing

Jamie

I don't know what possessed me the night of the opening. It was crazy. *I* was crazy, high on relief from what I'd done the night before, having kissed the drink goodbye.

It was the end of my lonely drinking sessions and the fuzzy-headed mornings that called for more whisky. Had I not stopped, how long would it have been since I'd answer that call and had a drink before breakfast? Just the thought made me shiver, to think of the abyss that would have opened in front of my Maisie's feet.

But I made it stop and I felt anew. That, together with the success of the evening, made me feel like I could reach out, made me fearless.

I know it's a cliché, but . . . it felt right. It felt like it couldn't go wrong.

But it did.

It was only that night that I'd realised the depth of Eilidh's wounds. When she came into my arms and I held her, I felt as if I had come home. And then she went away.

I'm going to leave her alone. That's what she asked of me, or something along those lines: leave me alone, why are you tormenting me? And the last thing I want is to hurt her. But I couldn't believe that awful, awful thing she'd said, 'I'm no good.' It just seemed so absurd to me that she could say something like that about herself. She's so precious to me and still she thinks she's no good.

I didn't see her on Sunday and then spent the whole of Monday bumping into things and breaking delicate moulds, until I gave up and went home early. There they were, Eilidh and Maisie, sitting on the sofa, doing Maisie's reading for the next day, their heads close and Eilidh's arms around my daughter's wee shoulders.

She blushed when she saw me and hurried to leave. I wanted her to stay but I was afraid she'd think I was trying to put pressure on her, once more. That she'd think I was some kind of . . . I don't know, that it was easy for me to put myself forward, that I played the field. First with Gail, then with her. When really, it was Gail that came forward, not me. As for Eilidh, it had taken me a huge amount of courage to lead her out into the night like that and open my heart. But how could she know that? A man with a daughter from a woman who disappeared. A man who needs to fill his solitary nights.

Never again I would speak to her that way, never again.

When I came in, she threw her jacket on hastily and moved toward the door. I put a hand on her arm, to stop her for a second. I had something to say.

We stood on my doorstep, the twilight lilac

and pink behind her, the pinewoods black against the sky.

'Eilidh, I just wanted to tell you . . . if you want to stop looking after Maisie, I understand.'

She looked up at me, her eyes full of dismay. 'Do you want me to?'

'No, not at all! Not for a moment! Maisie is so happy with you and I . . . I am . . . ' I stumbled. Shit. Whatever I say now, I thought to myself, it'll come out wrong. I know it. Words are clumsy, they build barriers, when a touch, just a single touch, can reveal the truth in a moment. But I couldn't touch her, no matter how much I wanted to.

'I really, really want to keep looking after Maisie,' she said in a low voice. 'I enjoy Maisie's company very much.'

The way she said it, I had to smile.

I love the way she speaks, all dramatic. I love the way she says 'very much'. And the way she says 'so', as in, 'I'm so, so hungry,' or what she said last night, 'It's soooo cold!' I love the way she looks at people straight in the face, straight in the eye, and the way she smiles, because it feels like the sun has come out . . .

I realised I was standing there, staring at her like a fool. I shook myself.

'I'm sorry I embarrassed you.'

'It's ok. Bye.' And she was gone. That's it. She practically ran out.

I felt a wave of despair, in spite of me. Like . . . like life was passing me by.

'Daddy, can you listen to me reading?'

'Of course. I'll listen to you reading and then

154

I'll make us some dinner.'

'Our dinner is in the oven, Eilidh and I made shepherd's pie, she put a apron on me and I mixed the potatoes and made them soft!'

Big breath. You won't be sad, Jamie McAnena, your life is thawing.

'Come on, darling, let me hear how well you read.' And we sat on the sofa and cooried in together, until I noticed: on the worktop, beside the kettle, a carton of milk and just one mug. The one that Maisie had given me last year for Father's Day, after Shona took the girls out to get gifts for Fraser and me. Eilidh always has that mug out and ready when I get home, she knows it's my favourite. But normally, she has another one beside it, for us to have a cup together before she goes. Since that awkward day when I practically threw her out, the cup of tea at the kitchen table has become sort of a tradition.

That is, until tonight. Only one mug. Looking . . . well, looking like half of something.

*   *   *

The night of the opening, after Eilidh had left, I just wanted to go home. But I couldn't, because Silke was counting on me to schmooze the guests. I'm not very good at schmoozing at all. I even hate the *word*. But I wanted to help Silke. She had made a success of the opening, and though my business didn't really need more advertising, I was happy to be part of it, for her, and for the other local artists.

So I went back in, feeling thoroughly awful, and hid it well.

There I was, networking — well, standing silent and smiling, really — when Emily Simms came looking for me.

'Would you be so kind as to tell me more about your work?' she asked skilfully, leading me towards one of my sculptures in a slightly secluded spot. I realised she wanted to speak to me alone.

'I won't ask you how it went. That would be nosy, wouldn't it?' she said, a hand on my arm. She had warm eyes and a lovely, wise face. She looked . . . serene. Something in her demeanour made me want to talk, which doesn't happen often.

'Not well,' I said and took a sip of the tea Silke had put in my hand when I had come back in from the cold.

'I'm sorry,' she said and looked at the cup of tea in my hand, while everybody else was drinking alcohol in one form or other. She *knows*, I thought.

'So . . . yeah, are you up here for long?'

'No. I just came for one night. I came to meet you. I've been keeping an eye on your work for a couple of years now and I suggested to a few of my Australian friends that they do the same. They are very keen to get to know you better, and so am I.'

'Well, that is very flattering. Thank you.'

'I think there would be good chances for you to exhibit in Australia, all over the country. Do you think we can talk about it tomorrow? Silke is taking me for lunch in the local pub, then I'm driving back down.'

Exhibit in Australia? I was speechless.

'I'd love to. Sure. Thanks.'

'Better go now, it's a long drive tomorrow. Oh, and Jamie . . . '

'Yes?'

'Can I be frank? I don't want to embarrass you . . . '

'Sure . . . '

She smiled and her face wrinkled up cheerfully, like it was used to smiling often. 'I'm nearly sixty now. I have quite a bit of life experience and I think it's always worth it to take a risk. Even when it doesn't pay off immediately.'

And with that, she walked away.

I finished the night on Silke's sofa, eating chips, and the awful sense of cold and loneliness left by Eilidh's rejection was softened and smoothed by Silke's companionship. Something about Silke seems to unknot me, to ease me into myself.

We sat together and chatted and ate, and I just hoped with all my heart that it would all work out for her, that Fiona would soon find the courage to bring their love into the light.

'Hopefully Eilidh will see sense, too,' she said, her German accent made thick by tiredness, her pink hair resting on the velvet cushions.

Yes, my life was thawing after all.

Thawing and changing. Turning upside down, even.

Over lunch the next day, Emily asked me whether I'd be interested in setting up a few

157

exhibitions in Australia and then touring the openings.

I was half excited, half daunted. She said I'd need to be there for about four months and I'd be travelling constantly, so it'd make sense for Maisie to stay behind. But I couldn't possibly leave her for so long. If she came with me, she'd miss out on her schooling but learn a lot on the way. It'd be a crazy life for a five-year-old, but better than being separated from me for such a long a time.

This was the opportunity of a lifetime, but I couldn't just say yes straight away, there was too much to consider.

I told Emily I'd get back to her, that I needed time to think, and saw her off with a mixture of excitement and a sense of . . . disquiet. Changes unsettle me, even good ones. Like my father, I always try and preserve the status quo. I had to speak with Shona and see what she thought.

'So, where were you last night? I heard you coming in at dawn!' She was sitting at the breakfast table, still in her dressing gown even though it was past twelve o'clock. Very un-Shona.

'I was with Silke.'

Shona looked shocked. 'Seriously?'

'No, not what you think. Silke's gay. Hers is the worst kept secret in the whole of Scotland. Everybody knows. The thing is, nobody knows about her girlfriend, so that's why they're trying to keep it quiet.'

'Who?' asked Shona conspiratorially. You can trust Shona with anyone's secret, so I told her.

158

'You are joking! Fiona? Well, good for her! Except . . . well, you know the Robertsons. They are very . . . '

'Bigoted?'

'I was going to say conservative. They are good people. Just not used to things being . . . you know, different.'

'Well, we'll see how it goes. Anyway, Silke and I are not having a relationship. In spite of what Gail says.'

'Did Gail think that? Not anymore anyway. I met Helena at Sharon's yesterday and she kept trying to prise information out of me about you and Eilidh.'

I looked away. 'I thought Helena was a friend of Eilidh's.'

'Some friend. The whole clan is out to get her now. Gail is in a bad way apparently, she's talking about going to New York for a year, they've got family there. They are furious with you, too.'

'They would have been more furious had I married her and made her miserable. I don't love her — can't they just get that? We went out for six months, it's not like I led her on for years!'

'I know, I know, just let it go. Don't get yourself upset over it.'

'I'm not. Well, maybe a bit. You don't look so good yourself — you look a bit pale. Did you not sleep well? Are you feeling ok?'

'I didn't sleep much last night, actually. I'm shattered today. Would it be OK if I give Fraser a ring and stay another night? I'll get a good night's sleep and drive up tomorrow.'

159

'Of course, don't drive tonight if you're not up for it. I'm sorry I left you looking after Maisie this morning.'

'Not at all, you had to go and meet that Emily person . . . what's her name again?'

'Emily Simms. She asked me . . . ' I took a big breath. 'Well, she asked me to go over to Australia for a few months. Set up a few exhibitions, attend the openings and all that. All over the country.'

There was a moment of silence.

'For a few months? What about Maisie? I mean, it's wonderful, but . . . what would Maisie do?'

'She'd come with me. I don't think we should be apart for that long.'

'No, of course not, you'd have to take her with you, you'd both suffer otherwise, I think.'

I nodded. She didn't speak.

'It's a wonderful opportunity,' I said tentatively. 'The sort of success I never dreamt of.'

'That's because you never really dreamt of success at all. Success never seemed to be high in your list of priorities. Money, even less.'

'Success would mean having to work less and being with Maisie more, and money would mean giving her the best chances in life.'

'Like what?'

'Like the best university, the best . . . I don't know. The best of everything. Ok, I know what you're doing here.' I smiled.

Shona smiled back and shrugged her shoulders. 'If you feel you want to go, I don't think that ultimately she'd suffer. You'd look after her, she'd be fine and she'd learn so much and see so much . . . It's just that I'm not sure you'd enjoy doing it. Being away from home for all that time, having to schmooze and meet lots of new people, networking and making contacts — you'd have to socialize an awful lot. I don't know, I think you'd be a bit . . . well, like a fish out of water. But then, it's only a few months . . . '

'You say being away from home would be hard but what's keeping me here? You have your own life up in Aberdeen, my pals are all married, we have a million cousins with an average age of seventy . . . *who* keeps me here? Nobody will be devastated if I go away for a bit.'

'I will. But that's beside the point. You know what I think? There's something you're not telling me. I don't know . . . It's like you *want* to get away from here.'

'Well, I think there's something *you* are not telling me. You've been strange this weekend, I can't quite put my finger on it.'

'Don't try and distract me. This is not about me.'

'Well, no, but I'll do you a deal. I'll tell you if you tell me.'

She hesitated, and looked at me open-mouthed for a second. Then she blurted out, 'I'm pregnant. Again. I'm not enrolling in college next year — it's back to sleepless nights and nappies for me . . . I really . . . I really wanted to do this, you know? Become a nurse. I got married so young, started having babies . . . This was *my* time . . . '

'Oh, Shona . . . ' I put my arm around her

161

shoulder and brushed her blonde hair away from her face. 'I'm sorry.'

'Don't say that! Don't say you're sorry. It sounds awful, to say that about a baby . . . '

'It does, but I can hardly say congratulations if you say you're devastated.'

'Can you bloody believe it? We had an accident. An accident! I'm on the pill, I didn't skip a day, I didn't throw up or anything, but still, it happened! It's not even like we do it that often, with the girls and stuff, I'm always knackered — '

'SHONA, please, I don't want to hear about that. Whatever happens, I don't want to hear about my sister's sex life!'

'Sorry . . . '

'Does Fraser know?'

'No. I found out for sure only this morning.'

'Well, maybe it'll be a son . . . '

'Don't say that! It sounds awful, to say that and then if it's a girl, it's like she's less wanted than the other three.'

I laughed.

'What's so funny?'

'I can't say sorry because it's not nice to say that about a baby. I can't say that maybe it's a boy in case it's a girl and she feels less wanted. It doesn't exactly sound like you're unhappy about this baby.'

'DON'T say that, don't say I'm unha — Oh. Yes, I see what you mean . . . '

'I know you're disappointed about the nursing but you can always do that in a few years. It's just a delay. I know it's not ideal — ' She opened her mouth. 'I know, I know, don't say it's not ideal in case the baby takes offence!'

We both laughed and she dried her wet cheeks.

'Thank you.'

'You're welcome. Congratulations.' I gave her a hug.

'Your turn now. And don't try to change the subject.'

'I asked Eilidh to go out with me, she said no.' Shona's face fell.

'*No?* But why?'

'Maybe she doesn't like me, I know it seems impossible to you that someone might not like your baby brother but — '

'No, it's not that. She does like you. Maybe it's too soon . . . '

'Yes. Whatever. I'm leaving it. For good. I don't want any more . . . I don't want any more heartache.' The words came out with difficulty. It's not easy to talk about feelings, not even with my sister.

'Oh, Jamie. It's all so complicated, isn't it? Our plans are going all over the place . . . a new baby, and maybe Australia, and Eilidh not working out . . . '

'What do you mean Eilidh not working out? Were you counting on us getting together?'

'You don't really understand women, do you? Of course I was counting on it!'

'Oh well. I'm always the last to know.'

'True. Anyway, it's all so confusing. I wish someone . . . well, I wish someone could look after us . . . sort everything out . . . '

We looked at each other.

'I'll look after you. I'll make you a nice dinner and a cup of tea and then off to bed.'

'You sound like Mum.'

That made me smile.

18

Ballet Classes

Eilidh

Those ballet classes had become the cross of my life. That woman kept asking me, over and over again. Four times in a week. I *had* to make her stop.

'Jamie, do you have a minute?'

'Of course. Tea?'

'Sure.'

'Are you staying for tea?' A wee voice came from behind the sofa. Maisie had built a den with a sheet in between a chair and the back of the sofas, and had furnished it with cushions, her Rose Cottage and her ponies.

'No, darling, not tea as in dinner, just a cup of tea,' I answered.

I saw Jamie opening his mouth to say something. Probably trying to reiterate what I had just said. He surely didn't want to spend any more time with me, after that awful night.

'Oh, OK . . . ' he said.

We hovered around the kettle until the tea was ready, then sat on the sofa. Maisie was having a tea party of her own with the ponies.

'More tea, Maisie? Yes, thanks, Pinky. I'll have

a scone and jam and chips and popcorn, thank you.'

'Right. What's up?' he asked. He looked tired, he was pale and had a five o'clock shadow. He had been very busy, even busier since the opening.

'Well, I'm being harassed by a mum at school. She's saying that all girls but two go to dance classes on a Saturday morning, one of them being Maisie. She says that Maisie is missing out, that I should take her. But I know that the two of you enjoy your family time at the weekend, and I'm not sure if you want to miss out on that.'

'I never knew about the dance classes . . . I can't ask you to do that as well. I'll take her. Though it'll be horrific.' He smiled, a twinkle in his eye.

'It *will* be. I'd be dreading it myself, it must be a stronghold of the mummy mafia.'

He laughed, a deep, wholehearted laugh.

'The mummy mafia?'

'You probably never noticed. Men don't notice these things.'

'Funny you say that. Shona just said the same to me last weekend. About something else.'

'Shona was right. Anyway, don't worry yourself about the nippy mums. They'll be all over you. They just love you, Jamie!' I rolled my eyes.

'Of course they do,' he said with a wink and we both laughed. It was good to be talking to him like that, without any . . . misunderstandings.

'I wouldn't mind taking her though. It

wouldn't be a problem for me at all. She'll look really, really cute in her ballet costume!'

'Come with us, then,' he said, looking me straight in the eye.

I hesitated.

'Look, I know you don't feel . . . I know you don't want . . . ' He started fumbling, and blushing. I just wanted to rescue him.

'It's ok, seriously . . . '

'What I mean to say is, we can be friends. Like we used to be when we were kids. I . . . I want you in my life. Even if not the way I'd like it to be . . . I still want you in my life.'

'What's for dinner?' piped Maisie from her den. We both jumped.

'I'm sorry, I couldn't cook for you today . . . I'm afraid there is no dinner!' I said, grateful for the interruption. We were straying onto dangerous ground.

'No problem, really, you don't have to do that anyway.'

'But I want to. I enjoy cooking. It's just that today . . . ' I shrugged my shoulders.

'Oh, I know what you're trying to say — no food in the cupboards.' He smiled. 'I've been so busy, with the opening and then the orders coming in . . . '

'Don't worry, I'll bring some stuff down from the shop tomorrow.'

'You don't need more work.'

'It's no hassle. Seriously.'

'Thanks. I always keep some money in here, help yourself.' He stretched to reach a biscuit tin on the top shelf.

'Daddy! I'm hungry!' The blonde top of a head appeared from behind the sofa, followed by a wee face.

'Chinese?'

'Naughty!' I smiled.

He laughed. 'Sorted then. Now, where's that menu . . . ' Jamie started rustling in a kitchen drawer.

'By the way, I haven't heard from Shona in a while. I texted her to ask her what she thought about those classes, you know, a mother's opinion — I hope you don't mind.'

'Not at all, she's the official authority on all things girly,' he answered, taking out a stash of menus and brochures. 'It's in here some-where . . . '

'Thing is, she said she'd call me and she didn't. It's not like her, especially where Maisie is concerned. Do you know if something's up?'

'Well . . . I'm not sure. I think she . . . I think she might have stuff going on right now . . . '

'I see.' Jamie *knew*, but didn't want to say. 'Well, tell her I'm always there for her if she needs to talk, or if she needs a hand or something . . . '

'Will do. There it is. The one and only Glen Avich Golden Palace. What would you like?'

Shona

So here I am, standing in front of the mirror in my Marks knickers and bra. Unmistakable, the signs of pregnancy. Bigger boobs, for a start, all

168

veiny and swollen and a bit painful. Shiny hair, glowing skin, but blue shadows under the eyes — due to tiredness, morning sickness or sleeplessness, or all of the above. And the bump, the tiny bump that is not quite a real, proper bump yet, but it's too big, too tight and solid to be just too many cream cakes.

The first time I got pregnant it was like a train had hit me. I was constantly sick, couldn't keep anything down, couldn't sleep, I couldn't even think. My brain had gone. Honestly, it was hell, so much so that I had to remind myself constantly why I was going through all that, that there was a prize at the end of it. The hormones made me moody, low and incredibly irritable. I cringe when I think of the time I harassed a shop manager in Kinnear because they weren't packing my frozen goods fast enough! Me, the usually mild mannered, extra polite Shona, who had been brought up to never, never, never be rude. Worse was to come when I screamed at Fraser for two hours solid, all the way down to the Borders where we were going on holiday. The poor man must have feared for his life, two weeks stuck in a cottage in the middle of nowhere with a woman possessed.

I became slightly cheerier when the morning sickness subsided and I could eat again. The colour came back to my cheeks. Then came the first kick. I'll never forget the feeling: a flutter, like a butterfly or a bubble going 'pop' inside me. That was the first time I felt that she was there, my baby, that we were *together*. I started chatting to her and I knew when she was sleeping, when she felt like having some exercise, when she wasn't comfortable and wanted me to move. She'd tell me all that, with kicks and movements and . . . well, telepathy. I know, it's not telepathy in the literal sense, it's just that she seemed to speak to me without words. In any case, however it happened, I knew.

Labour was . . . How can I put this? Well, when it's your first baby and you're talking to women who've been through all that already, they say something along the lines of: 'Yes, labour is a bit sore, but you forget all about it and you have your lovely baby in the end . . . '

It's all a pack of lies. It's not 'a bit' sore and you don't forget about it — that's just a conspiracy started by women to preserve the human race. Labour is *hell*. It was a day and a half of pure, endless agony and I did not forget a thing. Neither did Fraser, who nursed a mangled hand — the one I was holding on to for dear life — for a few days afterwards. He tried to wiggle free but I didn't let him.

'Darling, do you mind . . . could you release my hand for a wee minute . . . ouch!'

'Do you think that's painful?' I screamed at him. 'YOU DON'T KNOW PAINFUL! YOU BAS-TARD . . . AAAAAAAWWWWWWWWWWW!!!!!!'

Funny thing is, when a friend of mine who was expecting her first asked me about labour, guess what I said? 'Well, it's a wee bit sore, but you forget it and then you have your lovely baby in the end . . . ' and so the conspiracy continues, and the human race doesn't come to an end. And though I didn't forget the pain, the end

170

result was so amazing, so incredibly joyful, that I couldn't wait to do it all again.

Alison Elizabeth Boyd was gorgeous, all tiny and scrunched up and soft, with eyes that were two dark pools of otherworldliness. I had been in love with her since I knew she was there, then I had fallen for her all over again when she started moving. But when she was born, it was different. It was like a wave of the most intense love I had ever felt in my life. It was a tsunami, really. I was breathless with it. I held her and didn't put her down for about six months.

'I didn't know love until you were born,' I whispered to her one night when we were alone, tears of pure emotion rolling down my cheeks. Those moments you'll never, never tell anyone about. Like when I used to take her babygro off and her vest and nappy, and let her kick on a towel on our bed, just to enjoy the sight of her pink, soft, perfect little body, and feel that if I died there and then, it'd have all been worth it just for that moment.

It was bliss. And it was terror. All my radars were up, watching for dangers. When she was in my arms, her delicate head could have hit something. For the first few days, I froze every time I walked through a door. Her bath could have been too hot or too cold. I could have nipped her by mistake while changing her nappy, with those frightful adhesive things at the side of it. And worst of all, she could have stopped breathing in the middle of the night. The world around us was full of dangers and I had a painful, physical need to protect her. I felt so fiercely protective that I could have *growled*.

It took me a couple of years to relax a bit and by then, I was pregnant again, with Lucy. My feelings for her weren't less intense but they were entirely different. A lot less painful, a lot less frightened. Lucy slotted into our family without a bother, a happy, settled baby who ate and slept and hardly ever cried, and Alison loved having a sister.

A few years later came Kirsty, the baby of the family. I suppose I should have been a bit blasé about it all by then but Kirsty blew me away, with her black hair, like my dad's and like Jamie's, and her sweetness, her sheer . . . Kirstyness. And that was it. Our family was complete.

And then you came.

My college brochures and forms are in the paper recycling, and you are growing, silently, waiting to land and turn my life upside down.

I'm scared. I worry that a baby who comes like this, unplanned, unexpected, might end up being . . . less wanted. And I can't bear to want one of my babies less than the others. I can't bear the thought of not being blown away by all the things you'll do — the first step, the first word — like I've been with the girls.

I'm scared I won't love you as much, as naturally and easily as I do your sisters. Jamie thinks that's impossible. That's your uncle Jamie, you'll like him, he's great. As for your dad, well, he doesn't know yet.

Your sisters are away for a sleepover and I've prepared a lovely dinner for your dad and me, so we can get a bit of peace and quiet, and talk.

172

About you, of course. Oh, here he is.

The keys turn in the door, his steps are up the stairs. He comes in and looks at me, standing in my underwear.

'Hi . . . sorry, I'm not dressed yet . . . '

'Oh my God . . . '

'What?'

'Oh my God . . . '

'WHAT?'

'You're pregnant!'

He's standing there with his mouth open. For heaven's sake, SAY something!

'How . . . how did it happen?'

Oh God. He's not happy.

'What do you think?'

'Yes, well, I know but . . . you're on the pill . . . oh, who cares!' and he smiles, and he holds me, and he strokes my hair and says, his voice muffled into my neck, 'I love you.'

All my fears disappear in one big swoop and I know I'll love you, my darling little unborn baby, as much as the others. But not like the others. You'll have your own special kind of love, like they all do, the one that only you and I share.

Just please, please, let's skip the morning sickness this time.

19

Far and Away

Jamie

I thought and thought and thought about it. Then thought about it some more. To leave Maisie behind was not an option, four months away from her would just be unbearable.

I could take someone with me, like Emily suggested, someone that could look after Maisie and help her with her schoolwork as well. Obviously, Eilidh was out of the question, too awkward with all that had been going on between us. I didn't know anyone else but I didn't think it'd be difficult to find someone to take the job. A four-month tour of Australia, looking after an easy-going, sweet five-year-old would appeal to many people.

I knew I was going to miss Shona but we'd be back just after the birth. As for being away from Eilidh . . . well, that's why I wanted to go, really. I couldn't shake off my feelings. This arrangement we had . . . to meet every night when I got home and every Saturday for the dance classes . . . it was getting impossibly hard for me. Like some sort of torture.

After our talk, she'd started putting two mugs out again and there we were, sitting on the sofa with Maisie at our feet, and I could smell her scent and feel her as she occasionally brushed against me, and I felt like a hand was squeezing my heart. I'd speak to her, and it wasn't enough. I'd see her, and it wasn't enough. When we talked, I never wanted us to stop talking. When I was with her, I never wanted to part. I wanted to hold her in my arms and never let her go. But nothing, nothing could ever be enough, because I wanted to kiss her, and touch her, and make love to her. I'm not ashamed to say it, why should I be?

What happened to me? Only a couple of months ago I couldn't allow anyone in. I was determined it would just be Maisie and me. I resented Gail coming into our lives; I just didn't want her there.

And then, Eilidh arrived and she *destroyed* all my walls, just brought them down, turned them from stone to pebbles to sand, and I was . . . exposed.

Her blue eyes, her hair that is just the colour of chestnuts, a dark and warm and shiny shade of brown, her creamy skin with a hint of amber, maybe her Jewish ancestors? Her voice, her laughter, the way she walks and stands, so small and vulnerable and yet somehow strong. Like she has a backbone of steel, yet she doesn't know it. All of it, all of her, was all I could think about. She haunted me. My heart soared whenever I saw her and then it sank when she had to go. I lived for the moments we spent together.

I *had* to go to Australia. It was the only way. It'd just be torture to keep going on like this. I

175

never thought I'd want to leave Scotland but somehow, Scotland and Eilidh were merging, they were turning into the same thing, into all that is home to me.

★   ★   ★

'Hello, it's Jamie McAnena here, can I speak to Emily, please?'

'Speaking. How are you? I hope you have good news for me.'

'Well, I've decided to go for it.'

'Oh, I'm so pleased!'

'But I don't have anyone to come with me and look after Maisie, as yet. So that has to work out before I can give you a definite yes.'

'I might be able to help you with that. I spoke to my niece, Emma. She's a primary teacher, she just qualified last July, and is doing supply in different schools. She's thinking of teaching abroad, Singapore maybe, but she'd be happy to take four months out to tutor Maisie and look after her. She's a lovely girl, she's only twenty-one and she's great, though I know I'm biased!'

'No, it sounds good. Great, actually. A teacher would be ideal.'

'Exactly. Emma could speak to Maisie's teacher so that she could keep up with her classmates and not miss out on a whole year.'

'And where is Emma based?'

'London, like me. Come down to meet her — you can stay with us. Or we'll come up and see you, if you like. My husband can't wait to see

Glen Avich. I told him it's just beautiful.'

'I don't mind. We can drive down, or if you want a wee break, come and stay with me.'

'No, it's three people, maybe four because my sister, Emma's mum, would love to come up, too. We'll check in at the Green Hat. Goodness, so much to discuss . . . I'm so pleased you've said yes. As soon as you give us the green light with Maisie's arrangement, I'll contact the Australian side of the deal.'

'Ok. Thanks, Emily. Just email me or phone when you're coming up.'

'I will. I'll speak to you soon. Oh, and Jamie . . . '

'Yes?'

'You've made the right decision.'

'Yes. Thank you. Bye.'

Had I?

Emily had mentioned Sydney, Melbourne, Perth, maybe New Zealand, too. Places I'd never thought I'd see, places I'd never thought Maisie would see at such a young age. She'll learn so much.

Emily had also said we should ideally have everything ready by March. Less than four months away. It all seemed so sudden. Christmas was three weeks away and then March would come before we knew it. I had to tell Maisie. Knowing her, she'd be delighted. She's not a timorous child at all, I knew she'd take it all in her stride. The only thing was, she and Eilidh had grown so close . . .

I had to tell Eilidh. And of course, I had to tell Shona. But in a wee bit, after the shock of her unexpected pregnancy subsided.

I wondered how Eilidh was going to take it. On the other hand, I didn't even know if Eilidh would be here when we came back. I knew that she was thinking of going back just after Christmas, then she'd told me she'd stay at least until next spring. Clearly, she didn't want to go back to Southport, but who knows?

The fire was dying; the TV screen was flickering. There was a warmth in the air that night, like an Indian summer. My living room seemed a bit alien, a bit strange, as if things had somehow moved around, switched places. Like everything had changed slightly.

Soon, my home would be a hotel, a different one every couple of months. Goodness. Me, going on *tour?* I'm just a blacksmith, not a popstar or something. Life *is* unpredictable.

I wasn't sure if I was really excited or really terrified. A mixture of both. I finished my glass of sparkling water with lemon, switched the TV off and headed upstairs.

And then, it happened. The curtains at the far end of the room flickered as I went.

When it first started happening, as I realised it wasn't my cat Mischa doing it — she'd still be out for her nightly hunting — it freaked me out, my heart always skipped a beat and the hair at the back of my neck stood on end. But it happened so often — not every night, but nearly — that it didn't scare me anymore. I'd come to expect it. A wee flicker, the way curtains quiver and flow a bit when someone walks beside them . . .

Mine is a very old house and a lot of people were here before us. There's a long, long line of people behind each and every one of us. If there's a trace of them left, it would not surprise me, it would not frighten me.

I walked upstairs, brushed Maisie's forehead with my lips, gently touched her blonde hair, and made sure she was warm and cosy under her white duvet with the wee lilac stars. Like every night, I marvelled at her sweetness, at her innocence as she slept, and I thought about how lucky I was that God, or life, or whatever power there is, had sent her to me. I got into my bed, cold, big and empty, and like every night, in spite of my best efforts, Eilidh's face came floating in front of me, behind my closed eyes.

Elizabeth

He's going.

He's going and I know I won't be here when they come back. There's only so much I can do, there's only so long I can resist before I'm pulled away, before my soul is called back, made new and sent to the wheel of life again.

I know I'll never see my darling son again. My beloved Maisie.

I won't stop him. I must let him go. If things with Eilidh are not working out the way I hoped, the way he hoped . . . still, he's living his life. He stopped drinking alone, he started opening up. He's alive again. Eilidh did work a miracle, though not the way I thought she would.

179

Who knows what'll happen when he's in Australia. He might meet someone. He might stay. Who knows. I won't be there to see. But I have to trust that he'll be ok, and that Shona will be OK with her fourth child — it's another girl. I'll hold on until she gives birth, I'll be there to bless my new granddaughter.

And then, I'll go. I hope, I hope with all my heart, that I can come back to Scotland. More than anything, I hope that when I'm someone else, Scotland will still be my home.

Jamie

Eilidh was right about the mummy mafia. They *were* scary. At the dance classes, I got very, very quiet and Eilidh just smiled and said nothing. They seemed to have a uniform: tight jeans, black jackets, flat shoes in different animal prints, huge bags and huge wedding rings. And they all seemed to drive enormous jeeps. The classes were expensive, the equipment was expensive, the costumes for the shows — three each — were extortionate, and therefore only a 'certain kind of people' could take their daughters there.

The wee girls seemed a nice bunch, though, and they were funny and cute in their wee pink ballerina costumes. Maisie, of course, was the prettiest. She'd put her arms up gracefully, practice going up on her toes, cock her head on one side and smile, and I was bursting with pride. Eilidh did her hair in a bun on top of her head, kept in place by a knitted pink . . . thing. Not sure what it's called. Tea cosy for hair, really. Peggy knitted it. Maisie was the first one to have it, then they all followed suit, mobilizing grannies and great-aunts to knit one for them.

There was one boy in the class too, looking mutinous as he was made to jump about in tights. He clearly hated it, but his mum had no daughters and she wanted to be part of the golden mummy circle, so he had to be there. Poor wee guy, I overheard him once saying to his mum that all his friends go to tae-kwon-do on a Saturday morning, but he was blanked. They did tae-kwon-do just next door, so the girls in pink mix in the foyer with the — mainly — boys in white. The boy in tights would chat to his friends and look longingly at their costumes, clearly dying to join them.

It made me wonder if I'd ever have a son.

For the third Saturday in a row, Eilidh and I were watching Maisie from the sidelines, trying to keep ourselves to ourselves, but it wasn't to be.

'Hiii, Jamie!'

Keira's mum. Quick, hide.

'Listen, I was wondering, why don't you come up for lunch next Sunday?' she asked, looking straight at me and ignoring Eilidh.

She had very long, very red nails.

'I can't, sorry, I'm very busy these days and I'll be working at the weekend, too.'

'Oh. Well, maybe we can look after Maisie for you, and you can collect her and stay for dinner?'

'It's so kind of you to offer, but my sister will

181

come down more often, she and Eilidh will manage between them.'

'It must be hard for you, without any help,' she whispered sympathetically. I could see Eilidh's eyes narrowing, her cheeks getting redder.

'Eilidh is a great help,' I said, smiling and gesturing to her.

'It must be hard,' she reiterated. 'Well, maybe another time?' she said, still without acknowledging Eilidh.

'No, I don't think so.'

Shit. Did I just say that aloud?

Eilidh looked flabbergasted. So did Paula. She shot me a surprised look, said something about being in a rush and left.

'Very diplomatic,' Eilidh said, eyes wide with surprise, but her lips curling into a reluctant smile.

I was mortified. 'I shouldn't have said that . . . It just came *out* . . . Keira is her best friend . . . '

'Actually, Maisie is cooling it off. She says Keira is always bossing her and gets into trouble with the teacher a lot. And she's not nice to Ben.'

'Who's this Ben?'

'Oh, here we go, the jealous dad!' Eilidh teased me. 'Her new best friend. He's lovely. A really nice boy. He does tae-kwon-do in the afternoon.'

'Do you think Maisie might want to switch to tae-kwon-do?'

'Not in a million years. It's all the pink gear, you see. And the hair accessories, they clinch the deal. God, I can't believe what you said to that woman!'

'Neither can I, to be honest. She deserved it though, blanking you like that.'

The girls were dismissed and ran towards us, clumsy and sweet and funny the way wee girls are, like a gaggle of pink ducklings.

'Well done! You were great. Right baby, come on, I'll help you change,' said Eilidh, hugging Maisie briefly. They seemed so close . . . I've got to tell Eilidh about our plans.

'Can I treat you both to lunch?' I asked, as they came out of the changing rooms, Maisie back in her civvies — denim dungarees — her long hair loose on her shoulders.

'Yes! Can we go to the red restaurant?'

The red restaurant is a carvery between Glen Avich and Kinnear. Maisie loves it.

'Is that ok for you?' I asked Eilidh.

'I'm not sure . . . Maybe I should go back, Peggy will be on her own.'

'Well, I was hoping to . . . I was hoping to chat to you about something. Tell you both at the same time . . . '

'Sounds serious!' She laughed but she looked a bit worried.

'No, no, it's nothing bad, just something I need to tell both of you. Well, *ask* Maisie, really. Because if she doesn't want to . . . '

'Want what?' Maisie piped in. I looked at Eilidh.

'Ok. Ok, I'm coming, let's go.'

After a lovely lunch, which I didn't enjoy for nerves, we got to the pudding. Chocolate cake for the girls, a coffee for me.

'So . . . thing is, I've been asked to go and

work in Australia for a bit. It's a country far, far away, across the sea,' I added, for Maisie's benefit, 'and I'd like to go. For a few months only, then we'll come back.'

Deep breath.

'Can I come with you, Daddy?' Maisie looked nonplussed.

'Of course, of course, darling. You'll come with me and we'll travel around together, and a teacher will come with us so you don't miss out on schoolwork. You'll see lots of amazing places.'

'Ok,' she said, before putting a big morsel of cake into her mouth.

'It'll be great. We'll stay in really nice hotels and it'll be a great adventure!' I said, a bit over enthusiastically.

'Ok, Daddy,' she repeated, shrugging her shoulders.

Oh well. That was easy.

Then came the hard bit.

'I wanted to tell you together because . . . well, Maisie deserved to know first, you know, being her who's going, but then she would have told you and I wanted to be the one . . . '

'That's great, Jamie, really. Such a wonderful opportunity.'

'Yes, it is an opportunity . . . and we'll only be away for a few months.'

'So when are you going?' she asked, looking into her cake.

'This spring. March.'

'So soon?' she gasped but composed herself. I knew she'd miss Maisie terribly.

'It's five months away . . . and you'll see a lot

of Maisie until then . . . '

'Of course. Of course. I'm not even sure I'll be here when you come back. I mean, maybe I'll have gone back to Southport . . . '

For a second, I couldn't breathe.

'Yes, I understand . . . '

'Well, here's to your . . . well, I can't call it move, can I? You're coming back . . . '

'Emily . . . you know Emily Simms, I told you about her . . . she calls it a tour.'

'A blacksmith on tour?' She laughed.

'I know . . . it sounds a bit . . . X *Factor*, doesn't it?'

'Just don't go trashing hotel rooms! To your *tour*,' she said with a big smile, raising her glass of juice. We joined in.

'To the tour . . . '

'What's a tour?'

Eilidh and I laughed, and Maisie laughed, too, though she didn't know why we found it funny. Then we finished our meal, though Eilidh only picked at her cake after that, and on the way back, she was very, very quiet.

I wanted to say to her, had things been different, that night, had she said yes . . . But I didn't, there was no need, she knew.

'Remember to pack your bags,' said Maisie, as Eilidh was getting out of the car. Eilidh froze. So did I.

'Eilidh isn't coming, darling, it's just you and me.'

Maisie's face fell.

I knew it'd been too easy.

Eilidh smiled as if nothing was happening,

185

tapped on Maisie's window and waved cheerily, but I looked into the mirror when we drove away and I saw that her face looked . . . forlorn, that's the only way to put it.

Maisie was quiet, too.

My heart sank.

'Daddy?'

'Yes?'

'See when we go to Australia?'

'Yes?'

'Will Granny come?'

I was silent for a minute.

'Your granny? Darling, you know Granny is in heaven . . . '

'Not at night, at night she's on my bed.'

I didn't answer. I have to admit, I was a bit freaked out. She didn't say anything else about it and I didn't ask.

20

Let Nothing You Dismay

Eilidh

'Hi, Mum, it's me.'

'Hi, Eilidh, how are you? You're phoning an awful lot these days.'

Yes, well, sorry. Trust my mum to say something like that.

'I thought I'd let you know that I'm staying up here for Christmas.'

'Well, that's fine, but you can't expect us to come up. Peggy can't put up all of us and it'd cost Katrina a fortune to check into the Green Hat.'

'No, of course, of course I don't expect you to all come up.' God forbid.

'Will you not miss the kids? They're your nieces and nephew, after all.' She sounded reproachful.

Yes, I missed them. I missed my nieces and nephew, though Katrina never let us get properly close, never gave us time to get to know each other. But I love them to bits — Jack and the twins, and wee Molly . . .

'Yes, of course, but I'm not ready to come back. Not even for Christmas.'

'Katrina told me you were very cold with her

187

when she phoned to invite you.'

No point in saying anything. My mum never listens if I say something even remotely critical of Katrina. And they have the same sense of diplomacy, so Katrina's hurtful comments are their idea of being honest. Somehow.

'I was thinking, maybe you and Dad would like to come up . . . just the two of you . . . maybe not for Christmas, but around that time . . . '

'Us? No, darling, I'm sorry, but we just can't. We're spending the festivities with Katrina and the kids and then going down to Cornwall to see Jim and Laura.'

'Oh, of course. I shouldn't have asked.'

'We need a proper holiday, you know.'

'Yes, of course. Of course you do.' Deep breath. 'Have you spoken to Tom recently?'

'Yes, he calls a lot. We reassure him you're ok. I asked him, you know, about that girl. They're living together.'

Oh. A pause, as I was trying to start breathing again.

'I'm sorry, Eilidh. Good riddance, I say. I don't know how I bring myself to speak to the guy! Your dad wants to go and punch him straight in the face!'

The thought of my peace-loving dad punching anyone defied belief.

'No, don't do that! Ok? I'll sort it. Soon. Don't worry. I'm ok. I'm ok . . . about it.'

'As I said, good riddance. Have to go now, Eilidh. Must call Laura. Bye.'

She'd spend hours on the phone with Laura

but always cut me short. No point in feeling hurt about it, that's just the way it is.

After Christmas, I was going to sort out the whole thing. Speak to Tom, get the ball rolling about the divorce.

Divorce. God. What a harsh word. I was positively dreading it but it had to be done.

Peggy walked up to me. 'Eilidh, dear, I couldn't help overhearing what you and your mum were saying. Margaret and Sandy are coming for Christmas dinner. I'd love you to stay.'

'I'd love to, if it's ok with you.'

Peggy's face lit up and it warmed my heart. 'It's a pleasure. You know, with the girls not coming back this year, it's so good to have you here. Sandy and Margaret are on their own, too — James is staying down in London with the in-laws — so it'll be the four of us. Are you sure you don't mind being with us oldies?'

'Oh, it'll be wild, Peggy. We'll be dancing on the tables and disgracing ourselves!'

Peggy laughed. 'Oh dearie me. You're such a *character*.'

'Is it ok if I cook? I'm thinking of something alternative. Not the usual turkey, you know . . . something more . . . I don't know, something to stretch us a bit. As chefs.'

'Chefs? Oh dearie me.' Peggy 'dear me's a lot when she's excited. 'Sounds great. I'll have to make the trifle, you know; Sandy and Margaret don't care much for Christmas pudding but they love their trifle.'

'Great. I'll get a panettone, too. Traditional Italian dessert.'

'Italian? Oh dearie me . . . ' Again? Clearly, things were getting out of control. 'I can't wait to try it!' She giggled.

'I'll make blinis with salmon and crème fraiche for a starter and . . . what about duck? Roasted duck with veggies and potatoes?'

'Sure, dear, whatever, I trust your good taste. And I could do with a change. I've had years of turkey. Surprise me. Wait till I go and phone Margaret and tell her all about our plans.'

I smiled. Then an idea took shape in my mind; a thoroughly wicked, un-Eilidh idea.

Our credit card. Mine and Tom's.

Maybe he hadn't cancelled it.

Oh goodness me. Thoroughly dishonest.

Still, the man was living with his girlfriend. He'd had a girlfriend on the side for years while I was going through all that . . . maybe he even saw her while I was in the hospital . . .

Right. I'll do it.

'You going darling? Will you be back for lunch?'

'No, I'm spending the day in Aberdeen, Peggy, do you mind? I'm going Christmas shopping.'

'Don't mind at all, my love, I'll just sit here and watch the *Coronation Street* omnibus, warm my bones a bit.' She gestured to the fire.

'Sounds like a plan.' I got ready as quickly as I could and walked out in the freezing air. As I was walking to the station, I checked the timetable. Great, only twenty minutes to wait. I was getting more and more excited with every step. On the train, though, I started having second thoughts about the credit card. Oh God, what was I doing? But then, we were still married. After all, I wasn't going to ask for anything or want anything, he could keep it all, I didn't care. But this shopping trip, oh, he owed me this.

Hills and moors flew past my eyes as I leaned on the window, sipping a coffee from a paper cup. Maybe he had cancelled the card. But I didn't think so. It wouldn't be like Tom, knowing that I wasn't working, to leave me stranded. My mum told me that he'd asked many times if I needed money but the answer had always been no. I could easily live on what Peggy paid me. It wasn't much but then, I didn't need much. I didn't want anything from Tom, just my freedom and a fresh start.

I knew that I had to sort myself out, secure a house, put some money aside. My savings pot was pretty small but I had my profession. I could find work in a nursery and keep lodging with Peggy until I had enough money for a deposit on a house. Get a mortgage. Have my own wee place, a full-time job. A life. It was all in front of me, a million possibilities, and I felt strong.

Aberdeen was freezing, freezing and shiny and beautiful. The shops were all decorated for Christmas and the streets were full of people wrapped up in hats and scarves. I've always loved Christmas. Even with the thorn in my side of not having children to enjoy it with, I still loved it. The trees, the smell of spices, the darkness of winter broken by the Christmas lights, the shop windows all lit up and festive. In the nursery, we used to do lots of wee Christmas crafts, and the nativity play for the pre-schoolers, and I enjoyed it all.

I had a smile on my face as I entered Station Square and walked towards Marks and Spencer. Peggy was in for a treat.

'Delivery, please. Yes, next Thursday is fine. Peggy Watson, Holly Cottage, Glen Avich. No, no house number. Thank you.'

Duck, one.

Potatoes, three packets.

Mixed veg, three packets.

Panettone, two.

Smoked salmon, two.

Assorted ingredients for further cooking, lots.

Shortbread, five boxes (to give to our friends).

Whisky bottles, five (one for our table, one for my dad, one for Harry and Doug, one for Jamie, one for Fraser).

Courtesy of Mr Tom Davies.

I handed over the credit card resolutely, defiantly, but my heart was in my throat. Maybe I should have checked it first. Imagine the scene.

A very, very, very long time after, a whirr. The card had been accepted.

Ha. Revenge.

But then I felt guilty.

I walked out quickly and found a small side street. I took my mobile out. How could I hide my number? I didn't want him to call me whenever he pleased. I scrambled about a bit until I figured out how to do it — God knows how I managed, I'm useless with those kinds of things.

The phone was ringing.

'Tom, it's me.'

'Eilidh! Oh my God! Eilidh!' I heard a commotion in the background. Probably the girlfriend. 'Are you ok?' He was breathless, like talking to me was a real shock. Which indeed, it was. For both of us.

'I'm great, thanks. Just to let you know, I want a divorce. Hire a solicitor please. I don't want anything from you, so just make it quick.'

'What? A divorce?' He was whispering.

'Well, what were you expecting? To live with both of us?'

'No, no, but . . . It's all so sudden . . . '

'Sudden? It's been going on for years. I've always known.'

'Eilidh, it's complicated. Look, we can't do it like this. We need to talk.'

'No, we don't. Hire a solicitor, I'll phone after Christmas, sign whatever you want.'

'Eilidh . . . '

'Oh, and something else, I used our credit card to buy Christmas dinner for myself and my family. My Scottish family, I mean. Thanks.'

'Keep the card, Eilidh, you need it . . . your mum told me you work in that shop in Glen Avich. Come on, you can't live like that.'

'I think you'll find that I can. I'm cutting the card up right now,' I said, bending the thing over and over again until it was useless, then throwing it in the bin.

'Ei — '

'Have to go. Bye.'

I clicked the phone closed. My heart was racing. I did it.

193

'Well done, pal.'

'Yes, well done!' Voices piped up from around the corner. I took a step and saw two wee, frail old women in woollen hats and overcoats, one of them clutching the handle of a trolley full of groceries. My deserted alleyway wasn't deserted after all.

'You told him. Good girl,' said woman number one.

'Yes, good girl!' Woman number two.

'I'm sure he deserved it.'

'Yes, he deserved it!'

'Thanks, girls!' I said, and headed to Debenhams for more shopping. With my own money, thank you very much.

An hour later, I had bought presents for everyone, small ones, but I was satisfied. I got books for my nieces and nephews and the new Nigella Lawson for Harry and Doug. They love cooking, like me. I got a soft, warm cardigan for Peggy and the most adorable, sweetest little necklace for Maisie, with a little silver star because she's playing a star in her nativity play.

I was trying not to think about her going. I shouldn't have said that thing about not being here when they come back. Of course I would still be in Glen Avich. Every day that went by, every week, every month, took me further away from Southport. Some might think I was crazy, to go and live in a tiny village in the Scottish Highlands, but that was the only place where I felt I belonged, and considering that I didn't have anything else in my life, I had to follow that feeling. Scotland was to me like a lighthouse during a storm.

I was lost in thought when I saw them. Again. Had it become some twisted habit, was she following me every single time I went to the station?

'Hi Helena, hi Gail. How's things?'

'Hi, sorry, must dash . . . ' said Helena. Of course.

Gail had a face like thunder.

'So, Jamie is going,' she snapped at me, with Helena trying to gently steer her away.

'Yes, he's going to Australia.'

'I'm sorry it didn't work out between the two of you,' she said, sounding nothing but. Her face was all twisted and horrible. Jesus. Single white female.

'There was nothing to work out in the first place. Enjoy your shopping.' I walked on, boarding the train they had just alighted.

'You don't seem to be able to keep anyone, do you, Eilidh? Your husband left you, too, didn't he?'

I stood, framed by the train door, frozen.

'Gail, that's out of order!' Helena looked genuinely shocked.

For a second, I thought I was going to slap her. But I stopped myself.

Gail looked shocked, too.

'Look, I'm sorry, maybe I went too far . . . '

'You did, Gail,' I said icily. 'And when Jamie hears how mean and nasty you can be, well, if you had any hope left . . . '

Her face fell.

'Bye, Helena. See you around.'

'YOU NASTY BITCH! YOU LITTLE SHIT!'

God Almighty. It's Shona's voice. But Shona, talking like that?

'YOU TAKE IT BACK!'

It *was* Shona! She jumped down from the train — literally, she jumped — and grabbed Gail by the sleeve.

'TAKE IT BACK!'

It couldn't be Shona. It must have been her evil twin.

'Fine, fine, I take it back! You're crazy!'

'Don't you dare ever, EVER go near my brother AGAIN, understood?' she growled, with a voice straight out of *The Exorcist*.

But Helena and Gail were gone, clearly terrified.

I saw a guy in a uniform looking at us, a ticket controller or something. 'It's ok, we're fine, thanks!' I waved at him, smiling nervously. 'Come on, Shona . . . '

'Jesus.' *The Exorcist* voice again. 'She's out of control, that one!'

Ehm, ok. *Gail* is out of control.

We found seats on the train and I took a deep breath. 'Shona! What possessed you? I've never seen you like this!'

'Eilidh . . . you're like a sister to me,' she said and her eyes welled up. She was behaving like she was in an opera. I fully expected her to start belting out an aria and wrap herself around red velvet curtains with roses in her hands. 'I can't stand that NASTY BITCH

196

talking to you like that.'

'Shhhhh . . . Shona! What's wrong with you!'

'Why? What?' she said. 'What's wrong? Nothing's wrong. It's the hormones. I get a bit emotional when I'm pregnant, nothing to worry about.'

'You're pregnant?' I whispered, flabbergasted. Her face fell.

'Oh. Oh, I didn't think . . . ' She took my hands. 'I'm sorry . . . I don't want to upset you . . . with all you've been through . . . '

'Don't be silly! Come here!' I smiled and hugged her. I couldn't go through my life in envy and bitterness. 'It's wonderful news!'

'Yeah, well, unexpected really.'

'How far on are you?'

'Four months.'

'That's great. You need to watch your temper, though — you were possessed. I'm quite scared of you now.'

'Yes, I know. Fraser lives in terror. If I'm not shouting, I'm crying. Everybody is tiptoeing around me. Well, it's the least they could do. It's me going through HELL for nine months! Choccie?' she added, handing me a huge Mars Bar.

'Er, no thanks. Goodness, if you eat that amount of chocolate for all nine months, you'll give birth to a Mars Bar. Not to be insensitive or anything . . . '

'It's all I can keep down. I throw up everything else. I've actually lost weight, believe it or not. If Fraser says to me again, 'So when is the glowing stage?' I'll thump him.'

'Yes, I do believe you will. Oh, Shona. You're so lucky. Four children . . . ' I felt a tiny wee bit sad. I tried not to but I did.

'Yes, I *am* lucky,' she said and patted her tummy in a gesture that broke my heart.

'So, what were you doing in Aberdeen? I mean, before you met those two harpies?'

'Christmas shopping. Got something for Maisie, as well. Look.'

I opened the Accessorize bag, carefully undid the pink tissue paper, and showed her the silver necklace.

'It's gorgeous . . . Oh, Eilidh, she'll miss you so much when she's in Australia.'

'So will I.'

'I hope you don't mind me saying this but . . . you know you could stop him, if you wanted to . . . '

'I know. I know. But I just . . . It's complicated.'

'I know, you've got a lot to sort out.'

'I do. Yes. But even after it's all sorted out. Well, it's still me. And I can't . . . '

'I'm sorry, I shouldn't have brought it up. Don't get upset.'

'Yes, well. I just wish people would stop talking about Jamie and me.'

'This is Glen Avich, it's impossible to make people stop gossiping. They also talked about Silke and Jamie.'

'I heard that. But it's not true.'

'I know.'

'You know?'

'Yes.' We looked at each other, mute, in loyalty

198

to Silke and her secret.

'So . . . ' I said quickly, changing the subject. 'What will you do for Christmas?'

'Christmas is in my house this year. Jamie and Maisie are coming up, and Fraser's family.'

'Goodness! That's an awful lot of cooking!'

'You're welcome to join us.'

'Thanks but I'm staying with Peggy. I can't be bothered going down to England and her daughters can't make it back from Canada, so . . . '

'And Hogmanay?'

'Harry and Doug are coming up. We're having a party in Silke's house — the people she's staying with are going away.'

'Sounds good. If I manage to arrange something for the girls, Fraser and I could come, too, if that's ok?'

'I'm sure it is, Silke would be delighted.'

'Well, it was lovely to catch you,' she said, as we alighted the train and stood on the platform, the sky darkening behind us. 'Sorry for not returning your call before. Went through a bit of a rough patch with this . . . news, you know . . . ' She touched her tummy again.

'It's ok, it's all sorted anyway. See you soon.' I hugged her and breathed in her lovely, fresh Shona scent — of clean hair and soap.

That night, I dreamt I was pregnant. I dreamt I was having a boy. I woke up in the middle of the night, a rush of happiness invading me, then leaving me, ebbing away like the tide. It was just a dream.

There was no baby. It was still just me.

21

Families

Jamie

I've always loved Shona's house — warm, welcoming, full of noise and full of life.

From the outside, her family life looks chaotic, with three wee girls running around, stray clothes and toys all over the place, a flurry of school runs, dance lessons, swimming, trips to the dentist's and birthday parties to attend. A day with them would make your head spin. But if you look carefully, you'd notice that everything runs like clockwork, that underneath the apparent chaos, there's a strict routine. In the mornings, everybody's up and ready by half eight, the girls themselves having cleaned the kitchen from breakfast debris. Every evening, it's homework, chores, dinner, bath and then getting ready for the next day, laying out uniforms and sports kits. The girls have phased bedtimes, so that Alison gets a bit of time alone with her mum and dad, being the eldest. Then lights off, no getting out of bed allowed. My sister is a bit . . . how can I put it? Bossy, to say the least.

The weekends are just as organised, with classes and clubs on a Saturday and family time on a Sunday. Sunday afternoon, in particular, is sacred: the girls play, draw or watch DVDs in the living room and Fraser spends time with them all, while Shona catches up with her ironing. It's lovely to join them on these afternoons — to sit on the sofa with the girls at our feet, the familiar smell of the rose-scented ironing water, the gentle chat intermitted with the puffs of steam from Shona's iron. It's like . . . well, it's like being home — just like the home I knew when I was a wee boy.

Whenever Maisie and I go and stay for the weekend, we slot comfortably into the routine, happy to be bossed around in exchange for the sense of security and peace. And of being mothered, which we both miss, in different ways.

One weekend, Eilidh came up with us for the day. On the way back, in the car, she was very quiet.

'Did you enjoy today?'

'Very much. It was lovely. Actually, it made me think.'

'Of what?'

'It made me think of my own family.'

'Of course. You must miss them.'

'No, that's not what I meant.' A pause, as she was gathering her thoughts.

'It made me think how little peace there was in my own family. Always some . . . conflict going on, in one way or another. I can't remember a single day like the one we had today. It keeps . . . surprising me. You know, when I see the way some families live — like Shona's, like yours when we were little. The sense of . . . harmony.' She was looking for the right words. 'It's difficult to explain. For us, Christmases, birthdays, all occasions, really, were always such a strain.'

'I remember. I mean, I remember your mum always being quite hard on you.'

'Yes.' She seemed lost in thought. 'The funny thing is, they don't seem to *like* me much. My parents and my sister. I'm not sure why. When I was a wee girl, I used to wonder, am I really so unlikeable?' She spoke matter-of-factly, as if she had accepted it.

'Oh, Eilidh . . . That's awful.'

'Yes. It was. It is. With my gran around, things were ok for a few years. When we went back to England . . . I couldn't wait to get away, to go and live on my own.'

'Did you live on your own as a student?'

'Well, I shared a flat with Harry after we left school at seventeen. That was good.' She smiled at the recollection. 'But I always felt I had to . . . I don't know, look after my parents. I felt terribly guilty for leaving home. I would have gone back probably, had I not met Tom.'

I didn't say anything. I didn't want her to feel I was being inquisitive, or prying, although I was dying to know more about her husband.

'You see, Tom is a very kind, gentle man. Never raised his voice, never put me down. It was such a relief, after years of being everybody's favourite whipping boy.'

'Are you . . . are you in touch now?' I felt like the words were choking me.

'We've only spoken once since I left him. He's living with his new . . . his new partner.'

'I'm sorry.'

'No, it's ok. Really, it is.' I looked at her as she said that. Again, she looked as if she had accepted it. 'I haven't had feelings for him for a long time.'

'Are you not angry at all? I mean, he cheated on you . . . '

'I am, I am absolutely furious . . . But I hope there's happiness in store for both of us, though it seems quite . . . quite impossible now. No point in wishing him misery, we've had enough of that. Our marriage was sort of . . . empty. It was truly finished by the time he started seeing that girl.'

She was looking out of the window, her lovely profile silhouetted against the darkening sky. Once more, I wished I could hold her. All that talk about misery, all those things she said about her family, I wanted it all to go away, I wanted her to be happy.

But it wasn't for me to do that, it wasn't me she wanted.

Maybe Australia will help. Maybe it'll take her out of my heart, out of my soul. Maybe when I come back, I'll be free. She said that when we return, she might not be here.

A world without Eilidh.

We managed before, we'll manage after, Maisie and me.

'Look, oh look, the moon, it's so white tonight! It's really, *really* beautiful!' She was smiling, enraptured. Beauty makes her happy, it seeps deep into her in a way I've never seen with anyone else.

'*Really, really, so, so beautiful.*' I smiled. When

she gets excited, she sounds like a wee girl. The moon is so, so beautiful and she is so, so . . . Eilidh. My Eilidh.

★ ★ ★

Christmas day. We were all sitting around Shona's table, Fraser's parents and brother there as well, and his brother's wife and son. Everywhere I turned, there was something shiny and glittery hung up by Shona and the girls. A lovely smell of roast goose and cloves and oranges filled the air.

Fraser stood up with a glass of champagne in his hand.

'Well, I suppose some of you know already . . . '

'I know!' Alison piped up.

'Know what?' said Kirsty.

'Mummy's going to have a baby!'

Delighted *ooooooohs* rose from all around the table, a flurry of congratulations and handshakes and hugs.

'Mummy has a baby in her tummy?' said Kirsty, just to make sure.

'She does and I knew it before anyone else!' Alison answered proudly.

Shona took Kirsty on her lap and stroked her hair away from her face.

Everybody was smiling, everybody was happy. Maisie was chattering excitedly with her cousins. She was so pretty, so sweet in her blue pinafore, cream tights and shiny black ballerinas, her hair in a French plait expertly done by her auntie.

To think of sitting here on my own, how

. . . impossible it would be. Maisie is my own wee family inside the family.

When we were having pudding, her little hand slipped into mine as Fraser, dressed as Santa, made his entrance.

'Is there a Maisie here?' he boomed.

'I'm here,' Maisie said in a wee voice, all solemn.

'Here, Santa, here she is, my daughter,' I said proudly. Don't know why. It just came out. Daughter. I tasted the word, I savoured it.

Shona laughed. I realised it was a bit of a strange thing to say. I blushed, and I was quiet for a while after that.

Eilidh

Peggy looked delighted as her eyes swept the table, her cheeks flushed from the fire and the cheeky sherry she and Margaret had after church.

'Eilidh cooked it all, apart from the trifle but that was quick and easy really, she did all the hard work.'

'She's spoiling you, isn't she?' said Margaret, smiling.

'She sure is, Margaret, she's a great lassie, aren't you, pet?' She stroked my cheek and I swallowed, a bit choked.

'To think I stole her from her mum this year! She's here with me instead.'

To think my mum wasn't that bothered.

'Well, we're not giving her back. We're keeping

205

you!' said Sandy affectionately.

'What a blessing for you, with the house and the shop, as well.'

'A real blessing, Margaret. I just wish Flora were here to see her back.'

'Don't we all wish that. If she was sat here with us now — she loved a party, your gran! And her singing! I never heard a voice like hers.'

I smiled at the memory. Sandy and Flora used to entertain everybody with their singing. Unfortunately, neither Katrina nor myself had inherited Flora's lovely voice.

'True, Sandy, very true. Never heard a voice like Flora's. But Eilidh here, she might not be a singer but she can cook! Flora wasn't one for cooking.'

'She wasn't, no . . . ' Everybody agreed on that. I laughed. My gran's cooking is legendary and not in a good way. I was the only one that actually enjoyed her meals, out of sheer loyalty.

'Well, Marks and Spencer gave me a hand here, I must admit!'

The meal was great, though I say so myself, and then we sat companionably in front of the fire. It was the best Christmas I'd had in years, so peaceful and warm. And then the phone rang. Peggy's daughters had phoned that morning, so in all likelihood, it was . . .

'Rhona! Merry Christmas to you, how are you all? Good, good, there she is!'

I wished I didn't have to speak to them. But that would have been rude. Also, I wanted to, for some weird reason. Tom had always said it's sort of masochistic, the way I look for my family, my mum in particular, only to be hurt over and over again. I can't help it.

'Merry Christmas, Mum!'

'Merry Christmas, Eilidh. Wait, here's your father . . . '

Oh, ok.

'What?' My dad was fumbling with the phone. 'Yes. Yes. Eilidh? Merry Christmas.'

'And you, Dad, are you having a good time?'

'Yes, good I suppose, you know I don't believe in Christmas, anyway.'

'Yes, I know.' I know. I had been reminded every year as a wee girl.

'What did you — ' but he was gone already.

'Hi, Merry Christmas, Eilidh, how are you?'

'Hi Katrina, yes, all is well, having a good time here with Peggy.'

'God, Eilidh, at thirty-five you spend Christmas on your own with your old auntie, that's not normal. You should have come down, at least to give Mum a hand. Yes, coming, coming, darling!' A wee voice in the background. Molly. 'The kids are great. Such fun. Oh well, I'll let you go . . . you must be having a riot!' She laughed.

I said nothing. What was there to say?

'Eilidh?' My mum. 'Well, it was good talking to you.'

Talking to me? But you *didn't*.

'And you, Mum. We're having duck, what are you having?'

'Turkey, and steak for your father — he says turkey's dry, he's so fussy.'

'Margaret is here, they . . . '

'Must go darling, need to phone Laura. Merry

207

Christmas again, kiss to Peggy.'

'Oh, yes, of course. I'll let you go. Have fun.'

'Well, I don't know about fun. I'm not feeling that good, really, I haven't eaten a thing, my stomach's in a knot. Bye . . . '

For a change. My mum's ailments had no rhyme or reason, they were just meant to give everybody a reason to worry, not to enjoy the moment.

'That's a shame . . . ' But she had already put down the phone.

God.

I took a deep breath. I'll never, never get used to it. I'm sure Katrina didn't want to be there either. Imagine being able to spend Christmas with your family and actually have a good time. Tom's mum had died when he was barely twenty, his dad had remarried and they weren't close, so I couldn't seek refuge with my in-laws either. But my brother-in-law's family were lovely, so at least Katrina had a good one every second year. Though *they* probably didn't, being lumbered with her.

Maybe that's why she was being so horrible about me, making it out that I was so sad and pathetic for spending Christmas like I was. She didn't want to be there either, my dad in a mood, my mum doing her 'I'm not feeling well' routine and putting herself to bed in the middle of it. I nearly felt sorry for my sister. Nearly.

I went back into the living room. Peggy was sitting peacefully by the fire, a cup of tea in her hand — 'Enough sherry for me, dear!' — having a blether with her old friends. Margaret, with her paper hat on, was eating Celebrations and chattering excitedly about her son and her daughter-in-law, and how funny her grandson was with his wee English accent. And Sandy, his brown eyes full of kindness and a bit of mischief, sat gently making fun of 'the girls'. The window framed a cold and wintry Scotland, magical as ever. Home.

I sat down happily and as I unwrapped a chocolate and sipped my tea, Katrina's bitter words dissolved in my memory, weak and meaningless. They'll always be able to hurt me — my parents and Katrina. I love them, therefore they'll always have power over me. But not today, not right now.

My phone beeped. A text.

Merry Xmas from all of us baby, H, D and our families.

I thought of them and I thought of Maisie wearing her silver star necklace, and I smiled to myself.

Elizabeth

It would take too much energy to exist outside of Glen Avich, so I can't be with Jamie and Shona today. I'm sitting with Peggy instead, with her and my old friends, invisible, perched on the arm of the sofa.

'Remember when we had the jumble sale — we were about fifteen, weren't we — and Beth

Ramsay came and bought a gift for each of us?'

'Yes, she was always lovely, Lady Ramsay, a real heart of gold. Her family used to help out a lot, you know, in our time, when Glen Avich was a lot poorer, a lot of people were struggling . . . '

'She was great with the McAnenas, remember? When James died in Spain and Mary and wee James were left alone.'

'Aye, so they were. Poor Mary, how she struggled. She raised James all alone, and such a fine boy he was.'

'And a fine man he became. Elizabeth was lucky . . . '

'And so was James, with Elizabeth!' Peggy says. That makes me smile. Peggy has always been such a loyal friend.

'I wish she were here too, don't you, Peggy?'

'Oh, aye.'

But I *am* here. You can't see me but I am.

'Jamie is just like his father, isn't he?'

'Aye, the very image. And quiet, just like James.'

'He's doing great, he's going to Australia, isn't he, Eilidh?'

'It looks like it.' A shadow passes on her face.

'Is he not going out with Gail anymore?' asks Margaret.

'Not for a while, no. That poor lassie is quite low, I've heard. Her mum came to the shop a wee while ago. Gail is talking about going away for a bit. But maybe now that Jamie's going . . . '

'Well, you can't just stay with someone 'cause

they'd get upset if you left. The lad did the right thing. Better than be stuck for the rest of his life.'

'Like you, Sandy?' laughs Margaret, a twinkle in her eye.

'Aye, like me!' Sandy laughs, rolls his eyes and looks at her warmly.

'That wee girl, Maisie, she's just the apple of his eye.'

'She is, she's a wee doll and a real looker, like her mum.'

I feel Eilidh tensing up.

'Would you believe she's gone without looking back? Leaving her daughter behind? Unheard of . . . '

'She was stunning, no wonder Jamie fell for her.'

'Enough of that, Sandy!' laughs Margaret.

'Well, sorry, but she was!'

'Was she?' says Eilidh, trying to give the impression that it's just an idle remark, just making conversation, but really, I can see she's listening hard.

'Yes, tall, blonde, lots of airs and graces . . . '

Wrong. Janet could come across as pretentious but she was just very, very shy. She preferred the company of her canvases and paintbrushes to that of people.

'If I could live on top of a mountain and paint, I'd be happy,' she told me once and I had tried to ignore the fact that she hadn't mentioned Jamie and Maisie being on top of the mountain with her. Anyway, no point in thinking about that now.

Sandy's still talking. 'About time Jamie finds

someone else; that wee girl needs a mum, especially since Elizabeth is gone.'

Silence from Peggy. Eilidh stands up quickly. 'Anyone for tea?'

I smile to myself. She has feelings for him. If only she could let go of her fear . . . She thinks she can't allow herself to be happy, that she's not good enough for Jamie. She says to herself it's because she can't bear children, but I know it's deeper than that. Her family has made her feel so unlovable for years and not even Tom, a man that I know was kind and loving to her, could change that.

She's terrified, I can feel it. She's terrified to let herself go and take another blow. She couldn't survive any more pain, she knows that, and she's keeping herself away, safe, protected. My hope is that when her wounds are healed, she'll feel strong enough to take a risk. I don't know if it'll ever happen or if it does, if Jamie will be around, or if I'll be there to see it. But I hope so, for her sake as much as ours. She's so full of love, full to the brim, but with no one to give it to. I see the way she cuddles Maisie and strokes her hair, and how the two of them snuggle up, very, very close to each other, like they're both starving for affection. Maisie gets plenty of affection from Jamie but a five-year-old can never have enough. And Eilidh, well, she needs to be *touched*. It's a fundamental need for us all, the physical proximity of someone we love. Without it, it's a terribly, terribly cold existence. Enough to make you wither and wilt like a plant without water.

I see Jamie and Eilidh together and I see them gravitating towards each other, trying to get close without quite managing. I see Jamie looking at her when she's not looking. I see Eilidh steeling herself to a lonely life she doesn't *have* to live.

I see many things and nobody sees me, so I'm free to look.

I see Fiona crying in her room, taking off the necklace Silke gave her before flying home for Christmas.

22

First Footing

Eilidh

I was making the bed in the spare bedroom
when I heard the car pulling up. I ran down the
stairs and flung the door open.

'Harry! It's so, *so* good to see you! Oh, I
missed you!' I said, giving him a bear hug. I
pulled away to look at him. He was beaming. I
hugged him again.

'You look great, Eilidh . . . You look like
. . . well, the old you!'

'You look great, too,' I said and I meant it. He
seemed in great form, his brown eyes shining.

'Hi baby!' Doug came out of the car, laden
with bags. We managed to hug anyway.

'God, I'm gasping!' he said.

'Cup of tea?'

They laughed. 'Cup of tea? We are celebrating!
Where's the pub?'

Half an hour later, after a quick visit to say
hello to Peggy in the shop, the three of us were
sitting on the red velvet sofas of the Green Hat, a
whisky glass each in front of us. Yes, me too. I
know, quite naughty, being early afternoon, but
there you go.

I looked at my friends affectionately. Harry

was wearing a tweed cap on his bald head, a big tartan scarf and a corduroy blue jacket. All ironically, of course — he was playing 'country gentleman'.

'I love your cap!' I said, patting it.

'Yes, you know, when in Rome . . . '

'Harry, do you see anyone wearing a tweed cap?'

'Ok, I see what you mean, but I couldn't resist.'

'I had to talk him out of wearing tartan trousers. He looked like Tiger Woods,' said Doug, who, on the contrary, was ultra-stylish in Diesel jeans and a designer-looking top. Doug has this thing about him — it looks as if he's smiling all the time, even when he's not. People are drawn to him and his calm, easy-going good mood. Doug is a man without an agenda. He's happy with himself, happy with the people around him and the world seems a lot brighter when he's around.

'Really, Eilidh, you do look like the old you,' said Harry. 'Maybe it's the water up here or something. Your eyes are shining again and you put on weight. God, you were scrawny!'

'Yes, I've been eating constantly since I arrived here. If I don't stop, I'll be huge before I know it.'

'I'd say that's a long way away! Remember, you used to sit in front of my gorgeous ravioli and just look at them and go, 'I can't . . . ' It was awful.'

'That's all in the past. I'm never going back there. Did I tell you Tom is living with his girlfriend?'

'You did, yes.'

'Thing is,' Doug intervened, 'she doesn't seem to be making him very happy. I saw them in the centre a while ago. He didn't look good.'

My heart jumped. I was ashamed to be feeling a kind of malign satisfaction.

'Nothing to do with me,' I said coldly.

'No, not anymore. I mean, the two of you, you just weren't right together. And cheating on you for years, really, the man's a bastard.'

'Too right,' said Doug and we all took a sip of our whisky.

'Now. About Jamie.'

'Shhhh . . . Everybody knows everybody here! Keep your voices down!'

'*Sorry*,' whispered Harry dramatically. 'So, what's the story there?'

'No story. Nothing to report.'

'Do we believe her, Doug?'

'We don't believe her, Harry. You mention Jamie or Maisie — or both — in every single email. Something must be going on.'

'He asked me out, I said no.'

'WHY?' they both shouted in unison.

'Shhhhh!!!!'

'Why?' they hissed.

'Because I don't want a relationship. I don't want the heartache again. And anyway, I'm not even properly divorced.'

'You're separated.'

'Yes, we separated not even six months ago.'

'Listen, you don't need to marry the guy! Can you not just have a bit of fun?'

I looked at them.

216

'No, of course not. Eilidh and fun — two strangers. Eilidh only does soul searching and complicating simple things . . . '

'Exactly. You know me. I'm too neurotic.'

'But you have a touch of Highland tragedy. Perfect combination. Anyway, we are here now, we'll see that you have some fun.'

'Don't get me into trouble!'

'Us? No, course not,' Harry said.

'Jamie's coming to the Hogmanay party, isn't he?' asked Doug.

'Don't know. Maybe.'

'Leave it with us.'

'Yes, leave it with us.'

'We are not sixteen, guys! 'My pal fancies you!' and all that! Stay out of it!' I exclaimed — but I was smiling. God, I missed them.

★ ★ ★

'How do I look?' said Harry, giving a twirl.

'Dashing!' said Peggy, laughing. 'Never seen the likes!'

Harry was wearing velvet trousers and a skin-tight silk shirt. He was doing 'ironic seventies disco', apparently. His dress sense was getting more and more gay stereotype every year, much to Doug's amusement. Doug was wearing jeans and a stripy shirt. He had decided against a kilt, though he claimed his great grandfather hailed from Dundee. As for me, I had the same dress I'd worn at the gallery opening and my hair up in a loose bun.

'You look lovely, pet.'

'Thanks, Auntie Peggy. So do you.' She did look lovely, in her blue woollen skirt, a white shirt and her grey hair freshly done. She was going to a party herself, at Margaret's.

'Now, have some dinner before you go. I won't let you go out on an empty stomach.'

We all sat around the table in our fineries, eating ham sandwiches and drinking tea — 'Nothing that can stain,' Peggy had said.

'Thank you so much again for having us, Peggy. It's great to be here with Eilidh.'

'Not at all, not at all, dear. Any time.'

I smiled. Peggy, Flora, Elizabeth — their doors seemed to have been always open. Their warm, easy hospitality was, to me, Scotland in a nutshell.

We all kissed her on our way out. The sky was dark already, it was bitterly cold and we hurried along through the streets of Glen Avich.

Silke's house wasn't far from Peggy's. She was lodging with an elderly couple in a terraced whitewashed house on the other side from St Colman's Way.

'This is beautiful!' said Doug, as we were making our way through the village. 'And the air . . . it's so fresh.'

'Mountain air,' I said.

'It's a fantastic place. No wonder you wanted to come back.'

The windows at Silke's house were all lit up and the orange-yellow glow looked warm and inviting against the dark surroundings. We knocked at the door.

'Hello, welcome!' Silke gave us all a big hug,

as if she'd known Harry and Doug forever.

The living room and kitchen were full of people, some I knew, some I didn't. Some had instruments with them — great, that was going to give Harry and Doug a taste of the Highlands.

I was so happy that night. Everything was perfect — absolutely, totally and completely perfect. The whisky flew, and we danced and sang and listened to music.

And then Jamie arrived, on his own.

'No Shona?'

'She didn't feel up to it, she said she'd stay in to watch the girls, Fraser didn't want to leave her.'

'But you came out.'

'But I came out, yes. I wanted to see you.'

I swallowed. I was a bit tipsy. So was he.

'Come and meet my friends.' I took him by the hand and led him to the kitchen, where Harry and Doug were in deep conversation with Silke about the state of the arts in contemporary Britain. Really, I'm not making it up.

'Everybody, this is Jamie!'

'Well, nice to meet you.'

'Yes, very, very nice to meet you.'

They grinned.

I could have killed them.

Jamie looked embarrassed; he could guess he had been the subject of discussion.

'You came!' said Silke and hugged him tight.

'How you doing?' he said, giving her a tight squeeze.

'Been better. What can you do?'

'What happened?' I asked, worried.

'Fiona and I broke up.'

'You did?' said Doug, genuinely concerned. I had told them a lot about Silke. 'That's a shame.'

'Did everybody know?' said Silke. 'Oh well. Doesn't matter now.'

'Oh, Silke . . . ' I went to give her a hug. 'I'm sorry . . . What happened?'

'She wanted to keep it secret. I couldn't take it anymore.'

'You and Fiona broke up?' said a blonde girl who had just come into the kitchen. I'd never seen her before. 'Oh, I'm sorry!'

'Well, she sure was doing a good job keeping it secret!' said Harry.

'Everybody knows, Silke,' said Jamie. 'Nobody seems to mind. I mean, it is the twenty-first century, even in Glen Avich.'

'You don't know her family . . . Anyway! They're playing through there, let's go.'

We all went through and Jamie and I stood beside each other.

I could feel him beside me. Every bit of my body was aware of his presence.

The music, the whisky, the warmth . . . before I knew it, I had slipped my arm in his.

Suddenly, without warning, he took hold of me. He led me out of the living room into the corridor and I didn't protest. He kept his eyes on me as he opened the door and stepped out into the darkness, his hand still holding my arm.

He put his hands around my waist and without a word, he kissed me. For a long time. Slowly, slowly, like we had all the time in the world. I felt my knees giving way and I held on to him.

I could have kissed him forever.

Then he pulled away. He looked at me and cupped my face with his hands.

'Jamie . . . '

'Shhhh. No. Don't talk. Please.'

I stood quiet as he looked into my face, our eyes locked. I was frozen. His grey eyes were full of desire and completely serious.

Then he let go of me.

'I had to do it. I had to kiss you. Sorry.'

'Don't say sorry,' I whispered. I felt like I was going to fall. I wanted him to hold me again. But he didn't. He turned away.

'Don't go,' I said.

'I have to go.'

'Why?' I didn't understand. Why was he walking away like that?

'Because . . . to be near you like this, it's driving me crazy. I can't wait to go Australia. I can't take it anymore, to see you every day and . . . Well. Happy New Year.'

He walked away. Just like that.

I licked my lips. I could taste him.

I went back inside, my head spinning.

'Where's Jamie?'

'Gone home.'

'You ok?'

I nodded.

I don't remember a single thing after that. Dancing, alcohol, the bells, whatever. I walked back like a zombie, crashed into bed, and the thoughts I had . . . oh, the thoughts I had after that, I can never say.

The next morning, well, afternoon more like, we were all in the pub, looking ghastly. No, not hair of the dog, we're not that bad. We were having a pub lunch. Morag and Jim, the landlords, looked in great form as they carried big plates of steak pie and mash from the kitchen to the hungry revellers. They were probably the only people in Glen Avich without hangovers. Even Peggy and Margaret looked pretty bleary-eyed.

The steak pie was gorgeous, hearty and juicy. I just prayed that Jamie wouldn't decide to come to the pub. I could not have looked him in the eye.

'Look, there's your friend there. Hi Jamie!' cried out Harry, waving conspicuously.

Of course.

'Hi, happy New Year! I've been first-footing people for the last two hours. Mind if I sit?'

He didn't even look embarrassed. He definitely wasn't tongue-tied. It was like nothing had happened. Oh well. Clearly, it didn't mean that much to him, in spite of what he said. I was seriously annoyed.

'Hi, happy New Year!' Shona, Fraser and the girls.

I gave Maisie a big cuddle. 'Happy New Year, baby. Did you celebrate last night?'

'Yes. We had a party.'

'We did face painting,' said Lucy.

'Auntie Shona did my face. I was a butterfly.'

'Yum, steak pie!' said Shona.

We sat companionably. Nobody knew about last night, so nobody acted any different. Jamie was still pretending nothing had happened. It's not like I was expecting flowers or whatever. It was just a kiss, even a bit of a drunken kiss, I suppose. An exceptionally good kiss, an amazing kiss, a perfect, mind-blowing, tender, gorgeous kiss, but still just a kiss. Better stop recalling it, I was blushing.

God. The things I thought about last night . . .

'Eilidh?'

'YES?' I jumped.

'You ok?'

'Yes, fine, right as rain. Anybody seen Silke?'

'She texted me this morning,' said Jamie. 'She's got about twenty people asleep all over the house.'

'When are the Duffs coming back?' asked Shona.

'Next week.'

'Oh well, then. Plenty of time to sort the house out. I'll go give her a hand later on. How long are you staying?' she asked Harry.

'Just another couple of days. Back to work soon, I'm afraid.'

My stomach tightened. I really didn't want them to go.

'Back soon, though,' said Doug.

I smiled. The best Hogmanay ever.

I looked at Jamie. His black hair was standing up on end, he was wearing an old t-shirt and his jeans were ripped. Really ripped, not fashionably ripped.

What's going to happen now?

Jamie

I thought, what the hell, I have to feel her lips, I *have* to kiss her. Didn't even consider the possibility of her pushing me away and making a fool of myself. I suppose the whisky helped, having temporarily gone back to it to celebrate Hogmanay.

Kissing her felt like diving into warm waters. Like having been on barren land for a long, long time, dry and parched, and then just diving into the blue, diving into her.

I'm going away in eight weeks time.

She can ask me to stay.

I pray she asks me to stay.

What's going to happen now?

23

Secrets

Elizabeth

Secrets are not a good idea. They eat you up inside.

If you have something precious and fragile and you keep it locked away like a little plant trying to grow in the darkness, well, it'll die and your secret will turn into regret. Love needs to be in the light of day. A secret love will eat itself and die, or eat your heart and kill you.

I saw Fiona sitting on the doorstep of her parents' house, ripping her necklace off, the one that Silke gave her when they first got together. A few weeks have passed now but part of Fiona is still sitting there, still stuck in that shocking, earth shattering moment when Silke said, 'No, we're not going to be together.' Only half an hour later, she'd had to dry her tears and pretend nothing had happened because her parents had come home and she couldn't tell them, not for the world. So she'd put on a brave face — more of a dead-inside face, really — and got on with it.

But as a ghost, I see all sides of reality, layering one on top of the other, separated by thin, opaque veils that, to us, are easy to lift. A honeycomb of moments at every corner, the stories of the people of Glen Avich lingering everywhere, for us to read like a book.

I see that part of Fiona sitting there still, holding the broken necklace, her small frame shaken by sobbing. A few weeks on and this shadow of reality doesn't show signs of fading — she's slightly translucent and, of course, invisible to the living but she will not disappear any time soon.

Some people stay stuck in a moment for the rest of their lives. Like Beryl. She's about my age, if I were alive. One Beryl comes and goes, between her house in Glen Avich and her daughter's house with her grandsons in Aberdeen. She's been working in a factory for forty years, watching her daughter grow up, going on the occasional holiday and growing old like we all do. But since I died, I can see the other Beryl. The thirty-year-old woman running out into the street, invisible hands holding her back, eyes wild as she sees her three-year-old son lying in the middle of the road, no more breath in him.

They often cross each other, the two Beryls. One coming home from the supermarket, locking the car, holding a bag of groceries, brushing past the frozen thirty-year-old Beryl who screams silently and falls on the ground, over and over and over again.

I think I was stuck for a bit myself, when I lost the baby boy in between my children, but I managed to be whole again after a while. Jamie's birth healed me.

Beryl will be like that until the day she dies

but I know Fiona won't. I know that her love is deep and real, and that although her heart is broken now, it will heal one day and the only trace of what happened will be a scar . . . It will still be painful, it will hurt every time the memories come back to haunt her, but she'll get through it.

But I still hope that however Fiona decides to shape her future, she finds the courage to bring the little plant into the light before it fades and dies, because I know that's what she wants.

I believe we all only love once. Except sometimes, the one we are meant to love is not the one we think. Sometimes we lose someone, we think our life is over and we get frozen in the moment of despair. But it can turn out that, in spite of all that anguish, our true soulmate is actually still out there. Life can give us another chance — once the one we thought was our soulmate is gone, the real one comes along.

Sometimes, though, the one we lost *is* the one we were meant to love and we spend the rest of our lives trying to accept, to adapt, to make do. Trying to pretend that friendship, companionship, lust, children, work, whatever, can replace the once-in-a-lifetime love. It doesn't really work, not completely, but a life like that can still be happy.

I look around me and I wonder who's hiding a lost love, whether in bitterness or in acceptance, trying to make the best of what they have. I wonder who never met their true love. You see, since I'm dead, I don't believe in coincidences anymore, I see fate writing all the harmonies of the symphony of life, and us playing our little parts, or leading parts, in a way that's never random. I see fate's web superimposed on our reality, a million tiny connections and paths that we unknowingly walk along. Every turn we take opens up a different path in front of us, and choice after choice, we get exactly where we are meant to be. But sometimes people become so lost that they need a bit of guidance. That is when they call out, and we listen.

Janet wasn't Jamie's soulmate, even if he thought so at the time. Tom wasn't Eilidh's. James was my once-in-a-lifetime and Fraser is Shona's. And Silke? Is she Fiona's soulmate?

I don't know yet and I might not be around long enough to know. Other ghosts will be here after me to read the stories of Glen Avich, in this parallel world we inhabit, a world of signs and whispers and memories, where all the thin, nearly inaudible voices that are lost to the living sound like screams to us and get to be heard. We are the ones who are meant to listen to the words unspoken.

Eilidh

The holidays were drawing to an end. I'd spent most of the last few days sitting lazily in front of the fire, watching the black branches of the trees across the road making a lace against the sky, everything quiet, everything asleep.

Around me, Peggy watching TV or knitting a wee outfit for her cousin's new granddaughter,

228

down south . . . the laptop beeping once in a while, as Harry and I chatted via email . . . occasional visitors, mainly distant relatives, home for the holidays, bringing Roses and Celebrations and staying for tea before they went 'up the road', back to wherever their lives took them, away from Glen Avich.

Every morning, the ground shone with frost, the grass matted down, silvery and crunchy underfoot. By early afternoon, the morning frost had disappeared but the evening one was on its way already. The air started turning again, chilly and thin, a hint of darkness in the sky. The short, blink-and-you'll-miss-them winter days.

Since the sweet, maddening, perfect kiss on Hogmanay, everything in my life had been suspended — painful memories of the past, decisions for the future, the strange relationship with Jamie — everything was frozen and waiting, just like the land was. I knew that this peaceful state couldn't last forever but still, I was enjoying the moment, enjoying every day as it came, like a string of pearls, one after the other.

One day, I had the house all to myself and I felt it was the right time to take another step towards freedom.

With shaking hands, I called him.

Thank God, it's ringing. It'd be awful to try and muster the courage to phone him back again and go through all that hands sweating, heart in mouth, not breathing ordeal.

'Hello?'

'Hi, it's me.'

'Eilidh . . . ' He sounded different.

229

'Are you ok?'

'No, I'm not ok.'

'What's wrong?'

'Oh, Eilidh. Please let me see you. We need to talk.'

'Tom, we can talk for days, it won't change things. What's there to say anyway?'

'I made a terrible mistake. She's gone. You've no idea how my life has changed. She isn't . . . she wasn't *you.*'

'She was good enough to keep you warm while I went through hell!' I blurted out and regretted it immediately. There was no point. The cut had been made between us, so deep it was irreparable. It couldn't be stitched, it couldn't be undone. There was no 'Tom and Eilidh' anymore.

'Do you care for me at all, Tom? Do I still matter to you?'

'Yes! I want to give us another chance . . . I want to make it work.'

'If you care for me, you need to let me go. I can never go back to Southport, I can never go back to my old life.'

'We're not tied to Southport! We can move. I can come up to Scotland, get a job in Aberdeen or Edinburgh . . . '

'Tom.'

A moment of silence, a deep breath.

'Yes?'

'Are you going to help me? Are you going to contact a lawyer and we'll see what we need to do to get a divorce? Or are you going to stall us?' My voice was shaking.

'I don't want . . . '

'Tom, listen to me. I'm barely out of the woods here. I can function again, you know? I get up in the morning and I'm not in despair, for the first time in years, apart from when I was pregnant.' Tears sprang to my eyes. I still had tears left then, thought I'd cried them all by now. I must have filled a loch by now. Loch Eilidh.

'Please help me now. You need to let me go. Please.'

Silence.

'I wish I could say no. I wish I could insist and insist until maybe I break you and you come back. But I don't want to break you, I want to help you like you asked me . . . but, Eilidh, I can't agree to this if I don't see you once more. We must talk face to face . . . you can't hide up there . . . '

'I'm not hiding. Contrary to what you might think, people actually have real lives here, too, just like in Southport or London.'

'Ok, ok, sorry . . . I mean you can't hide from me. You need to see me and talk to me . . . '

'I'll do that. Come up. When you're ready. I'll tell you to your face that our marriage is over.'

'I can't tell you how many times I've regretted the whole Carol thing . . . '

Carol. So that was her name. I wondered if she loved him. I wondered if she was heartbroken. I hoped so. I hated her. I wish I didn't, I wish I was better than that. But I hated her.

'It wasn't . . . *Carol*.' Her name was like bile in my mouth. 'It was us. Both you and me. Need to go now. I'll phone you . . . '

'This weekend? I'll drive up Friday night . . . '

For a second, I couldn't breathe. My heart was beating so fast I thought I was going to pass out. Panic. But I knew I had to face it . . . I had to face him.

'Not this weekend, I . . . I can't. The following one, if you're not too busy.'

'Too busy? Are you crazy? I'll be up in two weeks time, then. Your aunt's house?'

'Yes. You can get a room in the Green Hat. The number is in my address book, by the phone in the hall . . . '

I could see it, in my mind's eye. The hall, the house. All that I used to know.

'Will do. See you soon, Eilidh.'

'Yes. Bye.'

I was glad. I was so glad it was nearly over. We'd separate, then divorce officially, then no more Tom. I was glad.

Then why was I crying so hard I thought my heart would break?

I looked up and out of the window. In the space of a few minutes, while I wasn't looking, the air itself had turned white, the sky had given way and innumerable little white flakes were falling. Everything grew quiet. I sat and watched the snow in silent grief.

Jamie

A Christmas card? Janet didn't do Christmas. Every year, she puts money in Maisie's account and I get the statement in the post, that's her Christmas card to Maisie.

I was always happier when Janet was out of the way. A part of me always worried that she'd come back for Maisie. I worried so much that I even went to see a lawyer in Aberdeen, just to know where I stood. Thankfully, the lawyer reassured me that no judge would ever take her away from me or from Glen Avich.

Still.

I fought the temptation to throw the card into the fire. If Janet was trying to make contact with Maisie, I couldn't hide it from her. What would Maisie say if one day she found out I'd hidden or destroyed her mum's letters? That I hampered her mother's attempts to get in touch, to make amends? It was addressed to me, though, not Maisie.

I knew I had to read it. I ripped the envelope open.

Dear Jamie,
I just wanted to let you know that I'm moving to New York. I'll still look after Maisie financially . . .

Look after Maisie? She never looked after Maisie. Her idea of 'looking after' is quite different to mine. Well, to the rest of the world's, really.

. . . but my contact details will change. Actually, I'd rather you didn't contact me at all. I'm getting married and I'd rather keep this part of my life a secret. I know I can trust you.

Merry Christmas,

Janet.

And Merry Christmas to you. From me and from your secret daughter.

24

The Empty Cradle

Eilidh

The snowfall had been long and heavy for the first time in years. By the time Maisie was back at school, a thick, white blanket was covering everything. Every morning, we'd wake up in a magical landscape and nearly every afternoon, a bit more snow fell and kept falling into the night.

I was so tense and anxious over the conversation I'd had with Tom, I often couldn't sleep. I sat up half the night, watching the snow falling, falling, falling. I was counting the days to him coming up, not because I wanted to see him, but because I dreaded it.

Two weeks to go.

'Can we go and show Daddy now?'

Maisie was putting her jotter into her bag, carefully. Hers was the best piece of work in the whole class, it had earned a sticker and a 'well done' in red pen. Maisie had asked if she could take it home to show her dad and Mrs Hill had agreed, with the promise that the jotter would be back the next day.

'Well, he's working now. Maybe we can show him later on, when he comes home?'

Maisie's face fell.

'But I don't want to wait!' she exclaimed, looking at me with puppy eyes. She knew it worked on me, every time.

'Ok then, let's walk up to the workshop but we'll only be five minutes, your dad is very busy.'

'Ok!' she said, jumping up and down in joy.

We walked up in the freezing afternoon, under a white sky. The snow was crunching underneath our feet and all noises were muffled. I was enjoying every step, it was like walking in a fairy tale. Maisie was blowing gently, to see her breath turn into a wee white cloud. She was wrapped up to within an inch of her life, her pink hat pulled down on her forehead and her scarf up around her chin, so that only her blue-grey eyes and her cold, crimson cheeks were visible.

We could see Jamie from the window, sitting at the drawing table, his back to us. Maisie tapped the glass gently and Jamie turned, his face lighting up as he saw us.

We walked round to the door and inside. It was my first time in Jamie's workshop. It was brightly lit, as the muted winter light wasn't enough for Jamie to work with. All around us lay Jamie's beautiful pieces, from everyday objects, like fireguards and little gates, to tables covered in exquisite jewellery and keepsakes.

Maisie ran to Jamie and gave him a cuddle.

'Look, Daddy!' she said, taking the jotter out of her bag.

'Oh, wow, let me see . . . ' I heard him saying as I walked on, going further back into the room.

'That's great, Maisie, well done . . . '

Their voices melted away as the room started

spinning around me. I blinked, once, twice. I couldn't believe my eyes.

The cradle.

My cradle.

The wrought-iron cradle, the one that Tom had brought home that day, when my world was still in one piece. The one he'd insisted we put in the nursery, in spite of my fear. I could hear his voice again: 'It was made somewhere in the Highlands . . . '

I couldn't breathe and I felt faint, so I ran out, I ran out blindly, into the milky light and the frozen air, I slipped in the snow and I didn't see the car driving up St Colman's Way.

★   ★   ★

'She came out of nowhere!'

'Eilidh? Eilidh!'

'Oh God, oh God . . . '

Voices all around me.

I could see the sky.

'Eilidh, my love . . . '

Shona?

The blonde woman leaned over me and put her hand on my forehead and I closed my eyes.

'Shona . . . ' I murmured and then I was under water, blind and deaf and swirling down, down, into nothingness.

Jamie

I don't understand. One minute Maisie and I were looking at her jotter and Eilidh was wandering about with a smile on her face, looking at my work — I was watching her out of the corner of my eye, hoping that she'd like what she saw — and the next thing I knew, Eilidh ran out as if she'd seen a ghost.

Then that awful, awful sound, the sickening thud of a body being hit and thrown and floored, Eilidh's body, my Eilidh's. I said to Maisie to stay there, not to move, to sit at Daddy's desk. She heard the tone of my voice and sat down at once, frozen.

Eilidh was lying in the middle of the road. She looked at me with empty eyes, she whispered: 'Shona . . . ' and I didn't know what to say. I could hear myself panting in fear and shock. I wanted to cradle her on my lap but in a moment of lucidity, I thought, don't move her, and I forced myself to leave her there, lying on the cold, hard asphalt in the muddy snow. I held her hand and I was mute, the words got stuck in my throat and suffocated me. The words were 'I love you' but I couldn't speak them.

Behind me, the driver of the car was calling 999. She was distraught and kept saying, 'She came out of nowhere . . . '

The ambulance came. By then, my neighbour Morag had come out, hearing the commotion, and I'd managed to tell her that Maisie was in the workshop, to look after her for a bit while I went with Eilidh. And we were away, sirens

238

blasting, breaking the icy air all around us, shocking Glen Avich out of its cottages and shops, people watching from the windows wondering, who is it, what happened?

When we got to the hospital, she was taken away and I couldn't see her again for a long time. They told me to go home, that I wasn't family, to go home to my daughter. I said no.

I phoned Peggy and listened to her crying.

I couldn't remember Morag's phone number, so I phoned my house and sure enough, Morag had taken Maisie home, Maisie had told her where I kept a spare set of keys, in the rosemary bush beside the door. She said not to worry about a thing, that Maisie was a bit shaken up but ok, she'd give her dinner and sit in my house until I'd come back.

I phoned Shona, she said she'd come down at once.

I got a call on my mobile from an unknown number. It was Eilidh's mum. Peggy must have phoned her.

I kept saying to her I didn't know how she was, they hadn't told me anything, they had just whisked her away, but she wouldn't listen, how did I not know anything, I was there, I should ask, I should *do something*.

'We're coming up,' she said and hung up.

I sat for hours holding an untouched cup of coffee. It'd started snowing again. I kept staring at the lamppost in front of the window, at the hypnotic dancing of the snowflakes in the orange light, surrounded by darkness.

Then a doctor came out and said Eilidh had

had to have an operation, that it was touch and go. Was I next of kin? Had I let her family know?

Her words blurred and my heart stopped beating, I stopped breathing, I existed in suspended reality as if it was me lying in intensive care, and I thought, please, God, please, please, please, save her.

Elizabeth

So that's what they were trying to tell me, the signs I've been feeling for a while. That's what I've felt coming, like the wind that announces the storm, when the air is full of electricity and you don't know where the lightning will strike.

I had tried to keep an eye on everyone, all my people here in Glen Avich, fearing it'd be one of them. It turned out to be Eilidh.

I was floating over the loch, in that stony corner where I love to be, when I felt this pulling inside, this terrible force wrangling me, taking me apart and then putting me together again. Human beings are solitary, independent entities whose bodies stand alone; ghosts are part of everything. I stood still for a bit, shaken, then I heard Jamie calling and I took myself over to him and I saw Eilidh lying in the street.

I knew she was alive or I would have seen her ghost beside her, stunned and shocked at being separated from the body. I knelt beside her and put my hand on her forehead.

Her eyes were open and they met mine. For a second, she could see me. I wasn't that

240

surprised, I know that sometimes we can be seen, especially by young children. Maisie sees me sometimes and sometimes I can even speak to her.

We looked at each other for a moment as I kept my hand on her, trying to give her a bit of my energy, to keep her strong. Then she closed her eyes and lost consciousness.

It was a huge effort to go to the hospital and sit with them all. Ghosts are bound to the place where they lived or where they died, and to go somewhere else takes a great deal of energy and concentration. It's nearly impossible.

I sat with Jamie, my heart wrenched with fear and compassion. This peace we feel when we die, this sense of detachment and serenity, never really leaves us — but we can still feel worry and pain and fear, though somehow more softly than when we were alive, as if the edge had been taken off.

After a while, Eilidh's ghost appeared. Floating against the far wall, the top of her head touching the ceiling. She looked terrified. I opened my mouth to speak and tried to reach her but I didn't make it in time because as suddenly as she had come, she disappeared.

Her body was strong, it was fighting hard to recover, to keep the soul with it. She wanted to live.

I decided to go and see Maisie, so I took myself to her room, where she was lying in bed, her magic lantern making lovely dancing shapes on the walls and ceiling.

I sat on her bed and touched her forehead, just

241

as I'd done with Eilidh. She was in deep sleep and didn't stir. I was exhausted from the journey away from Glen Avich and lost myself in the dancing lights for a bit, watching her sleeping, until I heard the keys in the door. Jamie was back.

He came in, pale, worn out. Morag was dozing on the sofa, bless her, and woke up with a startle.

'Sorry, Morag, didn't mean to wake you.'

'Not at all, don't be silly, I was just resting my eyes.'

'Maisie?'

'Sleeping like an angel, Jamie, no need to worry about her, she's fine. Any news?'

'No news. She's still asleep.'

'Poor lamb. Come here, take your jacket off . . . '

Morag is a mother of four and a grandmother of ten, she knows how to look after someone who's had a shock. In the space of ten minutes, she had Jamie on the sofa, a cup of tea in one hand, some fragrant toast in the other, and the fire revived.

'Maybe you could try and sleep for a bit . . . It's five in the morning, you can still get a couple of hours . . . '

'I'm not sure I can. I'll try.'

With Morag gone and Jamie on his way up the stairs, I couldn't resist. I had to tell him he wasn't alone.

I flickered the curtains, our secret sign. I knew he'd notice it.

And he did. He stopped for a moment, looked across the room in a daze and then went upstairs to try and get some sleep.

I dived into the sea of souls, into the sea of consciousness that floats in mine, until I found Eilidh's and I stayed with her, in her sleep, telling her stories like you'd do with a wee girl, telling her of when Jamie and Shona were children and all the things we used to do, soothing her frightened mind until I felt her thoughts calming down, unknotting, and settling in a sleep that wasn't death.

25

Falling

Eilidh

I watched them sitting in a green room with posters on the walls and plastic chairs. I watched them from the ceiling because somehow, that's where I was.

Jamie, white as a sheet, looking distraught . . . my mum and dad, crying . . . to see my dad crying, it was just . . . impossible. Shona was there too, a bit further from the others, sitting in a corner on her own. She looked very slim, no baby bump there, where's the baby? I was confused, my thoughts were all jumbled up.

Nobody could see me.

I was floating as if I had no body — actually that's the way it was, *I had no body*. Oh God, I thought. I'm dead. I really am dead.

What a shame. I'm only thirty-five, I thought in despair. I haven't done anything yet. I wasted so many years crying over what I didn't have, and now I'm dead and I can't change it.

One more chance, please give me one more chance, I cried inside, making no sound.

A man dressed in green walked in, I knew he was a doctor. He spoke to them and my mum hid her face in my dad's chest and cried. My dad's face looked all twisted and horrible, like he was being tortured. Jamie wasn't moving, he looked pale and distant. I knew they were grieving for me. I'm so sorry, so sorry, I tried to say over and over again. I'm so sorry for putting them through this. If only I hadn't run out, into the road . . . if only I hadn't slipped in the snow . . . if only I'd said to Maisie, no, let's wait for your daddy to come home . . . if only that cradle had been sold, if only that cradle had never been made, if only my cradle had been filled . . .

One more chance, one more chance.

Shona raised her head, she looked at me. She could see me! She opened her mouth to speak and I tried to reach her, but I was wrenched away with a terrible force, like the tide, like an all powerful current that pulled me backwards, and I felt nothing more and I saw nothing more.

But I could still think, in that deep darkness with no sensations, as desolate as the depths of the oceans miles and miles under water, where nothing swims, nothing moves, nothing disturbs the deep, solemn, barren peace.

I thought I was dead.

Jamie

The day after the accident went by in a blur. I woke up after a black, exhausted, restless sleep that brought no respite from fear. Maisie and I had breakfast together — I clumsily tried to hide my terror as I explained to her that Eilidh wasn't ok yet, she was still in hospital and the doctors

245

were looking after her. Maisie asked no questions, she's a wise child, she knew something bad had happened and she was trustingly waiting for us to sort it. As if we could.

I took her to school on autopilot — one foot in front of the other, a kiss and a cuddle, tried to be reassuring, 'See you later, sweetheart,' ignoring the looks of concern from all around. News of the accident had spread fast. I walked away from the school as quickly as I could and as soon as I was out of earshot, I phoned Eilidh's dad, Simon.

No reply.

Shit. Their phone was switched off. I needed to wait until they phoned me. Maybe they won't, I thought. Why should they? I'm not family, I'm not her husband or her boyfriend. Maybe they won't tell me, maybe she died and I won't know for ages. I felt tears prickling my eyes, a mixture of fear and exhaustion, everything swam and I leaned on the playground wall for a moment.

'Jamie . . . '

Shona's arms around me, her familiar scent, my mum's scent and my own.

'Come, come. Let's go to Peggy's.'

Peggy's eyes were red and swollen, she hadn't slept either.

'They phoned this morning. No change, really, still the same. The doctor said she might not wake up or if she wakes up, she might be . . . what's the word . . . brain-damaged. That's what Rhona said, brain-damaged.' She looked around, as if asking for clarification from us. Shona and I looked at each other, horrified.

246

I saw Shona opening her mouth. She was looking for something reassuring to say, something to make it better. One of those things my mum used to say when things were bleak, like when my dad got sick: 'I'm sure it'll be fine,' a mixture of stubborn optimism and sheer unwillingness to look at despair in the eye. Generations of women have used this to survive unspeakable hardships: it'll be fine, we'll be fine, it'll all work out. Put the kettle on, get on with it, keep faith, keep hope, keep your chin up. We'll be fine.

And sure enough, Shona and Peggy clutched each other's hands and performed the Scottish woman's ritual in the face of terror.

'She'll be ok, she's being looked after, you'll see, she's strong.'

'Ach I know, Shona, it'll be fine. I'll put the kettle on.'

And I sat, marginally comforted by their strength, like a small flickering light in this terrible darkness.

We stayed with Peggy until Margaret arrived, then walked home in silence.

Later on, at home, Shona was scrubbing an already immaculate kitchen — when she's anxious, she cleans — and I was pacing the room when my mobile rang. I jumped and answered quickly, my heart in my throat.

'Jamie? It's Silke. I heard about Eilidh. God, it's terrible. Any news, how is she?'

'She hasn't woken up . . . '

A moment of silence, followed by, 'Do you want me to come over?'

'I'm going to drive to the hospital later on, as soon as her parents take a break. Just so she's not on her own . . . ' I choked for a second ' . . . maybe you could come with me . . . Shona will stay here to look after Maisie and it'd be good to have you with me . . . '

'Of course. Just come and get me. Is she in Kinnear or Aberdeen?'

'Kinnear for now, I'm not sure what'll happen next.'

'Come any time, I'm ready.'

As soon as I put my mobile down, the house phone went.

'Hi Jamie, it's Simon. We're going to Peggy's to rest for a bit, Rhona is in a bad way, they had to give her medication . . . Peggy said you'd go . . . She said you've been a good friend to Eilidh since she moved up here . . . Thank you for that . . . ' He sounded terrible.

'Don't thank me. Please say to Rhona I'll do all I can. I'll be at the hospital in half an hour.'

'You see, her sister can't come up, she's got no one to leave her kids with. And Tom . . . well, I'm not sure Eilidh wants Tom around. I know he's still her husband but . . . I'm not sure if you know . . . '

'I know. What about Harry? Eilidh's best friend?'

'I'm going to phone him as soon as we know what's what. No point in just worrying him now. I mean, she's in a coma, nothing's changing . . . when she wakes up, I'll phone him.'

'Yes. Of course. When she wakes up.'

248

Silke and I drove in silence, the snowy winter landscape so beautiful it was heartbreaking.

★   ★   ★

No change.

We spent a few hours sitting in the waiting room. We were not allowed to see her.

We drove home in time to put Maisie to bed. I had to be there for that; she needed things to be as normal as possible. Shona was going to stay with me until Saturday — Fraser had taken a few days off to look after the girls. I was moved by their kindness.

The next few days were a blur, with Eilidh's parents and me taking turns to be there. She was lying on the hospital bed, perfectly still. She was breathing herself, though, and we clung to that — that she didn't need machines to help her, her chest rose and fell steadily. She reminded me of seaweed on the shore, ebbing and flowing with the waves. Her skin was creamy and there was no colour on her face, no colour anywhere on her, just a purple bruise on one side of her forehead.

I don't know how many hours I spent in that waiting room, thinking of her — the way she walked into my workshop, a few days ago, a million years ago, her cheeks pink from the cold, her eyes shining, so full of life, so vibrant. I still didn't know what could have happened that made her run out like that, into the road, without looking.

The doctors said there was no point in sitting on those awful chairs for hours, if there was any change they'd phone us, but we did anyway. We needed to make sure that, when she woke up, there'd be someone there.

★ ★ ★

'Were you there? Did you see?' asked Simon, his face grey.

'I was in my workshop. Maisie was showing me her work, Eilidh was looking at mine. Then she gasped and ran out. Just like that.'

'Did something scare her? What happened?'

'I don't know. It was all so sudden. I heard a thump and . . . '

'Did you say something that upset her?' He sounded exasperated. He needed a reason.

'Absolutely *not*. All I'd said to her was 'hello', then Maisie was showing me her jotter and that was it. If you think it's my fault, you're very, very wrong.'

'No, of course not. I'm sorry, I didn't mean . . . It's just that she was so much better. In the last few phone calls. Like the old Eilidh, before all that happened. I just can't believe . . . '

'What are you saying? That she *threw* herself under that bloody car? You're wrong again.' My voice was a whisper but had we not been in a hospital, I would have shouted. 'Eilidh is strong. You don't know her. She was rebuilding her life. She *is* rebuilding her life!'

'I don't know her? I'm her father! Of course I know her!'

'Eilidh is strong,' I repeated.

Later on, I went to my workshop. Everything

looked untidy, unfinished. There was no way I could go back to work yet, not while she was lying in that hospital bed.

I retraced her steps, trying to look at things with her eyes, from my drawing table, to the right-hand side where the jewellery is displayed, then further on, right at the back where I keep the finished pieces ready to be collected.

And then I noticed it: the cradle, the wrought-iron cradle ... I always have one on display, it's a popular piece and I've been getting orders for bespoke cradles from all over the country. Maybe that's what she found so upsetting. She'd told me that just before losing her baby, her husband had bought a cradle and that it felt like a bad omen to her, to put it in the nursery like that, empty and waiting, so long before the birth. She said they had got it from her husband's best friend.

I went home and checked the books. There'd be no record of it had they bought it ready-made but I kept a note of all orders and deliveries. It was a long shot but worth a try.

I'd made a couple dozen of them in the last three years or so and, sure enough, one was delivered to Southport, to a Dr Ian Pearce. Maybe . . .

Maybe.

There was no way of knowing, except asking her, and I couldn't do that, not in a million years. But I couldn't bear to have that cradle in my shop anymore, so I drove it at once to Kinnear, to the Oxfam shop.

Days and nights blurred until, finally, after what seemed like weeks but was only four days, Eilidh opened her eyes.

Eilidh

I rose up, up to the surface. The black, silent, cold depths of the ocean became warm waters, shallow sea. I started having dreams, one of which I'd had before but not in such detail.

I was kneeling on the floor, a wooden floor. I could see my knees. I was wearing a brown skirt and beige tights, those that were in fashion years ago. I could see the sun streaming through the window and dust dancing in it. From the window, I could see the rolling, pine-covered hills of Glen Avich beyond fields of green grass. In front of me, I could see the legs of two people sitting on the sofa. My arms were stretched out, open like in an embrace, and a blond toddler wearing brown dungarees was wobbling towards me with a look of intense concentration on his face. He's learning to walk, I thought. The boy made it into my arms and I held him — he felt soft and tender as he squealed with delight. I smiled and raised my head to look at the people on the sofa: Lord and Lady Ramsay, smiling back at me, praising the wee boy's feat. In a split second, I knew I was Elizabeth and the wee boy was Jamie. I kept holding him tight and wishing the dream wouldn't finish. But the whole scene blurred and everything melted away, leaving in its place a white ceiling and aqua walls. I was awake.

26

The Day After the
End of the World

Jamie

She was beautiful — pale, nearly translucent, like
mother-of-pearl. She was beautiful and she was
alive.

They had to cut her hair very short and it
framed her bruised face, soft and silky on the
white pillow. She had a line in her hand but no
more tubes in her nostrils, no more oxygen
mask. She lay in her hospital bed, the pillows
raised a bit, her head leaning on one side. Rhona
was sitting beside her.

I walked in and she smiled, a little smile that
was weak but very joyful, all at the same time. I
sat down, unable to speak. I didn't dare to touch
her — I felt I might break her.

'Jamie.' Her voice was thin and soft. She was
still smiling.

'Eilidh . . . ' I wanted to say, 'my love,' but I
couldn't because Rhona was there and because I
didn't know how she'd react, I didn't want to
upset her.

'I'm awake now.'

I smiled. 'Yes, you are.'

'I thought I was dead.'

'No, no, thank God, no . . . ' I went to hold her hand and then I stopped in mid-air and just touched her wrist lightly, awkwardly, for a moment. She raised her hand and clasped mine. I couldn't stop myself, I stroked her cheek and she closed her eyes.

'I can feel that. It's amazing, to be awake,' she said.

'I thought I'd lost you,' I whispered.

She looked at me with those clear, honest eyes.

'Has Shona had the baby?'

Oh my God, I thought. She's confused. Maybe it's a lot worse than it looks, maybe she can't remember . . .

'No, that's a few months away still.'

'I thought so. She's due in May, this is February . . . ' she said this slowly and deliberately, as if making sure she was getting it right. Thank God, I thought, for the millionth time that day. She's ok. 'But when she was here,' she went on, 'her bump was gone.'

'She was never here. She stayed in Glen Avich to look after Maisie. She never came to the hospital.'

'Yes, she did. She sat with you. She was there when I was hit.'

'No, she came down the day after. She was in Aberdeen when the accident happened.'

'But, Jamie, I saw her. She had her brown skirt, she was kneeling beside me and she touched my face when I was lying on the ground.'

I thought it was better not to upset her, so I

255

changed the subject. 'She'll come and see you as soon as you're stronger.'

'She was there, Jamie. I saw her.'

'She can't wait to see you — '

'You better go now, the doctor will be here soon,' intervened Rhona, sensing that Eilidh was getting agitated.

'No, Jamie, stay. Don't go, stay for a wee bit longer.'

'Of course. I'll stay as long as you like.'

How strange, she'd seen Shona, minus bump. She must have been delirious. Believe me, Shona's bump is hard to miss now, she's six months gone.

'Don't go,' Eilidh said again and she looked a wee bit frailer, a bit more tired than she did a minute ago. She closed her eyes.

No, I won't go. Of course I won't. What could ever keep me from you?

'You're leaving soon . . . You're going to Australia,' she said all of a sudden, as if she'd just remembered.

'Don't think about that now.'

'It's ok, your dad and I are here, we'll look after you,' said Rhona, leaning over her, but Eilidh didn't lose that frightened look.

'When are you going?'

'Well, we're due to leave next month, but . . . '

'Don't go. Stay with me.'

'Eilidh, be reasonable . . . ' said Rhona.

'I didn't want to ask you . . . I didn't want to stop you . . . but I am asking you now . . . stay with me.'

I was speechless. Rhona looked at me with

strange hostility. That took me by surprise, too.

'Eilidh, for heaven's sake, he can't just cancel everything at the last minute, the world doesn't revolve around you.'

I looked at Rhona incredulously. Even with her daughter in a hospital bed, she couldn't help having a little dig. But Eilidh ignored her; her eyes didn't leave mine. She had that look on her face, a vulnerable look, like a little girl, and yet, there was a strength in her that didn't seem to waver.

I thought, I'm not going anywhere.

'I won't go. I'll phone Emily tonight. I won't go. I'll look after you,' I said.

She took a deep breath and closed her eyes, her hand still in mine.

★   ★   ★

'I think you'll find that *we'll* look after her, Jamie. I don't understand who gave *you* the right . . . '

We were walking out of the hospital, Rhona having only just managed to keep her spitefulness from brimming over in Eilidh's room.

'Rhona, I don't intend to take over. I just want to help.'

'Some help. She got all agitated — '

'She thought I was going to Australia, she didn't want me to.'

'You always have an answer, don't you? Just like that sister of yours, like she knows everything. You might not be going but we are. Eilidh is coming with us. We're going back to

257

Southport and we'll see she gets the best care money can buy.'

'Have you asked her? Have you asked where *she* wants to be?'

'Don't you raise your voice with me, Jamie McAnena. She'll go with us because she has no choice. Who'll take care of her? Peggy?'

'I will.'

'Don't be stupid.' I flinched. 'I spoke to the nurse. Even when she can leave here, she needs specialized care. She won't be able to do much for herself for a few weeks, do you realise that?'

'I didn't mean I'd look after her myself. I meant I'll get a private nurse, for as long as she needs one.'

'And who'll pay for it? She hardly has a penny to her name, she won't take anything from Tom. And don't expect us to pay if she stays up here.'

'I'll pay, of course.'

'Yes, sure, you'll pay. For a private nurse,' she said sarcastically.

'Actually, I will.'

She stopped for a second, surprised.

'She's coming back with us,' she repeated.

'Ask her.'

I left Rhona standing in the hospital car park and drove away in a rage.

★   ★   ★

'She just wants to make sure Eilidh's well looked after . . . '

'No way, Shona. She's got an agenda, I'm telling you.'

258

'Jamie, it's not like you to speak like this. I think you're misunderstanding her. Give her a chance.'

'You should have seen her face.'

'The priority here is Eilidh's well-being.'

'Exactly. They want her back in their clutches. They'll eat her alive.'

'Jamie, what are you talking about? That's Rhona Lawson, we know her. She's all right, she's not a monster.'

'I just want Eilidh to choose where she wants to be.'

'I know. I know. Don't worry. Right, have to go. Must get girls ready for bed. I'll phone you tomorrow. Oh, and Jamie?'

'Yes?'

'I'm so glad you're staying.'

After I put down the phone, I sat on the sofa, both agitated and shattered, full of relief and worry all mixed up. At least she's alive and there'll be no long-term damage. That's what the doctor said. And she wants to be with me.

She wants to be with me! This called for a celebration. I poured myself a glass of sparkling water and squeezed some lemon juice in it. I looked at the glass in dismay.

This does call for a celebration, a real one. Not a lonely pouring of glass after glass but not sparkling water either.

I went to the kitchen and unburied my treasure. Twenty-five-year-old Lagavullin. Drinking it is like a long, lingering, passionate kiss. Fire and wind and peat and sea, all mixed together.

The fire was on, the lights all out but a couple of table lamps and the blue reflection of Maisie's night-light on the landing. No noise but the wind outside and the occasional shiver of fire, the way peat fire does, like a hissing shudder, not like the crackling of logs.

I closed my eyes to savour the first sip..

Then someone knocked at the door. Oh, no. Please no small talk tonight.

But thankfully, it was Silke.

'Hi. You ok? Wasn't sure you'd want company but I was driving by and I thought I'd stop for a moment.'

'Great, come in. I just opened a cracking whisky, you have to taste this. Come and sit down. I've got quite a few things to tell you . . . '

One dram later, I'd told her everything. About Eilidh asking me to stay and Rhona's reaction, how I was hoping Eilidh would choose to stay with Peggy and I'd get a nurse to look after her . . .

'Fiona could do it.'

'Do you think?'

'Yes, you know she's a qualified nurse, don't you? She qualified a wee while ago.' I love Silke's Scottish sayings delivered with a German accent. 'She found a post down south but didn't take it up because of me. Then she looked after Mary for a bit. I don't know what she's doing now, we haven't spoken since we broke up.' She was looking into her glass.

'Do you think I could phone her?'

'Sure, why not.'

'But if she accepts, would you mind having her around here?'

'I would love having her around here. God, I would just totally and completely *love* having her here. I miss her . . . You see . . . '

We were up talking until two in the morning. There was one dram of whisky for me, two for Silke, and the rest was milky tea. I wasn't taking any chances. The smiler with a knife, even in its beauty and infinite pleasure, will always be out to get me.

And I won't let it.

Elizabeth

It's always strange when the real person crosses paths with its memory, the shadow trapped in the traumatic moment. It's like seeing double. As if being a ghost wasn't surreal enough, we see all these things — many that I have no words to describe.

And now, I see one Fiona sitting on that step again, on the phone, right next to the other Fiona, the broken-hearted one, holding the necklace.

'Yes, we heard. Thank goodness. No, I'm not sure what I'll do next, I've just been helping my mum in the salon really. Yes. I'd love to do that. Will I be able to stay with Peggy? That's kind of her. Great. Give me a call when Eilidh gets out. Oh and Jamie? Can you thank Silke from me . . . I mean, so nice of her to get me this job. Yes, I do have her number. Yes, of course, you must

261

be snowed under, and of course, she'd like to hear it from me. Will do. No, seriously, I will. Seriously.'

One Fiona smiling, one Fiona sobbing, sitting side by side . . .

27

Revelation

Jamie

A summit had been called. A meeting on neutral ground, Peggy's house.

It was ten days since Eilidh had woken up and she was doing well, so well that the doctor said she could come home soon. But, whose home? Her parents wanted her in Southport with them, she said she wanted to stay with Peggy and I was fighting her corner. For both her interest and mine.

We were all sitting on Peggy's sofas, an untouched cup of tea in each of our hands.

'It's very simple really. She's a grown woman, she says she wants to stay, let her stay.'

'Jamie, you must understand. She nearly died. She has to be with her family.'

'Simon, Peggy is her family, too, and this is her home.'

'What are you talking about?' shouts Rhona, ready to turn it all into a fight. 'Southport is her home! She only came up here because she lost her mind.'

'She came here determined to build a new life and she did.'

'Look, Jamie,' said Simon, trying to sound

reasonable. 'It all comes down to Eilidh's safety, really. Where do you think she'll be better looked after, here with an elderly woman' — indignant noise from Peggy — 'and someone we barely know — '

'Your wife's family has known me since I was born!'

'Actually, I wasn't talking about you. I was talking about this nurse, this . . . Fiona. You're not even in the equation. You're not her family — what *are* you, her new boyfriend?' All pretence of civility gone.

'I'm not her boyfriend. But we've been close since she came up. I'm just trying to stick up for her — '

'Now everybody QUIET!'

Peggy?

'This is my house you're shouting in. I won't have you behaving like this under my roof. We're all going to calm down . . . Excuse me . . . ' The doorbell had gone.

The second Peggy left the room, Rhona started again.

'If you think you can do this, Jamie, you can think again. She's had a bloody breakdown, she was in hospital, now she ends up under a car, she's clearly incapable of making decisions for herself. She's coming to Southport with us, whether she likes it or not. Any doctor would say so — '

'Eilidh, under a car? What are you talking about?'

A tall, blond-haired man had entered the room and was staring at us, his eyes darting from

264

one person to the next. He looked shocked.

'Tom! What are you doing here?' exclaimed Rhona.

'What happened? What happened to Eilidh? Why didn't anyone call me?'

'Call *you*? You lost the right when you went off with that woman!'

'Can someone tell me what's happened?' Tom's hands were shaking. He was as pale as a ghost.

'Eilidh had an accident. She was hit by a car,' intervened Simon.

'Oh my God! Is she ok?'

'She is now. She's still in hospital. She's due to come home soon . . . '

'Can I see her?'

'Over my dead body, Tom, you'd just upset her and she's too weak right now,' growled Rhona.

'*She* asked me to come up. To discuss . . . our divorce.' Peggy had sat him down with a glass of whisky, his hands were shaking and he was pale, but he was remarkably calm.

'You can discuss things when she's better. Now is really not the time,' said Simon.

'I understand. I won't upset her. But if only I could see her — '

'You *can't* see her,' said Rhona and then turned to me. '*And* she's coming down with us.'

'It's her call, Rhona. She decides if she wants to see Tom and where she wants to be.' Peggy's gentle voice silenced everybody.

'Like I said, she's incapable. Any doctor would say that she can't look after herself, that she can't make decisions — '

'What?' intervened Tom. 'Eilidh can very well make decisions, Rhona. She sounded . . . fine when we spoke on the phone. She was determined. She wanted things to move forward, a fresh start.'

'And that's why she threw herself under a car?'

'She didn't! It was an accident!' I said, trying not to raise my voice. 'There was sleet on the road, she slipped and fell . . . '

'Rhona, on the phone with me last week, Eilidh didn't sound like someone who wanted to die,' Tom intervened, in a calm, authoritative voice. He had a subtle Manchester accent that made his voice pleasant to the ear. 'When we spoke, she was well determined to live. I believe . . . him . . . ' He looked at me. 'I believe that this was an accident.'

'I'm Jamie,' I said and awkwardly shook his hand.

Our eyes met and he knew. We both looked away. This wasn't the time to start locking horns and we both understood that.

'Rubbish. We'll speak to the doctor, they'll say she's not in her right mind and we'll take her with us.'

'I *am* a doctor, Rhona,' said Tom calmly. 'And I'll say that she is indeed in her right mind and that she can choose where to stay. I've known you for quite a few years now and I think you're using this suicide farce to get your own way.'

Silence.

'Are you siding with *him*? Her boyfriend?'

Tom winced. 'I'm siding with *her*. I've hurt her enough. She needs me now. I'm going to the

266

hospital, she'll choose whether to see me or not. I'll ask her where she wants to be and that you'll comply with.'

Nobody spoke.

'Thanks, Peggy. I'll see myself out.'

And he left.

Oh my God, I thought. What if she sees him and realises she still has feelings for him . . . What if the shock of the incident made her change her mind about the divorce . . .

An abyss opened in my mind and I needed some fresh air. I walked out with a muttered farewell to Peggy, away from the Lawsons and their power games.

Eilidh

I couldn't wait to see him. I couldn't wait to face the pain, the grief I'd feel looking into his face and knowing it was all over, then get on with the rest of my life.

People were surprised I didn't seem angry about the affair but the grief for my lost baby was so all consuming, it didn't leave room for anything else. I had no feelings left for him. Actually, no feelings left at all.

That night when I had knocked at Peggy's door, I barely had the energy left to exist. It was such a huge effort just to breathe, and to eat, and to keep myself alive. But as life started flowing back into me and I started feeling things again, the anger came. Not because I loved him — love had gone a long time ago — but for the sheer

267

humiliation. I was positively furious. With him, for cheating. With me, for putting up with it so that we could get on with our IVF.

But when he walked into the room, there was no anger. It was Tom, the Tom I'd known forever, his blond hair sticking up on one side as it always did, his eyes full of concern. It was my husband and all the anger somehow flew away.

'Eilidh . . . ' He came to sit beside me and held both my hands, as if nothing had happened, as if he'd never hurt me.

To my surprise, I held his.

'How are you feeling? I just found out now, I was at Peggy's . . . I tried to phone you but your mobile had been switched off for ages . . . '

'I'm so glad you're here . . . '

'You *are*?'

I nodded.

'Darling, you won't believe how much my life has changed. I'm on my own. It's over . . . you know . . . It's all over. I resigned from a few things, I'm ready to spend more time with you.'

'Remember the cradle?'

'Our cradle? Yes . . . '

'It was made here. I mean, in Glen Avich.'

'Oh, Eilidh . . . That is so weird . . . I can't believe it . . . When Ian gave it to me, he didn't tell me . . . What a strange coincidence that it's been made where your family's from . . . '

'I saw it in Jamie's workshop. It was like a nightmare. I ran out and didn't see the car. I tried to jump out of the road but I slipped in the snow . . . '

'Poor you. My poor Eilidh.' He smoothed the

268

hair away from my forehead, in a gesture so familiar it broke my heart. 'Your mum keeps saying you tried to . . . to harm yourself . . . '

'What? What is she talking about? I'd never . . . ' Of course. I should have known. What a perfect occasion for her to take control, seamless really. Eilidh is so unstable she even tried to kill herself. We must take control of her. I was so angry, I couldn't speak.

'I know, I know. Don't worry. Everybody knows she's talking nonsense. We'll get you discharged soon and back on your feet. We'll take a holiday, anywhere you want . . . '

I untangled my hands from his.

'Oh, Tom. No. I'm sorry. Nothing has changed . . . We're not getting back together. We can't . . . '

'Why can't we? I know you called me here to talk about the divorce but . . . With all that happened . . . '

'Nothing has changed. Please, Tom.' Our eyes met. He looked into my eyes, his blue gaze holding mine for a long time, as if he was searching my soul.

'Do you have feelings for Jamie?'

'Yes.' My heart stopped for a second. It was the first time I'd said it aloud. 'But Jamie has nothing to do with you and me. It's been over for a long time, before you . . . you . . . '

'Nine days.' He said and his face was bitter.

'Nine days? What do you mean?'

'Once, you didn't speak to me for nine days. And there was nothing wrong between us, really. I hadn't . . . I wasn't seeing anyone, we hadn't fought or anything. It was this baby thing that was eating you inside. We were living together and you didn't speak to me for nine whole days, apart from, 'Hello,' 'Night,' and, 'Would you like a cup of tea?' I counted. The tenth day, you spoke to me just before bed, about some stuff needing done in the house.'

'Oh my God, Tom. I'm so sorry . . . '

'Well, you know what? You should be. Because this is your doing as well as mine. I'm not attacking you, Eilidh, God knows I love you, if I could go back . . . But you did this too, with me. We destroyed our marriage. And for what?'

I took a deep breath. 'I saw two people in love, a few months ago. They were about to kiss and were looking into each other's eyes. It made me see . . . I never felt that way for you. And you never felt that way for me.'

He looked shocked. I could see at once I'd hurt him deeply and that there was no return from there.

'You're wrong. As far as I'm concerned, at least.' He stood up and covered his eyes with his hand. I started crying, too, and made no effort to stop the tears. Our marriage deserved those tears. The end of our marriage was a time to cry.

After a few seconds, he spoke again.

'I'll speak to your parents. I'll see that you're able to stay in Peggy's house. I'll see that your parents have no way to take you back to Southport . . . '

'Wait . . . ' He couldn't possibly leave like that. He couldn't leave *me* like that.

'What?' he said softly. 'What's left to say?'

I held my hands out. 'Tom . . . '

He held them.

'I'll give you a divorce, of course. I'll take care of everything.'

'No, it's not that . . . Tom . . . '

'No more, Eilidh. Please.' He let go of my hands and it felt like a part of me had been cut off.

He left, without looking back, he left.

'Thank you . . . ' I whispered but I'm not sure he heard.

28

The Words Unspoken

Fiona

Eilidh was sitting on Peggy's sofa, sipping her tea and emailing on her laptop. She looked serene and peaceful and smiled a lot. For someone who'd just been in a near-fatal accident, she looked very . . . *satisfied*.

I knew it had something to do with Jamie. They couldn't hide the feelings between them. I just hoped they'd finish their 'will we, won't we' dance and get on with it.

Still, she seemed pretty happy *all* the time, not only when Jamie was there or when he phoned.

'Eilidh, can I ask you a question?'

'Sure.' Her clear blue eyes met mine. No wonder Jamie fell for her, I thought, she's beautiful. Not in an obvious way, more in a . . . soulful way. Silke would have the words to describe it. She always does.

'You seem so . . . I don't know, contented. It's like this accident hasn't really affected you . . . '

She smiled and all of a sudden, her face was like a wee girl's.

'Just the opposite, actually . . . ' She looked thoughtful and put the laptop down beside her. 'It has affected me a lot. In a good way . . . '

I wasn't sure what she meant, so I waited.

'You see, I've spent a lot of time being sad. For one reason or another, you know, my family, not being able to have children, my husband, and so on and so forth. When I was in hospital, I thought I'd died. It's difficult to explain, I was in a coma but I could *think* and I was sure I was dead. Then I woke up . . . ' She gestured towards the window, as if to show me the world she was still here to enjoy. 'I feel like I've been given a second chance. And I'm just so relieved, so delighted, that I've been allowed to live . . . '

She brought her knees up and hugged her legs, wincing slightly. She was still in pain. I knew that, I was the one sitting with her through the night and helping her with all the things she still struggled to do by herself.

'And of course, there's Jamie . . . ' she added.

I blushed and looked away. I'm not good with this kind of talk, I get embarrassed. I know I'm old enough to be over this chronic shyness, I'm not a teenager anymore. But I can't help it.

She noticed my awkwardness and smiled, a mischievous smile, I thought.

'What about you, Fiona, do you have someone?'

She knew, of course. Silke's friends all knew. My desperate attempt to keep it secret hadn't worked, which is mainly why we broke up.

Mainly. And also the fact that I couldn't possibly be the kind of person who lives *that* way. Ok, I might have dabbled in it, it happened, but a life choice, no. I was going to get married and have children, like everybody else. I couldn't be the one that people whispered about, I couldn't be the one who lets her parents down, who lets her dad down.

Since I came back, I've seen Silke twice. Twice my heart stopped. She looked at me for a long time, waiting for me to speak. I saw that she still loved me, I saw it in her eyes, and I just wanted to run into her arms.

But nothing had changed for me. I still wasn't comfortable with people knowing. We were back to square one. I knew that I couldn't be near her, without . . . without giving in.

'Yes. I'm seeing someone.'

Oh God, I thought. I'm terrible at lying. How on earth was I going to keep this one going?

Eilidh looked taken aback.

'He was at college with me. He's from Aberdeen. We . . . we text and speak all the time.'

'That's great. Good for you . . . ' she said and looked at me for a long time.

'His name is Jack. He's great. He's my . . . ideal man,' I added, feeling my cheeks getting hotter and redder every second.

My ideal man. There was no ideal *man* on this earth for me.

There was only Silke and I'd just taken another little step further away from her because I knew that Eilidh would tell Jamie about this Jack I made up, and Jamie would tell Silke, and she'd move on.

Which was what I wanted of course, I wanted her to move on and be happy. Without me.

Eilidh

Jack? I didn't believe her for a second. She just made it up. Fiona was so transparent, so innocent. She couldn't lie to save her life. She looked very young, I thought, with her wavy brown hair down, her milk-white skin dotted with freckles, her deep, dark green eyes. Her cheeks were very pink, which made her look even younger.

I wasn't sure what she'd choose. I knew she still had feelings for Silke but she was fighting them with all her strength.

It was easy for all of us to say she should free herself, she should accept who she is. But it's such a difficult choice, to go against your family, to defy all their expectations and stand firm against their disapproval. Just thinking about it made my heart beat faster with upset — to be Morag and Hugh Robertson's daughter, to be brought up in the Baptist faith, going to the church and Sunday school every week, and actually sharing their beliefs and trying to live by them . . . and then falling in love with a woman.

I'd felt a lot better for a while now; Fiona's stay in Glen Avich was drawing to a close. I really didn't have the slightest idea what was going to happen with those two. This much I knew, though: Fiona could maybe manage to be strong this time and walk away, but judging from her face the night I saw her kissing Silke, she was too passionate, her blood flew too fast and warm in her veins, for her to deny herself forever. Sooner or later, I knew she'd fall in love again, and her falling will be sweet, too sweet to stop, too sweet to talk about it.

My head spun a little. Maybe it was the painkillers, or maybe I was just hungry . . .

All of a sudden, I felt restless. A sense of longing rose up inside me, I couldn't sit still anymore. It was a beautiful night, the world was pulsating all around me, it was early spring and my thoughts were flowing like a singing stream. I put my jacket on and said to Fiona that I was going for a walk, and I did mean to do that, to just go for a walk, but my legs had a will of their own; they took me up St Colman's Way, past the spot I nearly died, to Jamie's house.

Jamie

I wished I could just reach out and kiss her, like I did at Hogmanay. But I seemed to have lost my courage. In my mind, she was fragile now, like something that's been broken and put back together and needed to be handled with care. But when I was alone at night and I closed my eyes, the things I saw, the things we did together . . . it could never be this way for real, not now.

But, since the accident, she smiled and looked straight at me, she didn't look away like she used to, as if I wasn't meant to know what she was thinking, as if she had to hide from me. She looked like she was waiting, waiting for something that she knew was inevitable, something that was going to happen soon, as soon as I could reach out and touch her.

276

And then, one clear spring night, I came home to find her on my doorstep. I looked into her face and she wasn't smiling, her eyes were dark, nearly black in the twilight. I held her and she was shaking.

'Hi . . . come on in. Maisie's with Shona tonight . . . '

'I know.'

I realised at once why she'd come and why she was shaking. I put the fire on and we sat for a while, watching the flames flickering, watching each other tentatively.

Eilidh has this way of kissing, slow and steady, she doesn't change, she stays nearly still and doesn't stop until I can't take anymore. She did that to me that night and I tried to stop myself but I couldn't, it'd been so long . . . I held on to her waist like I was about to fall — and I did — I fell into her. And then she stroked my hair and looked at me with those dark, liquid eyes that I'd never seen before.

I took her by the hand and led her upstairs and we didn't need to be quiet. I held her gently, like a porcelain doll, until I couldn't take it anymore and I had to take her the way I dreamt of and she didn't stop me. She whispered, 'Keep your eyes open.' Our eyes were locked as we moved together and our souls were bared. We looked into each other's eyes as we came and it was raw and beautiful, and after that I knew that our ties could never be broken.

Eilidh

'It's been so long,' he'd said.

And so it'd been for me . . . I was frightened and I couldn't stop shaking. I was frightened and still, I couldn't stop and I didn't stop. I wish I could say it was him that led me — I knew it was wrong to do this, I was still married, it was too soon — but I couldn't deny it was me, it was me who came close to him, so close he just couldn't move away, and it was me who touched him so that it would have been torture to stop and so there could be no way back.

I'd been empty and longing for so long and I was coming to life again. I wanted him to look at me, I wanted to see his eyes as we melted into one, and I hoped, I hoped with all my heart, he'd never leave me. I should have whispered, 'I love you.' Instead, I whispered, 'Don't go . . . ' because I knew that if he left, I would survive, I would keep breathing, but I would never be alive again.

He whispered back, 'I'll never go,' and I couldn't talk then, I couldn't talk anymore but I thought it over and over again, don't go, don't go, don't go.

My heart was breaking with love for him and I was frightened because he had my life in his hands and when he said, 'I'll never go,' I didn't believe him. I knew by then that vows can be broken and promises can be forgotten, that all we have is hope that love doesn't fall through our fingers, like sand.

29

Don't Go

Eilidh

Maisie and I were sitting at the kitchen table. I was helping her with her reading and keeping an ear out for the phone. Tom was due to call me that afternoon, to arrange for me to go down to Southport to sign some documents. It had all been so quick, so smooth. I didn't want anything of his and I had nothing of mine to share, except a pot of savings so small it wouldn't have even paid for the lawyer. There were no children, of course, so no custody battles. Very straightforward, yet not painless. No, not painless.

A few days before, I'd received a letter from him with some documents attached. It was a statement from a fund opened by Tom, with me as its beneficiary. The letter said that I'd left my job to concentrate on undergoing fertility treatment, a treatment that took so much out of me, physically and emotionally, that it'd left me unable to work — that much was true. He argued that I'd done that for both of us, that he felt responsible that I had no provision for the future and that the time left in my working life wasn't enough to provide for my old age comfortably.

279

I felt a hand squeeze my heart and the little spark of affection I still had for him stirred inside me, a feeling I knew would go away.

I wasn't going to accept. In a way, I knew he was right in saying that I sacrificed many years trying to achieve something we both wanted. On the other hand, I didn't want anything from him. I felt sure that once I'd found a better paid job than helping Peggy and looking after Maisie, I was going to be able to look after myself into my old age, as far away as it might seem now.

I knew I'd be all right. My idea of comfort and Tom's are completely different: he seems to need an awful lot in order to find his life acceptable, while I'm happy with very little, which is something I inherited from Flora and that I'm very proud of.

I'd decided to take some time to think about it and see how events turned out. In the meantime, though, we had to get on with the divorce papers. That involved me going to Southport.

In a way, I was looking forward to it. I hadn't seen my nieces and nephews in a long time. And I couldn't wait to go back to my old house and get a few things I'd missed . . . my books and clothes, lots of bits and pieces that belonged to my old life but that I still wanted to carry into my new one.

I had one ear on Kipper's adventures, read by Maisie's silvery voice, and one on my mobile sitting on the table between us. Finally, the phone rang and we both jumped. It was Tom.

'Sorry, darling, you keep on reading. I won't be long. Hello?'

I sat on the stairs while Maisie obediently went on reading, occasionally raising her head to look at me.

'Yes. Yes, I'll be there first thing. I'm staying with Harry. I'm driving. I don't know how I feel about going back to Southport. Good and bad, all mixed up. Don't really want to leave Maisie and Ja . . . Peggy but they'll be fine without me. Yes. I'll see you then. Thanks for letting me know. Bye bye.'

His voice was as familiar as a brother's. I sat still for a few seconds, contemplating the fact that soon he was to be out of my life forever. Surreal. As if someone had told me that Harry or Katrina were to be out of my life. For a few moments, I felt lost.

I put the phone down and Maisie was looking at me. She was pale and had a strange expression on her face.

'Maisie? Are you ok?'

She shook her head.

'Are you not feeling good?'

She shook her head again.

That moment, I heard the keys in the door. It was Jamie.

'Hello, how's everyone?'

Before I could say anything, he saw Maisie at the table. With the instinct of a father, he knew something was wrong.

'Are you ok, sweetheart?' he said, kneeling in front of her.

'I have a sore tummy.'

'Why don't we go and lie down for a bit, then maybe if you feel any better later on you can have some dinner with us?' he said, taking her by the hand.

'I can't stay, Jamie, I need to pack. Can you phone me later to let me know how she's doing?'

'NOOOOOO! DON'T GO!' Maisie burst into tears and ran to me. Jamie and I looked at each other in shock.

I gave her a cuddle and held her trembling little body.

'You *can't* go!' she wailed.

'Baby, I've got stuff to do tonight, you'll see me tomorrow and then I'll only be away for a couple of days. I'll be back before you know it.'

She disentangled herself from me and looked me in the eye, pale and solemn.

'You won't be back.'

'What? Of course I'll be back, darling, you don't need to worry about that!'

But Maisie turned away without a word and ran upstairs.

Jamie and I were left, frozen.

'I'm sorry, I didn't mean to upset her . . . ' I whispered.

'She'll be fine . . . I think she's just worried you're going for good, you know, like Janet. Or my mum. I suppose she's got quite a history of people leaving her, in her short life . . . '

'Maybe I should stay the night . . . ' I blushed. 'I mean . . . '

Jamie laughed. 'I know what you mean.' He put his hands on my shoulders. 'I want you to stay the night and the night after that and all the nights to come, but let's do it on our own terms.

Go and sort out all you need to sort out, then we'll be free.'

Free. And a little bit lost. He must have seen something in my face because he held me tight, very tight, as if to state once more that this was where I belonged.

'Do you want me to come with you? I can come down and back in a day . . . '

'No, I have to do this on my own.'

He took my face in his hands and kissed me, a little bit harder than he normally did. With a touch of . . . possessiveness.

I went out into the windy, chilly spring night and Maisie's pale wee face haunted me all the way home.

Elizabeth

Nobody had seen that coming, not even me. I had no idea that Janet leaving and then me leaving had left such a deep wound in Maisie's heart. It was so awful to see her like that, pale and frozen with fear, lying awake in her bed.

Jamie and Eilidh had no idea of the depth of her terror. Seldom we realise how intense children's feelings can be, the intensity of their fear of being abandoned, of being left alone.

Jamie did all he could, brought her a cup of warm milk, tried to convince her to come back down, snuggle up with him on the sofa and watch TV as a special treat, though it was past her bedtime. He told her over and over again that she had nothing to worry about, that Eilidh was going to be back soon.

She didn't believe him.

Maisie is a happy-go-lucky little girl, more prone to joy than to sorrow, but she had inherited her mum's intensity of feeling and her emotions can be so strong that they shake her like a gale shakes a young tree.

Jamie went on about his night, had his dinner, tidied up and folded some washing away, and all along, Maisie was sitting on the stairs quietly, waiting for the right time to go.

I sat beside her and whispered in her ear, 'Don't go, it's dark, it's cold, stay here with Daddy and me . . . you don't need to be afraid, she's not leaving you, she'll be back.' But Maisie pretended not to hear me and then she said, with a strong, cold voice that I'd only heard in her mother: 'I don't believe you.'

She waited for the right time and, while Jamie was talking to Shona on the phone, she walked out, ever so quietly, out into the night in her pyjamas, and ran on into the street, a little pink figure against the darkness.

Running away from home. The ultimate cry for attention, the ultimate bargaining tool. But actually, I realised, that wasn't why she'd done it. I followed her as she walked up St Colman's Way, past the well and into the woods, and saw that she was looking for something.

'What are you looking for?' I whispered in her ear.

'The brooch.'

I knew what she was talking about. She was looking for Eilidh's brooch, the one that Jamie

284

had made for her when they were children. I recalled the conversation they had that day they went to the Ramsay's estate, while watching the red deer. How Jamie had told her that he'd made the brooch hoping Eilidh would stay but then didn't have the courage to give it to her, and she'd gone. He told Maisie that he'd hidden it in the woods behind the well, waiting for her to come back.

Sometimes we forget how children live in a parallel reality, a literal world that has its own logic. This is what Maisie had heard from her dad's story: I made a brooch for Eilidh so that she wouldn't go, had I given it to her, she would have stayed, but I didn't and she went away. In Maisie's mind, the logical consequence of this was that if she found the brooch and gave it to Eilidh, this time she would stay. The brooch with the deer on it had become magical, it had the power to bind Eilidh to them, and she had to find it. It'd cast a spell on Eilidh and make her stay.

She couldn't see that the spell had already been cast, that Scotland and Glen Avich and the little family of two had bound Eilidh and that she would never leave. In Maisie's experience, love or family ties hadn't been enough to keep the people she loved from leaving.

Maisie was digging with her bare hands, moving dead leaves and branches out of the way. She was cold, her lips were blue and her cheeks were white. I took myself back to Maisie's room and threw all her books down from her bookshelves, so that Jamie would come upstairs and see the empty bed.

It worked. I watched him jump up in fright and run upstairs to search for Maisie and then, when he didn't see her, he frantically searched the bathroom, then his room, then downstairs. He flew out of the door to bang at his neighbours' doors, all the way to Eilidh's house, and every single person he called came out to look for Maisie.

'Jamie?'

'She's gone!' His eyes were wide with panic.

'But how? How did she get out?' Eilidh's voice was cold with fear.

'I don't know. She was in her bed. I was downstairs. Oh God . . . '

They hugged briefly, then started searching again. The streets were echoing with Maisie's name.

I had to find a way to take them to Maisie.

I went to find the fox and whispered to her. She was so brave, so loyal, she ran among all those humans in spite of her instinct begging her to stay away. She stopped in the middle of St Colman's Way, yellow eyes shining in the darkness. Eilidh, Jamie and the others that were with them stood frozen.

'That's the fox I saw just before I had my accident. And that night . . . ' Eilidh whispered, putting a hand on Jamie's arm.

The fox was trembling with the effort to stay put, overwhelmed by the voices and the human smell. They recovered from the surprise and walked on towards her. She couldn't take anymore, her instinct overwhelmed her and she disappeared, as quick as lighting, into the bushes.

'Wait,' said Eilidh urgently. Jamie stopped.

The others were a few paces in front of them and Eilidh and Jamie were standing in silence, Jamie's torch pointed at the ground.

'Come on, let's go . . . ' Jamie shook Eilidh's arm and went to make a step, but tripped into a small, hard body. A pair of yellow eyes met theirs. The fox jumped aside, into the wood, but was still visible. Then she jumped back onto the road in front of them, then into the wood again.

'We need to follow her,' said Eilidh. Thank God, thank God Eilidh had understood.

Jamie looked at her.

Alice through the looking glass, I thought. They're about to step into my side of reality.

And they did.

Eilidh

I was upstairs packing when I heard the voices in the street. Jamie's neighbours, Malcolm and Dougie Ross, father and teenage son, were standing outside my window, a torch in Malcolm's hand, talking loudly to someone I didn't recognise. A brawl? Malcolm and Dougie? Unlikely. And then I saw Jamie, running down towards our house with a panic-stricken expression. I ran downstairs.

'What's going on?' Peggy came out of the living room while I was opening the door.

'I don't know. Something's wrong.'

287

'Eilidh! Maisie's gone!' he called.

I quickly put my jacket on and stepped out. 'Jamie?'

'She's gone!'

It took a minute for his words to sink in. How could this have happened?

'But how? How did she get out?'

'I don't know. She was in her bed. I was downstairs. Oh God . . . '

I held him in my arms. I knew he blamed himself. But how could he have imagined . . .

'Let's go,' I said, and we started walking, calling out her name. A few other men and women had joined us. I looked at my watch: past midnight. It's so cold and damp, I thought as we walked on. My little Maisie's in her pyjamas. Please God, please God, let us find her soon.

Please God, keep her away from the loch.

The familiar, comforting words of the prayers I used to recite with my gran at night came back to me and I found myself praying silently, for the first time since I'd lost my baby.

The loch and its dark, still waters . . .

Jamie and I must have had the same thought because he looked at me.

'I called the police. They'll take us down to the loch.' The last word was a strangled whisper. I felt my knees give way.

'Don't go thinking of that now, Jamie,' said Malcolm gruffly and he walked on, followed by a wide-eyed Dougie, shivering in his denim jacket.

That second, we all froze. A fox had stepped into the street and was watching us, trembling, her eyes reflecting the light of the torches.

A few seconds and the spell was broken. The men walked on. But the fox stood still. When she didn't move, I realised it was *my* fox, the one I'd seen that time I'd gone up the St Colman's way at three in the morning, the one I saw just before my accident.

I put a hand on Jamie's arm, to stop him walking on. I don't know why. Something told me to stop and *listen* to the fox.

But it was too late, the men had got too close and she'd gone.

We walked on, too.

But Jamie stumbled on something. I turned to catch him and a pair of yellow eyes met mine.

We both froze again.

The fox jumped aside into the woods and then onto the street again.

I was sure we had to follow her and I was ready to go myself if Jamie wouldn't follow. I stepped onto the soft earth, strewn with pine needles, and into the wood, and though I didn't know it at the time, I stepped into a different world.

A moment of hesitation, then Jamie followed.

We had to pick up the pace at once because the fox was fast and silent in front of us. With the light of the torch, we managed to follow the fox's movement, guiding us ahead. We were both quiet, as if by a silent agreement not to frighten her. No more crying Maisie's name, only our breathing and the soft rustling of us making our way into the wood.

We didn't walk for long, barely ten minutes. We came to a little clearing in the wood, a semicircle of flat stones on one side, a wall of trees on the other. All was perfectly quiet, the silence was unbroken. The fox climbed onto a flat stone and stopped as Jamie's torch beam trailed in front of her to reveal a little girl in pink pyjamas, lying curled up against a tree, asleep.

In somebody's arms.

It was a woman. For a second, I thought it was Shona, the same blonde hair. But there was something about her that made a memory stir in my mind. The memory of a warm kitchen, the smell of toast and the feeling of a hand around my shoulders.

And the last time I'd seen her, many years later — a brief encounter outside a theatre in Aberdeen, before we all went on our way, never to meet again.

Elizabeth.

She had her arms around Maisie and her face was hidden in Maisie's hair. Then she looked up, straight into Jamie's face and smiled.

She let go of Maisie gently, stood up and took a few steps towards us. Maybe I should have been afraid, it was a ghost I was seeing, but as she walked towards us, I just felt this incredible relief, like they were all back — Flora, my grandfather, all the kind faces that looked upon us when we were children.

'Elizabeth,' I said and her name was so sweet, the relief was so great, that the tears started running down my cheeks, like water from a well.

She put her hand out towards us and caressed Jamie's face, the same way she must have done a million times when Jamie was a child.

I looked at him and he was transfixed, his eyes wide in wonder.

He put his arms out to hold her and she came into his arms. He let go of the torch and it fell on the ground, spreading its light towards Maisie, while we were in darkness. I couldn't see anything anyway, so I closed my eyes. I felt safe.

Jamie made a soft sound in the darkness and I knew she was gone. He threw himself on the ground, in front of Maisie, and held her close. I could see them in the torch's stray beam. I shook myself and kneeled beside them, cupping Maisie's face in my hands.

Jamie had his eyes closed and was holding on to her like his life depended on it.

I broke the spell.

'We need to get her in the warmth . . . ' My voice sounded strange, like something coming from far away, like an echo in a cave.

Jamie opened his eyes and looked straight into mine.

Without a word, he stood up with Maisie in his arms. She hadn't even stirred, lost in the deep sleep that only children can have.

I took hold of the torch and suddenly, we were somewhere else. Not deep in the woods like I thought, but . . . just behind St Colman's Well. The calling of Maisie's name filled the air again and I realised it'd never stopped. I could see the little white lights, dotted all over the garden, just beyond the trees.

We walked towards the lights, in silence.

Elizabeth

I couldn't help it. I thought, if it's the last thing I do, I'll hold my son one last time.

And I did, I held him in my arms again, as my body held on to itself for a brief second before dissolving again.

It was like when he was born, the greatest happiness I've ever known. I let myself drift into the black waters, I didn't know where the loch ended and I began, and I was at peace. Because when I had to let go of him, I hadn't left him on his own.

30

Sea of Souls

Elizabeth

When my body stopped working and my heart stopped beating, I was left with an imprint of me, something that retained my features somehow, and still looked and felt like me. I was the shadow of myself but I could still touch and be touched, and if I wanted to, I could be seen. I was something fluid that could dissolve itself in the elements and then come back together, a body without matter, a body that could be itself and at the same time be water or stone or air.

I could turn into particles swirling in the sun, black waters lapping on the shores of the loch or a breeze between the trees. I could sit beside an owl, high on a branch in the darkness and contemplate the night in its company. I could swim with the otters and emerge among the reeds, their shiny black eyes looking straight into mine in a wordless conversation. I could turn to stone and when I did, I could feel the heart of the earth itself pulsating at the centre of each rock, vibrating with invisible heat and energy. The power of thousands and thousands of years, the time of the earth forming and shifting into what we know now, all that I could feel as I was the side of a hill, a pebble on the shore, a grey stone covered in moss in the middle of the woods. I could be fire and that was the silencing of all memories, the most powerful of all sensations as I burned and burned without pain, as I flickered with the flames in a swirl of orange and yellow.

And then, after having been air or water or stone or fire, I could be me again, Elizabeth McAnena's shadow, with her face, her memories, her senses.

But all that is changing now.

Since that night in the forest, since I touched my son one last time, I seem to have lost all that was keeping me *together*. I don't need to dissolve myself in the air or water, it's happening all by itself, and it's getting harder and harder to be me again. As if all the bits of me that once stuck together, like planets in a solar system kept in their orbits by gravity, had been freed and now followed their own course, too far from each other to be bound together.

And then, one day at dusk, I couldn't see anymore, I couldn't feel anymore. I couldn't hear anything but a rhythmic sound, like the sound of waulking, with the cloth hitting the table over and over again, and the sound is growing stronger, coming nearer and nearer.

As I struggle to think, a memory comes back to me, an evening of many years ago. Flora singing, the two of us wee girls, the rain tapping gently on the window and the glow of the fire. It's a winter night and all our families are there. Flora's voice marks the rhythm and matches the beating of my heart, she's slightly older than me and looks so pretty in her blue skirt and white socks, her wavy brown hair falling on her shoulders and her cheeks pink with the warmth of the fire. I long to be like her, grown up and lovely. I'm sitting on the carpet at my mother's feet and the entire world is perfect and everybody is there, my dear father, my grandparents, my brother, everybody is alive, nobody has gone yet.

Flora's song has a soft rhythm, the Gaelic words falling sweet out of her mouth like a waterfall . . .

And that's my last thought before I'm not me anymore. My last thought before the last bit of my consciousness is gone and all I know, all I hear is a heart beating, fast and fluttery like a bird's, and I realise it's my own heart beating again . . . Flora's song has turned into my heartbeat and there's something else, another soft drum, another heart somewhere in the darkness, beating slow and strong alongside mine, and I'm in the dark and the warmth, but I really want to remember who I was and remember James and Shona and Jamie and Maisie and remember Glen Avich and my mother, she had blue eyes and . . .

31

Not Now, Not Yet

Fiona

> Dear Silke,
> I'm so sorry . . .

> Dear Silke,
> I hope you'll understand . . .

> Dear Silke,
> I . . .

My love. My love. I have to go.

I scrape away these last few words, obliterate them, and the piece of paper they're written on joins the others in the bin.

I can't do this. I can't even speak to her. I can only see one way out and it's to go away, the farthest I can go.

I'm flying to New Zealand. My cousin works there as a nurse, she can help me get a job. I can stay with them for a few weeks, until I find a place of my own. I'll be in Auckland for a year or so and then travel on, maybe Australia, the Far East, wherever. I don't want to be anywhere else long enough to betray myself, for anyone to

296

know who I really am, *what* I really am.

I don't care where I go, as long as it's far from this little village, from this fishbowl. It's suffocating me. Everybody's watching, judging. Everybody will see how my eyes linger where they shouldn't, how I get animated and I blush when I shouldn't, how I'm not like everyone else.

Many people know, many people guessed. Maybe even my own parents. Just thinking about it makes me sick to the pit of my stomach.

There's nothing for me here. Maybe somewhere out there there's a man for me. Maybe I'll change and be *normal* again, like I used to be.

No, I've never been normal. I was always like this.

I remember Karen Roathie, the girl who used to live across the road . . . I never tired of looking at her face. I wanted to be close to her all the time. I used to sneak my hand into hers . . . When we went to secondary school, I tried to be beside her all the time. God knows how nobody picked up on it. She was so beautiful in her uniform, her long black hair brushing my arm as she sat beside me, her leg touching mine briefly, and me trying to get that little bit closer to feel that light touch again. I used to dream at night, imagining her soft lips on mine and the scent of her neck as I held her tight . . .

See? I've always been this way. God, I don't want to think about that. I want to forget all about it.

I don't care what happens now. I just want to be where I'm not watched all the time. Where I

297

don't have to feel so horribly self-conscious, like I'm trying so hard to hide and I don't quite manage, and sooner or later people will find out who I really am.

I don't even want to say goodbye to Silke. I know I've lost her, anyway. I hope she didn't cry. I hope she'll forget me, I hope she'll be ok, find someone else, someone who can bear to be like this, to be all wrong.

No, I'm lying. I am good at it, it seems, but only to myself. The truth is that I hope she remembers me. And I can't think of her with anyone else.

I can't be what I am. Tim got me watching *Doctor Who* the other night and I cried because it talked about a planet close to a black hole, a planet that by all laws of gravity and attraction should fall into the hole and disappear, but somehow it doesn't. It was called the 'impossible planet', and that's me, the impossible girl, the girl without a place and time to be.

I can't live being the way I am but I can't not be the way I am. I'm close to a black hole and sooner or later I'll fall in, and when I do, I don't want my parents and all Innerleithen to see.

I've got to go, the sooner the better.

★ ★ ★

Scotland looks very green from up here. Blue and green, its coastline ragged and perfect and lovely. She looks tiny, a small little place in a big world. I hope that I'll be back one day.

32

Lie Still, Don't Make a Sound and Listen

Jamie

And there she was again, white as a sheet, sitting on the sofa, hugging a pillow. She looked ill. Maisie was sitting beside her, quiet as a mouse: she could sense that again, as many times before, Eilidh wasn't feeling well.

As she heard me coming in, Eilidh sat up a little and smiled.

'In already? Sorry, time flew by . . . ' She looked at her watch. 'Oh my goodness, five o'clock. I've got nothing ready for dinner . . . ' She got up quickly from the sofa and just as quickly, she had to sit down again.

'Uh-oh . . . '

'Are you ok?' I ran over to check on her.

'Yes, I'm fine, I'm fine. Just a bit dizzy.'

'Eilidh, you need to go to the doctor. This can't go on. You've been like this for . . . for weeks!'

'It's just the change of season. And I got stressed when I went to Southport, you know, all that stuff to sort out . . . '

'I know, I know. Since you came back, you

299

haven't been the same.'

Is it really here that you want to be? With me? I wanted to ask. But it wasn't the time, not with Maisie looking at us, with a worried expression on her wee face.

'Just sit down and I'll cook you dinner.'

'No, come on, you're just in, you sit down and I'll cook.'

I shook my head, took her by the shoulders and gently sat her down.

'Promise that you'll go to the doctor.'

'Promise.'

*   *   *

Later that night, I phoned Shona. I was worried sick.

'She just seems . . . I don't know, really under the weather. And she's off her food. I keep asking her to go to the doctor but she refuses.'

'Maybe it's just like you said, she's under the weather. She's been through an awful lot in the past year, she needs a bit of time to build herself up again. Does she seem low to you? Or teary?'

'You know Eilidh, she's always a bit on the emotional side, but she doesn't seem down in the dumps or anything. Just a bit . . . absent. Like her head is somewhere else. I worry that . . . '

The words unspoken hung between us. That she'll go away, like Janet.

'Don't go worrying yourself now. You're just jumping ahead.'

I could hear Maggie's wee noises in the

background. Even if I was worried, I couldn't help but smile.

'Is that Maggie?'

'The very one. I wish you could see her right now, Jamie. She's unbelievably cute, she's got the stripey babygro on, the one I got from Jean. Listen, why don't you come and stay this weekend? With Eilidh, I mean. I can have a wee chat with her, see how the land lies.'

'I'd love to. I'll ask her.'

'I'll text her tonight, too.'

When I put the phone down, I felt a little bit lighter. Shona didn't seem too concerned, so maybe there was nothing to worry about. Shona is a bit like the cabin crew to me, you know, when you're on a plane and there's turbulence, and you look at the cabin crew and if they don't look scared, then it means there's nothing to worry about? Like that.

Still.

Eilidh

I could see the worry on Jamie's face and honestly, I was quite worried myself. I felt so weak, listless. I thought maybe it was the stress of going back to Southport, taking my stuff away from Tom's house. Seeing him again and knowing it was likely to be the last time we were in the same room. But that was a few weeks ago now. Surely I should have felt myself again.

I arranged an appointment with the doctor.

'And how do you feel in yourself? Mood wise,

I mean? You've had a hard year . . . '

'Yes, you can say that. I feel . . . ok. Since my accident, funnily enough, I've felt a lot better. I don't think this is in my head.'

'Well, sometimes long periods of stress can weaken your body, make you feel drained. Why don't we do a blood test and take it from there?'

Dr Nicholson has kind, clear blue eyes and as she looked at me, I knew that she was thinking something she was not saying. I found myself hoping and praying I didn't have to go through the whole thing again — the antidepressants, the hopeless counselling. I had all that after I lost my baby, it was awful, intrusive and it didn't work. Crazy, I know, but I hoped the blood test found something, I don't know, like anaemia, something a course of vitamins could fix. Anything but emotional stuff. I was fed up with emotions. I just wanted to live my life.

★   ★   ★

They found something, but it wasn't a vitamin deficiency. It was something different entirely. It was a different bathroom, a different floor I sat on and a different Eilidh who cried tears of joy, and I knew, I *knew*, that this time there would be a different outcome.

33

It's You

Jamie

I was awake in a fraction of a second. I bolted upright at once as she whispered, 'Jamie.' I had waited for many nights for it to happen, I had only half slept for a long time, listening out for any sign of it starting. Many times I had watched her sleeping, her rounded form under the duvet, her eyelids flickering gently as she dreamt. Often, if she was sleeping soundly, I'd slip a hand under the duvet and place it gently on her tummy, to feel our baby moving. I'd hold my breath and smile in the darkness, wondering what it must be like to feel those kicks *from the inside*. Wonderful and very, very weird, probably. Now that her due date had come and gone, she was so big we could make out the shape of the baby and I could not believe the miracle that was unfolding before my eyes. I was in awe of it as much as I'd been in awe of Janet's pregnancy, although back then the joy of it had been so dampened by her own distress. Eilidh had been so happy all throughout, very sick, very weak and uncomfortable, but glowing with hope and delight in her growing baby. We had been frightened, though, both of us, and every endless

303

drive to Aberdeen, where she'd chosen to be looked after, had an edge of fear to it.

Eilidh had barely moved beside me after whispering my name but I was already half out of bed.

She laughed and said, 'It'll take another wee while.'

We sat together in the light of our bedside lamps, whispering in excitement and terror, sipping tea and eating buttery toast. Shona had told us to try and get some food down us when it all kicked off, because Eilidh wasn't going to be allowed to eat throughout labour and I probably wouldn't feel like it.

'Mind you, your brother-in-law went for chips while I was labouring!' she'd said, glaring at Fraser.

'And a sausage in batter. I'd been through it three times by then. I thought, well, might as well eat 'cause it'll last a while,' he said, with a twinkle in his eye.

My stomach was in a knot as I tried to chew on the toast. I felt so charged I could have gone for a run. By dawn, Eilidh was in pain and struggled not to make a sound. She didn't want to frighten Maisie.

I loved her so, so much as she sat at the breakfast table, white as a sheet, eyes shining, keeping it together for Maisie. We had explained to her that when the baby was ready to come, Eilidh was going to have to sleep at the hospital a couple of nights, for the doctors and nurses to help her get the baby out. And she, Maisie, was going to stay with Aunt Shona and Uncle Fraser.

She seemed very calm about it but I knew she was apprehensive.

Half an hour later, we were driving towards Aberdeen, Maisie sitting in the back with her little *Charlie and Lola* backpack and an overnight bag. Shona and Fraser were coming to get her at the hospital to drive her home with them.

'You ok there?' I asked Maisie. Eilidh was silent. Very silent, very white, a film of sweat on her forehead. Oh God.

'Yes. You ok?' Maisie answered, a little shakily.

'Right as rain, my love!' I said cheerily. Well, I tried to be cheery, I probably sounded hysterical.

'You ok, Eilidh?'

'Yes.' She answered curtly. Her voice seemed to come from far away. Like she wasn't with us, like she was somewhere on her own, somewhere we couldn't reach her.

She's going into battle, I thought. And there's only so much I can do to help her.

As the automatic doors of Aberdeen Maternity Hospital closed behind us, with Eilidh leaning on me and breathing heavily, I felt dizzy. We were stepping into a new world, nothing was going to be the same again.

Eilidh

I was in so much pain, I couldn't breathe, I couldn't even scream anymore — and I had done a good deal of screaming by then. I was strapped to a monitor and in the haze of pain, I

305

could see it tracking my baby's heartbeat. It was strong and unafraid, resounding in my ears like a song.

An eternity of pain later, my baby's cries filled the room. Its voice was as old as the mountains and as strong as the tides, life flew through it without obstacles, like a rushing river. And I thought of my other baby, the one that passed, the one that couldn't stay, and for the first time I saw clearly why it had gone and why this one would stay. This baby was meant to be, this baby belongs here . . .

'It's a boy!' I heard Jamie saying.

'It's a boy,' I whispered back. Yes, of course, it's *you*. It was always you. I'd known you all my life.

He was placed in my arms, his head still covered in our blood, his scrunched face and his little fists, his little warm body wrapped in a blanket. He was beautiful and perfect and my heart sang with happiness, in a way I never knew before. I couldn't stop looking at his face, his hands. I couldn't stop breathing in his sweet baby smell, which was my own scent, too.

'What's his name?' the midwife asked me. I looked at Jamie. I wanted him to name our baby.

'Sorley. Sorley McAnena,' he said and it sounded like a blessing, like a prayer, like a song.

The midwives left, saying something about the golden hour and bonding. Not sure what they were talking about, what bonding? My baby and I have bonded since before time, we are one and always will be. Whatever, as long as they went and left us for a bit. Jamie and me and our son.

Our son. I couldn't believe I was finally saying those words!

When I could finally tear my eyes away from my baby's face, I looked at Jamie. He looked terrible, blue shadows under his eyes and all pale and flushed at the same time, but he had a big smile from ear to ear. I'd made him happy.

I felt so proud.

I raised my face to him for a kiss. He brushed my wet hair away from my forehead and our lips met over Sorley's little head.

And then something strange happened.

They say newborns can't really see, they can't focus, they can only make out shadows and silhouettes of this big strange world they've been thrust into. But my son, I think he looked at me. At us. His eyes were two black pools, like the eyes of an underwater creature blinking in the light of the surface. Like someone coming to a new place from far, far away.

He looked at me, he took me in, and then deliberately, his eyes moved to Jamie, as if he knew us already. Through my tears of joy I said, 'Look, Jamie, he's got Elizabeth's eyes.'

Epilogue

Time, The Deer

Eilidh

I think of the women behind me, my mother Rhona and her mother Flora, and Flora's mother Margaret, and Margaret's mother Anne, and on and on, a long line of strong women with their stories, their joys and their sorrows. Their blood runs in my veins and with their blood, their memories — they flow through me and make me who I am. In my blood and in my bones, from the cradle to the grave, through marriage and childbirth and loss, their lives are inside me. I hear their voices whispering and I feel their hands supporting me when I'm weak, their strength is my strength and their pride is my pride.

And my husband's mother, Elizabeth, I see her in Shona and in Maisie and in my own son. I know that she reached to us from beyond, she watched over us and led us home, Jamie and me. When I was in darkness, two years ago, I must have prayed without realising. I must have asked for help, because God knows I was lost.

Elizabeth heard my call and I'll hear our children's call when it's my time, and if they turn to the unknown looking for help, I'll listen when they say, 'Watch over me.'

308

We do hope that you have enjoyed reading this large print book.

Did you know that all of our titles are available for purchase?

We publish a wide range of high quality large print books including:
Romances, Mysteries, Classics
General Fiction
Non Fiction and Westerns

Special interest titles available in large print are:
The Little Oxford Dictionary
Music Book
Song Book
Hymn Book
Service Book

Also available from us courtesy of Oxford University Press:
Young Readers' Dictionary
(large print edition)
Young Readers' Thesaurus
(large print edition)

For further information or a free brochure, please contact us at:
Ulverscroft Large Print Books Ltd.,
The Green, Bradgate Road, Anstey,
Leicester, LE7 7FU, England.
Tel: (00 44) 0116 236 4325
Fax: (00 44) 0116 234 0205

Other titles published by
The House of Ulverscroft:

NIGHTWOODS

Charles Frazier

In the lonesome beauty of the forest, across the far shore of the mountain lake from town, Luce acts as caretaker to an empty, decaying Lodge, a relic of holidaymakers a century before. Her days are long and peaceful, her nights filled with Nashville radio and yellow lights shimmering on the black water. A solitary life, and the perfect escape. Until the stranger children come. Bringing fire. And murder. And love.